I Let Her In

ALSO BY SOPHIA SPIERS

The Call of Cassandra Rose
The Family Home
I Let Her In

I LET
HER IN

SOPHIA SPIERS

LUME BOOKS
A JOFFE BOOKS COMPANY

Lume Books, London
A Joffe Books Company
www.lumebooks.co.uk

First published in Great Britain in 2025

Cover art by Nick Castle

ISBN: 978-1-83901-613-4

To Byron, my rock,
who's always telling me to get off my phone.

Please note, all characters mentioned in the novel
are works of fiction.

PROLOGUE

The panic doesn't set in straight away, and for a split second I feel like the nightmare unfolding is happening to someone else. But reality catches up fast, shocking me from my trance-like state.

I'm the one in the stormy sea and *I'm* the one that can't swim.

A tide catches me in its web. A malevolent force pulls and pushes me under. Somehow, I manage to come up for air, but no sooner do I breathe than the sea whips and drags me away again. As I scream, I swallow and choke. The water closes in and my lungs shrivel into tight fists, burning like hot lava. My mind splinters, red and frenzied.

Air. I need air.

Up above the foamy sea, I see the shadowy boat bobbing up and down. My heart thrashes inside my skull. It's not far from me. Fresh blood pumps through my veins as survival mode kicks in. Instinctively, I work my limbs, desperately trying to propel myself up, battling the water knotting around me.

A lifeline slices through the surface; a hand reaches for me.

It's you. My saviour.

This gives me fresh hope and the momentum I need. Scrambling, I kick as hard as I can, stretching my arms as far as they'll go. I touch your fingertips, and when I do, adrenaline bolts through me. *I'm going to be saved.* Your hand grips my wrist, and

1

I'm whisked up. My head breaks the water and I manage to grip onto the side of the boat with one hand. Coughing and spluttering, I expel the sea out.

Everything calms.

It's blindingly sunny. The brightness burns the backs of my eyes. The gulls swoop low. Your features are smudged and fuzzy from the dazzling light.

I wait.

A cloud trickles past the sun, blocking it out. I stare into your clear blue eyes and a softness envelops me. You're beautiful and serene, exactly what I need in this moment. You part your lips and I think you're about to give me instructions, offer me reassurance, help me onto the boat, but instead you just smile. It's a bright smile. A smile that I've grown to trust. A smile that I've grown to love.

Time passes.

Pull me up, I beg with my eyes. *I'm losing grip. Why aren't you helping me?*

Confused, I notice you're holding a mobile and you're pointing it in my direction.

'Say goodbye,' you say, baring your teeth.

You begin to uncurl my fingers gripping the boat. First finger freed — I'm bewildered. Second uncoiled. *What are you doing?* Third finger goes. *I thought you loved me. I thought . . .* I'm dangling on a piece of string, with only one finger hooked. You force it open.

Terror rips through me as I slip away from you, sinking into the deep.

This time, I'm never coming back.

CHAPTER ONE

Frankie

'Close your eyes and breathe . . .' I instruct my students as the session comes to an end. I lie flat on my Pilaga-branded mat, spreading my arms and legs wide. 'Surrender yourself to this perfect moment of deep relaxation.'

Exhaling through my mouth, I close my eyes, but I can't seem to switch my brain off completely. My thoughts flit to the Instagrammable Stella dress that's on sale but is still clearly overpriced. I can get a taxi straight to the store after work and could be showing it off tonight. Stefan's Chelsea gallery is exhibiting the new Lynda Smyth show. It'll be an evening reserved for pretentious small talk with aloof artist types pretending not to give a shit about how cool, important and relevant they are. If it wasn't for Lynda, my oldest standing friend, I wouldn't be going. At least Stefan will be working, which means we're not obliged to spend the night together. What did he mean when he said, 'You're everything to me.' Everything how? We've got a good thing going, no complications, why rock the boat like that? I dismiss his comments as drunken talk.

Tonight, I'll show my face at the gallery for an hour then escape home alone, order sushi and catch up on some reality

TV. It's the season finale of *Love Conquers All*, and with only two loved-up couples left in the Majorcan villa, I'm not sure which pair will make it down the aisle.

My nails tap on my mat. My thoughts hop to the interview I have in twenty minutes on Insta Live with a young yogi from California. The interview is making me angsty for some reason. Usually these things don't bother me. I'm so used to them. Perhaps I'm feeling this way because I didn't sleep well. In fact, I haven't been sleeping well for quite some time. It's that damned recurring nightmare. Every night I dream of tumbling out of a boat into the choppy sea and drowning. Every night I wake panicked, in a cold sweat, unable to breathe. Every night I wonder who the other person on the boat is. According to various dream dictionaries, dying in a dream is positive and means new beginnings.

So why does it feel like doom is lurking around the corner?

Someone sneezes. I open my eyes and stare at the ceiling, noticing cobwebs in the corners. Everything about my Pilaga gyms should be high-end and spa-like, so the clientele can escape their world. God only knows, that's what they're paying for. I make a mental note to tell Mia, my receptionist-cum-manager, to find a new cleaner.

Sitting upright, I roll my shoulders out. The low winter sun floods through the windows into the large exercise studio and falls over the sea of bodies splayed flat on their mats. Everyone's eyes remain closed and their serene faces shimmer from the light pouring in. The bright sunlight illuminates the dust balls in the corners of the room. Damn it.

I clear my throat to give everyone an indication that the session has now ended. 'Well done, people. You've worked extra hard today.'

The students uncurl themselves off the floor and clap their appreciation. Smiling broadly, I nod a few times, ensuring I make eye contact with as many of them as possible. Another jam-packed class with no cancellations. Recently, I've had to increase the number of people to keep up with the demand. But it's not made much difference to the two-month waiting list. Not that I'm complaining. It's good for business. Great for business.

Pilaga, a blend of yoga and Pilates, is my brainchild, my baby — *the intelligent way to exercise*. It's the only way to exercise, in my opinion. Using techniques which I've mastered over the years, it helps realign, tone and strengthen the body. It gives me a thrill to see my clients transform their bodies and lives.

Light chit-chat fills the room. A bead of sweat trickles down my vertebrae. I don't like to wear much when I'm teaching; a Pilaga Lycra leotard is all I need. It's become a bit of a trend and most of the women wear similar. The latest range has sold out in all our gym shops, online too, and I've had to place another order, which I'm hoping will arrive in time for the Christmas rush.

The class gather their mats and the noise in the studio swells. There's good energy today. Amanda crosses the studio and approaches me. She's wearing our latest royal-blue number. She looks good in it. Her hair is tied in a messy bun and her face is creased with lines. Amanda's missed a few classes recently, cancelling at the very last minute. I must check with Mia to see whether she's paid the cancellation fee.

'Thanks for an amazing sesh, Frankie.'

'My pleasure, Amanda.'

'The tension in my body has completely disappeared. All that pent-up stress from the week — vanished!'

'That's what I like to hear. You worked hard.'

Truth is, she positioned herself right at the back in my blind spot so I couldn't see her.

'Off anywhere nice this evening?' Amanda asks, as a bead of sweat drops from her forehead onto her nose. She wipes it off using one of our branded towels.

'Going to an exhibition, then heading home to watch some TV. I've only just got back from skiing.'

'I saw your stories. You had fantastic snow in the mountains. I loved your pink jumpsuit. So retro. It looked great on you.'

'Thank you,' I say, feeling myself blush.

Even though I know my clients check my Instagram pages and my followers have grown in the last few months to a staggering 800,000, it still takes me by surprise when someone approaches me about my feeds. Especially Amanda.

'Where did you buy it from?'

'It was gifted to me by *This Sporting Life*. I'm sent free merchandise and in return I post them on my socials. Perks of my job.'

'Wow,' Amanda says with her mouth open wide.

I smile. A silence lingers between us. It's been a hard challenge over the years to keep quiet, but I've learned not to fill the gaps with inane conversation.

'You're so busy all the time, I hope you haven't forgotten about our next coffee date.'

'Of course not. As soon as I'm free.'

A while back, she pressurised me for weeks about going to her house for a drink. Finally, I caved in. Even though she lives one road away from mine, our lives couldn't be further apart. As soon as I entered her home, I knew it was a mistake. Two huge dogs jumped up on me, pawing at my Pilaga leggings. Three children, all under the age of five, curly blonde hair and mucky faces, were competing for my attention, waving their crayon drawings at me. Amanda had the TV and radio on at the same time and her mobile, on the loudest setting, kept pinging with messages. I was so claustrophobic from all the chaos, the bombardment of questions from her, that by the time my herbal tea had cooled down, I couldn't wait to get out of there.

'Anyway,' she says. 'I should shower. The hubby's coming home early so we can get our Christmas decorations up. I know, I know — it's only the first of December. But it's become a thing in our house. I promised to pick up mulled wine from Jeroboams and chocolate coins for the kids. See you next week.'

Amanda leaves and the studio empties out. I'm alone. I cross the studio, flicking the switch on the wall for the dehumidifier. Picking up my phone, I switch off my Café del Mar Ibiza mix which usually plays in the background during class and reposition my mat near the window where there's still some natural light. I sit down cross-legged and wait for the room to air from the build-up of stale deodorant and sweat, a smell only a group of bodies exercising hard can create. A smell that I've grown to love.

It dawns on me that I haven't posted any content all day and my twenty-four-hour story is about to expire. I flick to the camera on my phone, point it to my feet and take a snapshot, showing off my ombre-effect painted toenails. I upload the picture with the caption, *Always keep yourself grounded, folks.* It'll do.

Like. Like. Like. Like. Like. Like.

My socials flood with likes. Endorphins rush my system. I'm in a blissful bubble where hundreds of faceless people are validating me, making me feel good. In fact, they make me feel great. I scan the comments.

Your feet are so perfect.
Where did you get your pedicure from?
Are you out tonight?

Maybe I should buy that Stella dress after all. I refresh the page a few times, watch the likes climb to over a thousand and the comments grow. Slotted in between the usual comments, I notice the username *@ubitch666*. Curious, I expand the remark.

You think you're something special, but you're not. You're a nobody. And I'm going to prove it.

Hmm. My phone buzzes in my hand. *Lynda*. She never calls me at work. I dismiss the comment as jealousy and answer my friend.

'Hi, Lynda. You need to be quick because I have an interview shortly. You okay?'

'Sure. Sure. Yeah, I'm fucking cool. Yeah. You coming later?'

'Wouldn't miss your show for the world.'

'Franks?'

I pull my phone away from my ear. Three minutes until I go live. 'Hmm?'

'Do you remember back in the day? The King's Cross days, when we were—'

'What the . . . ? Lynda, why are you bringing this up now? Thought we agreed never to discuss it.'

'It's just—'

'Listen. I need a clear head for the interview,' I say, cutting her off. 'Remember, we're different people now. Better. Happier. Forget the past. Concentrate on your art show and your success.'

'You can't run away from your past forever, Franks,' she mumbles. 'It'll catch up with you in the end. It always fucking does. Trust me, yeah? Fucking trust me on this one.'

'Is everything alright, Lynda?'

'Nah . . . I mean, fuck. I dunno.'

She doesn't sound right. 'Do you have pre-show nerves?'

'Something's cropped up. Someone—'

Two minutes until I go live. Damn.

'What's cropped up? Who?'

'Forget it, Franks. Forget what I said. You're right. It's butterflies.'

Lynda's never jittery before a show. A text message pops up on my phone. *Are you ready?* asks Kelsey, the yogic guru from LA who's about to interview me in under one minute.

'I've got to go, Lynda. I'm sorry. I'll see you later.'

She terminates the call without saying goodbye.

I shake off her weird comments and inhale deeply, saying my mantra out loud like I usually do. 'You've got to fake it to make it.' Somehow, my words sound hollow.

Damn it, Lynda, why bring up the past now?

CHAPTER TWO

Bee

I pressed 'like' on my phone and stared at the image of Frankie's pedicured toes for a while. Perfect, just perfect. Her feet were small and tanned, the skin appeared smooth and soft to touch, how I imagined silk would feel on my fingertips. Switching my phone on silent, I placed it in my jacket pocket and fingered the letter inside.

A whoosh of air blew through my recently dyed-black hair, messing it up. I stepped back as the train to London hurtled into the station. I picked up the two bin liners filled with my clothes and boarded the train, squeezing past hordes of passengers. The snow had soaked through my ankle boots, making my feet wet. They were supposed to see me through the winter. I pictured my own ugly feet with toenails that had never been pedicured inside my boots. Dotty, my mum, painted her nails every Friday without fail. Her feet on the glass coffee table, pink foam separators in between her long toes, cigarette holder dangling from her mouth, like she was a 1940s film star. Hair pinned in rollers, a glass of Pinot Grigio next to the nail polish, which she'd always buy from Superdrug, not Boots, because it was better value.

Battling my way down the aisles towards the first-class carriage, posh commuters stared at me like I was polluting their air. I hoped for a quiet seat, at least for a little while until I got kicked off. I found an empty table seat and dumped the bin liners next to me, throwing my rucksack and the flowers I'd bought Charlotte, my ex-friend from school, on the table. She'd moved to London when her dad hit the lottery jackpot and bought her and her older sister a house in the East End. Some people were born lucky.

And some had to make their own luck.

As I settled down, I lifted the back of my hair away from my clammy neck and noticed my sweaty pits. I'd need to change clothes when I got to Charl's house. Problem was, she still hadn't replied to my text messages, all five of them, informing her that I was visiting. The fast train screeched out of Folkstone.

London would work out. *It had to.*

Doubt clouded my mind. I could hear Dotty's voice in my head. *Nothing ever works out for a girl named Bernadette!* she'd say, her cheeks hollowing as she puffed on her ciggie, her eyes smiling, cruelly. I often wondered if she'd given me that old-fashioned name on purpose. It was the sort of thing she'd do for a cheap thrill. But as I rocked from side to side, I couldn't help but grin. Little did she know, being six feet under and all, I'd decided to change my name to Bee after she'd died. And things *always* worked out for a girl named Bee. Which reminded me, I hadn't told Charlotte about the name change. I fired out another text, noticing that she still hadn't read the last ones.

I wasn't travelling to London for a jolly and a catch up with an old friend. I had more important things to sort out. Big things. *Life things.* It had to do with the address at the bottom of the letter which was inside my jacket pocket.

My face reflected back at me from the black-mirrored window. I had to do a double take because I wasn't used to the new hair colour and heavy black eye make-up. But despite the identity and name change, and small bursts of optimism, I found the same thoughts rushed my mind. Ugly, unwanted, unloved. It would take a while to shake off the old me.

A fly buzzed past and landed on the window. I focused on it for a while, blurring my face out. The fly skipped its way to the top of the window and buzzed all the way back down to the bottom, only to ladder up the window again, looking for an escape route. That's exactly how I felt living in the tiny flat with my stepdad Reg and Mum. Trapped. When the opportunity struck, I swatted the fly and squished it with my hand, killing it.

Two girls around my age crash-landed into the two seats opposite me, breaking my thoughts. They looked like they'd been plucked out of an episode of *The Only Way Is Essex*. Personally, I preferred the more natural look, like Frankie Fitz, social media star. Even though she had peroxide hair, Frankie didn't pump her face with Botox and fillers. The girls chatted. I tried my best to ignore them and contemplated moving seats, but I didn't want to face the walk of shame with the bin liners if I could help it. I sank into my seat, not wanting to attract their attention. Not that I needed to, they were too busy discussing the season finale of *Love Conquers All* to notice me.

'But isn't Jordano well fit, babes?' one said, sucking on a strand of red extension hair.

'Do you fink they're gonna win, hun?' The other clicked her fake nails on her phone.

'Nah, babes. It's gotta be Billy-Bob and Pete. The world loves a gay wedding, don't they.'

'Angela's yoga arms, though.'

'Oh, babes, I know. I want those arms. Don't want no bingo wings, do we? Think she's been doing that new exercise trend. Can't remember what it's called. It's when you mix — hang on . . .

let me fink . . . yeah, that's right, when you mix yoga with Pilates together. It gives you arms like hers. God, I'd die for arms like that. Wouldn't you, hun?'

Something came over me and before I knew what I was doing, I straightened myself up, opened my mouth and found words spilling out, in an accent I didn't recognise.

'Babes, you talking about Frankie Fitz?' I asked, cringing to myself. I'd no idea why I was deliberately trying to sound like them.

The pair looked startled.

I cleared my throat. 'Pilaga. Frankie Fitz.'

'Yeah, that's right, babes, how did you—'

'I know her, don't I, babes,' I said.

The girl with the long nails clocked the stuffed bin liners next to me. She poked her friend in the waist. The other girl turned to look. Simultaneously, they burst out laughing.

'Yeah right, hun. In your dreams.' They giggled. 'Come on, babes. Let's find another seat. Think she's homeless or somefink.'

A slight mist, the colour of weak blood, formed around my eyes, like it always did when I felt myself getting mad. My hand reached inside my pocket and I looked out the window, past the dead fly, past my distorted, ugly reflection. I crumpled the letter in my hand.

Breathe, Bernadette, breathe.

The ticket inspector stood over me. I didn't even bother trying to convince him I belonged; I just grabbed my stuff and battled my way back through the packed carriages where there were no more seats available.

In the end, I sat in the corridor next to the loos with the window open to air out someone's smelly dump. EarPods in, I waited for Frankie's interview on Instagram to start.

London was going to work out fine.

Frankie would make sure of it.

CHAPTER THREE

Frankie

Kelsey's delayed for some reason, and as time ticks on, my insides twist with nervous anticipation. *Will the online viewers like me?* Three minutes later than scheduled, Kelsey's sun-kissed face appears on my phone. My pulse races. I ask to join her live. She accepts. The screen on my phone splits into two parts. She appears on the top and I see my face below. She's a quintessential Californian with shaggy blonde hair, white veneers and layered bead necklaces. She's young. Very young. I make a mental note to keep a close eye on this up-and-coming social media starlet.

Kelsey slurps from her branded green juice, making sure it's in shot. Perfect product placement. I wonder how much she's been paid to promote Juicy Organic. I've seen their juices lined up on the shelves in health food stores around London. Maybe I should contact them? I'm sure they'd want to expand their reach in the UK. It's the game we play. Us influencers want fame, likes and an army of followers, and we need sponsors and endorsements to keep us on top.

'Frankie, baby,' she booms, like we're the oldest of friends. The juice moves out of shot.

The first time I met Kelsey was when she PM'd me on Insta asking whether I would do an interview. She has around 120,000 followers, which is great considering she's new to the scene. Kelsey's lucky, she's got youth on her side and has plenty of time to build her following. This interview will not only widen her reach in the UK but will help widen mine across the pond. I've been flirting with the idea of moving my practice abroad. She could be my ticket for expansion. *Maybe this is the new beginning my dream has been telling me about.* I can picture it now: a house in the Californian canyons, an infinity pool with views to die for, teaching Pilaga on the beach while the waves lap my feet and the sun prickles my skin. All that vitamin D from the sun and negative ions from the sea soaking into my body. Even though I hate being in the water, I'm not averse to the idea of living by the ocean. London can be so grey and stagnant, the air loaded with lead.

Kelsey stares expectedly.

I snap out of my fantasy. 'Hi, there! Thanks for having me,' I say, mirroring her enthusiasm.

She's infectious, I'll give her that, and a morning person like me. It's only 8 a.m. in LA.

'Here's an intro for those of you who've been stuck under a rock for the best part of a year and don't know who I'm about to interview. This is Frankie Fitz, the founder of Pilaga, the exercise craze which has swept the UK and is making ripples here in California.'

She looks down to what I imagine is a sheet of prepared questions.

'Frankie, am I right in thinking that by cross-training yoga and Pilates together, you've managed to create a unique full-body workout which tones and sculpts the body?'

Her question seems pretty bog-standard. I ease myself into the interview. 'In a nutshell, yes. You've described my practice perfectly, Kelsey.'

My eyes dart to the viewer counter: 488 people. The counter moves up to 490, 493. Down to 492, 491. I must hold their attention. I have to come across as sassy, interesting and alluring. The viewers need to want to know me. They need to want to *be* like me, the version of me that I put out for the world. Let's face it, *I'm the brand*. I'm what the followers are logging on for. They don't care about the mechanics of Pilaga itself. It's just another fad. Most people want to be a part of the 'it' crowd, the tribe, they want to associate themselves with whatever's trending and whoever's trending at the time. It's a hive mentality, and if you can tap into it and give them what they want, what they expect, or better still, offer them something they think they need in their life, then you're onto something.

My smile broadens, and I try to flirt with the camera and beyond, hoping I'm connecting to those tuning in.

'The Pilaga circuit is split into three parts. Firstly, we begin with Pilates-based exercises, involving movement that concentrates on building core and stamina. We move from one exercise to the next with no breaks, creating heat in the body. After that beautiful intensity, we use yoga poses for strength and flexibility. We slow things down in the last part of the circuit, so we're in a meditative state, creating a mindful energy throughout the body, which we call Prana.'

'Wow. Incredible. Am I correct in thinking that three sessions of Pilaga a week is equivalent to working out seven days a week for one hour?'

'Yes, you're right.' I nod, impressed. She's done her homework. 'Three sessions a week to keep your mind and body healthy is not a huge sacrifice to make. Plus, most students see results as quickly as six weeks.'

'Holy moly. That's insane.'

'Everyone needs Pilaga in their lives.' I wink to the camera, hoping I appear playful and not arrogant. Self-assurance is good, but as soon as your confidence crosses to a hint of narcissism, you've lost them.

'How did this all come about? When did you first have the idea for Pilaga?'

'Around thirteen years ago when I was, *ahem*, twenty-two years old.'

'Hold on. Wait. What? How old are you, Frankie? Like, *how old?* No way can you be thirty . . . hang on . . . thirty . . .' Her eyes dart to the sky as she does the calculations. 'Thirty-five. You look so young.'

'Thank you. You're very flattering. I try my best to take care of myself.'

'Have you always focused on health? Are your family in this line of business? For instance, my daddy used to teach yoga way back in the eighties, when everyone was doing Jane Fonda workouts.'

My gaze turns to the window so I can recalibrate. I have a tight sensation in my chest. No one asks about my family. I turn to my screen. The smile on my face now pasted on.

'Sadly, I don't have a family anymore,' I say, keeping my tone light. 'I'm self-made and have grafted hard to get where I am today.'

'Grafted?'

'Oh, sorry, Kelsey. My slang is coming through, I do apologise. What I mean to say is, I've come from nothing and have had to work my fingers to the bone to get to the top.'

Kelsey's eyes light up. 'Tell me more about your humble beginnings.'

First Lynda and now this!

I don't like where this conversation is heading, but the audience counter has crept up. Everybody loves a 'rags to riches' story. The bad girl turned good.

'You say that you don't have a family. Are your parents . . . deceased?'

'I left home when I was sixteen,' I say mechanically. It's as though the words coming out of my mouth don't belong to me. 'I spent my late teens and early twenties living a hedonistic lifestyle. I was a troubled soul with no prospects. But one day, I thought, *I'm not going to be defined by my past.* I wanted to make positive changes, so I cleaned myself up, started exercising and looking after myself. I worked bars and clubs at night and studied as much as I could during the day. I kept my head down, worked hard at reinventing myself and became the person I always wanted to be. I was determined to make something of my life . . .

'When I turned twenty-three, a year after the idea came to me, I took the plunge and opened my first ever studio in Islington with a hefty £100,000 business loan. You see, I had to make it work, I had no choice. Fast-forward twelve years later, I now have five other successful exercise studios under my belt in London.'

'You could say that you've made it!'

'I've found something I'm passionate about. Work has saved me from who I used to be. So, I guess, yes, I've made it. In a weird way, Pilaga has completed me. It's provided me with the family I never had. And I guess, subconsciously, I always wanted to feel like I belonged someplace, and Pilaga has done that for me . . .

'Now, work is all I need. I don't need anything else. Of course, my clients and followers keep me going too. Hearing their transformation stories spur me on.'

'That's very inspirational. Especially for our younger viewers. Holy moly. Tell me something, Frankie. You say, and I quote, that you're complete in every way and you don't need anything else apart from work.'

Number one rule, never give yourself fully to them. *Never give yourself to anyone!*

'So, I guess the next big question is, is there a special Mr or Ms Fitz in your life?'

I pause before I answer, hoping Stefan is busy setting up the gallery and not tuning in. 'No. Not at the moment. No, there isn't anyone special in my life.'

The doors to the main studio fling open. In comes Martha, our practitioner, the Bavarian beauty, long and towering, dressed in an orange Pilaga leotard which rides high. She's wearing her hair in a neat bun like a ballerina. I've been saved by her perfect time-keeping.

I point my camera at Martha. 'Say hello to everyone!'

She waves and places her mat at the front of the studio. A few clients trickle in.

'Kelsey, it looks as though our time is up. We have a class about to start and I have someplace fabulous to be and need to get ready.'

'Oh, the suspense is killing us. Where are you going this evening?'

'You'll all have to check my Insta later to find out.'

She laughs. 'Thank you so much for sharing your life story with us, Frankie. A fascinating insight into how you started out. *Fascinating.* I wish we had more time to talk. I'm sure the followers would like to know more. Maybe we can arrange a follow-up next week?'

The words 'not a chance in hell' catch in my throat.

My eyes flick to the counter at the bottom of the screen. The numbers have tripled. Kelsey's waiting for me to respond.

'Of course,' I say, forcing a smile on my face. 'I'd love to chat more next week.'

CHAPTER FOUR

Frankie

The White Noise gallery is in full swing when I arrive for the Lynda Smyth show, *Beauty in Violence*. I slip out of my taxi and step into a sea of art patrons and artist types wearing thick black rimmed glasses and t-shirts with kooky slogans such as 'You are your own brand' and 'Normal people scare me'. Scattered among them are the well-connected rich set with oodles of cash to burn on their next piece. These are the serious collectors.

Ambient music plays in the background as the room hums with people discussing the impressive works lit up on the bare brick walls. The occasional clinking of champagne glasses can be heard. Stefan, the gallery curator and owner, and my secret lover, is standing at the far end of the gallery with a clipboard in his hand. Next to him is Lynda, with her spiky girlfriend, Grace. Seeing Lynda gives me a sense of relief. In a packed room full of faces I recognise but don't know at all, she is my constant — we've been friends for almost twenty years. But seeing Grace irritates me. She's always been jealous of our bond.

'Frankie's my very best friend in the whole world,' she told Grace when we were first introduced.

'Oh really?' Grace said, linking her arm through Lynda's possessively.

'Yeah, really. I'd do anything for this fucking girl. Anything,' Lynda said. 'She's a real diamond. Pulled herself out of the gutter and helped me along the way too.'

Grace eyed me suspiciously. We walked the rest of the way to Lynda's show in silence.

Lynda looks scruffier than usual. Her hair's a wiry mess and she's in an oversized plaid shirt, flared jeans and dirty-looking trainers. It makes me worried seeing her this way. And after her strange, incoherent call earlier, it makes me wonder whether she's . . .

No, she can't be!

A man wearing a charcoal flat cap, a grey scarf and a tweed jacket strolls over to them, looking like he belongs in *Peaky Blinders*. He's tall, mysterious and has a strong presence about him. He shakes Stefan's hand and then kisses Lynda on both cheeks. This makes me chuckle. She doesn't do two kisses, finds it pretentious. We used to laugh about that years ago. Grace stamps her feet, looks to the ground. All of them turn to the huge oil on the wall. They have their backs to the room, admiring a painting of a semi-naked woman with a ripped blouse, sporting a bruise on one eye. Her right breast is exposed and scratched up. The piece makes me uncomfortable. It's raw. Bold. Unsubtle. Just like Lynda.

Taking my coat off, I hand it to the woman manning the pop-up cloakroom by the front door and place the gold plastic ticket she's given me into my clutch. Discreetly, I reapply my lip-plump gloss. My long Stella dress sweeps along the floor and my heels click as I head across the uneven concrete floor towards Stefan. Damn these galleries. A few people turn to stare my way. This gives me the injection of confidence I need. Even though I may appear self-assured, I always suffer anxiety when I first arrive at an event, especially if I arrive alone. *You've got to fake it to make it*, I tell myself, stopping to take a glass of champagne from a waiter holding a silver tray and ignoring the plate of delicate canapés. I take a swig and it fizzles in the back of my throat.

I approach Stefan and the group, gently tapping his shoulder. He spins around.

'Darling, you came!' Stefan's dressed in black tie, looking as sharp as Bond. He leans in to kiss my right cheek. 'So good to see you, Frankie.' He kisses my left. His lips linger a little too long. 'You look stunning tonight,' he whispers into my ear.

He smells good. I breathe him in then pull away sharply, realising that we're huddled too close and look too intimate.

'I wouldn't miss this for the world,' I say, smiling and looking around the room to see if I can spot Victoria, his ex-girlfriend. Thankfully, she's not here.

Vic doesn't know about us yet. No one knows apart from Lynda and maybe Grace. I guess I'm guilty of using Vic as an excuse to keep us a secret, telling Stefan that I'm protecting her feelings — which I am, of course, as well as protecting my own. She was one of my Pilaga students but stopped coming when she split with Stefan. A struggling artist turned wellness coach, she's been trying to build her presence online and has roughly 20,000 followers.

A while back, Stefan invited Lynda and me out to dinner. He became close friends with Lynda after her first successful show. That night, Lynda was sick and cancelled on us, but we went anyway. During our starters, he surprisingly broke down on me, saying he'd split with his on-again, off-again girlfriend, Vic. Just as pudding arrived, he professed his secret attraction for me. By the time we were ready to leave the restaurant, our legs had entwined underneath the table and we were holding hands. That day, I was feeling particularly low and, like a fool, I stupidly fell for his softness, his charm, his boyish, handsome looks. I fell for his vulnerability and his longing. I gave into my need to belong to someone, relying on somebody else to give me the comfort that I deeply craved. That night we slept together. And we've been sleeping together ever since.

I tilt my flute of champagne and take a sip, then turn my attention to Lynda. I have one of her earliest pieces hanging up on my wall in my basement kitchen next to my dining table. She gifted it to me just before she hit the big time.

'Congratulations on your latest show.' I give her a light peck on one cheek.

Her skin feels rough and she smells stale. Now I'm up close, I'm convinced something's up. Lynda's avoiding eye contact too. Weird.

'How are you doing tonight? Have the nerves settled?'

'Fine. Yeah. Fucking fine. You know how it is. The way these things roll.'

I want to ask her about our phone call earlier, but she's already turned her back. Hmmm. Now I'm really suspicious. Her body language is off, and she seems to be avoiding conversation. Usually, at this point in the evening, she can't wait to make a comment about the event being a waste of her time and how the art world is full of sycophantic vampires. I step back to catch Grace's attention, waving at her with my free hand. She sighs loud enough for me to hear as I approach.

'Hey,' I say.

'Do you know who the dude is standing next to Lynda?' Grace asks, pointing with her head towards the smartly dressed man wearing a flat cap.

'No idea. Why?'

'I dunno. They seem pally. I've never seen him before.'

Good God, is she getting jealous of this guy too?

'I'm sorry, I don't think I know him. Maybe he's an art dealer. Ask Stefan.'

'Fine.' She's about to strut off when I stop her. 'Look, Grace. Is everything okay with Lynda?' I whisper.

'Why shouldn't it be?'

A trickle of annoyance rushes through my body. I pull her aside, away from the group.

'You know why.'

'Not now, Franks.'

'Is she using again, Grace?'

Now it's Grace's turn to avoid my eyes. If there's one thing we both have in common (the only thing we have in common), it's our need to protect Lynda from her addiction to heroin.

'It's not the right time to talk.'

That's all the confirmation I need. 'Uh-huh.' I look around. I don't press further. She's right. It's Lynda's big night.

Grace resembles an awkward teenager as she stomps off towards the canapés, where the street artists collectively known as the Drayton Twins are. I compose myself and step back into the group. I put my arm around Lynda's waist and squeeze. It breaks my heart seeing what a hold the drug has had on her over the years. I'll call her tomorrow so we can chat properly. Not that my chats make a difference when it comes to her reckless decision making. I wish they would.

Everyone in the art world knows about her on/off addiction, but no one ever discusses it openly. Of course, nobody in the art world cares about her drug use, because let's face it, if the artist can produce pieces this good while high, and you so happen to have one hanging on your wall, why would you care? And if, for arguments sake, she dies of an overdose, it's even better. A dead famous artist is much more valuable than a living one. It's the tragic truth in this cut-throat industry. She's a commodity.

But when I look at Lynda, really look at her, I see who she is, hiding behind her art pieces, behind her mask. I see the broken woman I used to know when we were living in bedsits in King's Cross. Lynda's art became her saviour. She'd probably be dead by now if it wasn't for her work.

As would I.

I swipe my murky past from my mind and down the rest of my champagne in one gulp.

The man in the flat cap turns to look me square in the eye. His face is masculine. With his chiselled jawline, stubble and thick brows, he's familiar somehow. I tilt my head, smile politely, trying to place him. He doesn't say anything about having met me before, so I guess that he has one of those faces. He extends his hand and introduces himself simply as Sol. Electricity buzzes through me as we hold hands and I have that strange déjà vu feeling again. His devilish eyes draw me in. Dark, almost black, intense. Dangerous. How does he know Lynda? I want to ask, but I'm tongue-tied.

Silence lingers. I pull my clammy hand away and look to the painting in front of us.

'It's stunning, isn't it?' I blurt, desperate for something to say.

Stefan, Lynda and Sol all turn in unison to look at the oil. What an odd moment.

'You've captured feminism in the modern day brilliantly, Lynda,' Sol says animatedly.

The familiarity I sensed moments earlier disappears. He's just an intense guy.

Stefan delicately takes me by the elbow. 'Let me introduce you to the Habibs. They're a fabulous couple who've recently moved here from Dubai. They're dying to meet you. Farah would like to have some private sessions with you at her house in Kensington,' he says, eager as ever.

'You know I don't do home visits. I don't have the time.'

'I know. I told her, but she's very persistent. She said she could pay a full day's wages. Anyway, let's go and say hello.'

We approach the uber-stylish couple. The Habibs are talking to a Twitch gamer and skits TikToker named Vortex who's young enough to be my son. He looks out of place in his get-up, wearing a baseball cap the wrong way around, vintage Michael Jordan trainers and ridiculously baggy jeans hanging below the bum, revealing his white Calvin Kleins. Yikes. At least his underwear's clean. Up close, he looks even younger than I first anticipated and is pale and spotty. With a kiss of the teeth and a few *you get me, bruvs*, I see he's worked hard trying to shift his public schoolboy image and swapping it for a 'road-man' image. I would put money on the fact that he lives at home with his mum in Chelsea, filming his gaming and skits in the basement.

It's easier for the younger crowd to find fame online. All you need is one post to go viral and that's it, you've made it. Fame at your fast-typing, selfie-taking fingertips. But these successes are fickle. The social media landscape was different when I first qualified as a personal trainer. Back then, I was posting workout videos on YouTube. These videos did okay. I noted an opportunity on Instagram, the 'visual' app, and I soon realised that it was a platform I could sell my exaggerated lifestyle on. And so, I learned how to edit video and styled my posts like an ad campaign. All my content was aimed at the invisible viewer, explaining how I could make *their* lives better, how I could help them achieve *their* goals, give them a taste of what I had. I always made sure I interacted with followers' comments and liked the posts that they shared from my pages. My exercise shorts became popular. By the time I opened my first Pilaga gym, success was inevitable.

The Habibs are delighted to meet me. They talk quickly and loudly, speaking mainly about themselves. These people are next-level rich, billionaires who have everything at their disposal, including people. They tell me about their various properties around the world, numerous classic cars, private jets (not one, but two) and their extensive art collection. They're hiring a celebrity chef to cook for a charity function they want to host in London in a few weeks — maybe I could join them, they say. The couple even invite me to their villa in the south of France for the summer. Vortex is left out in the cold and is being ignored. He mosquitos around us for a while, pulling faces, but soon wanders off to annoy poor Lynda, who is looking frazzled.

The chat is drying out. My face aches from smiling and my feet are killing me from the heels. I'll stay for another hour. It'll give me enough time to work the rest of the room and take a selfie with Lynda so I can post it online. I can't let this fabulous dress go to waste.

* * *

On the taxi ride home, the streetlights give off a sepia glow and dazzle in the snow. The streets look like a deserted movie set and it's unusually quiet for a Friday night. I take the opportunity to upload the best picture I have of Lynda and me onto my story. We're standing in front of the woman with the battered eye and exposed breast. The painting is striking. My dress is on point and Lynda's sporting her 'heroin chic' well, appearing more rock n' roll rather than down and out. The outside world would never know that she's using again. I tag her and say, *Great night, fab show. Congrats, Lynda Smyth.* I'll call her tomorrow.

The likes come flooding in. Refresh. Refresh. Refresh.

I check my messages on Instagram. I don't usually scan them, mainly because I get so much junk mail and a ton of dick pics, but I want to see if Kelsey has sent me a follow-up after our interview.

Waiting for me is one from *@ubitch666.* I would normally delete something like this without giving it the time of day, but I remember the handle from earlier and curiosity gets the better of me. I open it up.

You may have all your followers fooled, but you can't fool me. I know who you really are.
A fake.

I look outside the cab window, trying to convince myself that it's just a bitter person with nothing better to do than to stalk influencers online. But their words run through my mind, *I know who you really are. A fake.* Back on my phone, I click on the user's page and notice that it's a private account. They have no followers and are only following one person — me. I'd have to send a request to check their posts. Coward.

I delete the message. There are so many haters in this world. I catch the taxi driver's glare in his rear-view mirror. I can't quite read his expression. The dazzle from the car headlights on the opposite side of the road illuminate his eyes as he looks at me. Is he scowling? Feeling uncomfortable, I rearrange myself on the seat.

'Everything okay, madam?' the driver asks, sensing my momentary unease.

I clear my throat. 'Yes, thanks.'

'Nearly there.' His voice turns calming and reassuring. The driver indicates left, turns onto Essex Road in Islington. I forget about the message and think about what I'm going to order instead. I'm starving.

I'm dropped off outside my house. My road is quiet, the crescent moon is low and the Christmas decorations on the Georgian houses flicker. I pull my coat tighter around my chest. It's freezing and the snow is turning to black ice under my heels. I teeter up the front steps to my white stucco townhouse, cursing under my breath, hoping I don't slip backwards and fall to my death.

Inside, I peel my shoes off, checking the soles. They're not ruined. In my room, I put them away in their silk bags and place them on the top shelf inside my wardrobe. As I'm getting changed into my nightclothes and ordering a sashimi mix, I think about that troll's message and how easy it would be for a lunatic to locate me. I pull my kimono dressing gown cord tighter and pad over to the window to peer outside. Hiding behind the original shutters, I look across the street. There's no one there. Of course there isn't. I pull away from the window and close the shutters in the bedroom and then go around the entire house making sure all the shutters are closed. Something I wouldn't normally do.

Settling in for the night, I try my best to forget about Lynda. There's no use in worrying. Grace will keep an eye on her tonight. Time fades as I check my likes and comments, scan the people who've interacted with my pictures, seeing what else they've liked and commented on. Comparing other posts to mine. Always comparing, forever. Thankfully there's nothing more from @ubitch666.

I scroll quickly, fingers firing like bullets, swiping from page to page, image to image, my brain processing information like a supercomputer, only stopping for a brief second if something catches my eye, absorbing the image on my phone and moving on to the next.

I check Kelsey's Instagram page. Her follower count has grown. She's posted a new picture. Her bare feet in the sand. Hmm. *Is she copying me?* I flick to a picture of her face and stare at her clear complexion for a while.

When I'm done with socials, I pick up the remote and repeat the same process with my TV, scrolling various viewing platforms I subscribe to. Amazon, Paramount, Apple, Netflix. Flicking through my algorithms and AI 'just for you' recommendations, I notice the latest Netflix series, *The Devil Inside*, has hit the number one slot. It's currently sweeping the nation thanks to a couple of young TikTokers posting about it. The series is low budget with no A-list stars attached, but since the influencers brought awareness to it, it's gone stellar. Such is the power of social media. I take a snapshot of the opening credits and post on my stories with the caption, *Netflix and chill, that's me for the rest of the night.* Maybe I'll watch it after *Love Conquers All*, which is about to start.

The doorbell buzzes.

I approach the window and bend the shutter in half to look outside. There's a shadow leaning against the trunk of the bare tree across the street. I move in closer and squint my eyes for a better look. It's as though they're staring straight at me. I can't make them out properly. Another buzz makes me yelp out loud. My hand goes to my chest. I look to my right and see the delivery guy holding a white plastic bag with food containers inside. My sushi.

'Just a minute,' I shout out loud.

When I look across the road again, the shadow is gone.

CHAPTER FIVE

Bee

I'd arrived at Charlotte's much later than I'd hoped. A plastic Christmas wreath was hanging on her flaky red door in Hackney. Her house was a small Victorian terrace, more shabby than chic, but still nice. Still a home. Pots with dead plants and overgrown weeds lined up in a neat row on the cracked red-and-black path tiles. Her neighbours were playing loud music. I checked the time: 9.45 p.m. She still hadn't responded to my messages. She hadn't even read them.

Hoping for the best, I dropped my bin liners on the snow-covered floor and rang the doorbell. Nothing. I tried the door knocker then the doorbell again. Nothing. When I peeped through the letterbox, it was dark inside with no signs of life.

What the fuck was I going to do if she wasn't home?

I waited, hopping from one foot to the next. Next door's music got louder. I was desperate for a wee. Feeling frantic, I pounded the door with my fist and rang the bell a few more times. Moments later, the light switched on in the hallway and the door opened. Charlotte stood in front of me in stripy pink pyjamas and a frayed dressing gown. She had dark circles under her eyes, a crusty nose and cracked lips. She was holding a ton of used tissues in her hand.

'Surprise!' I thrusted the now wilted flowers in her face.

Charlotte took them without looking. I bit down on my bottom lip, trying not to get cross. They cost me ten quid. Money may not have meant much to her, seeing as she was rolling in it, but it did to me.

'What the—' She coughed without covering her mouth, spewing her lurgies into the air.

As I stepped away, my right foot sank into a puddle of snowy mush. The last thing I needed was to get ill. I had things to do in London.

'What are . . . Why are . . . What are you doing here, Bernadette?'

I winced at the sound of my old name. Letting it slide, I reminded myself that she hadn't read any of my messages yet. She didn't know about the name change. She didn't know that I needed a place to crash.

'I sent a few texts explaining.'

Charlotte felt around in her dressing gown pockets with her free hand. 'I don't know where my phone is. I've got a bad cold and I've been sleeping on the . . . never mind that. What are you doing here? What time is it? What's going on, Bernie?'

'I've decided to visit London and do some Christmas shopping, maybe live here for a bit to see whether I like it or not. You know, things at home, with Mum, well . . . She died recently, didn't she. She died of cancer and it was awful, like. And I had to get away from Folkestone, away from home, and thought maybe a break in London would do me some good. A change of scenery is exactly what I need to help me get over the death and stuff.'

My hand fondled the crumpled letter inside my pocket. I'd hoped she'd understand having a mum that had passed away when she was fourteen.

'That's a lot to take in,' she said, not revealing much of an expression. Not one I could read, anyway.

'I was supposed to stay at my friend's house. Actually, I was supposed to cat-sit while she went skiing,' I lied. 'She let me down at the very last minute, didn't she, as her trip was . . . uhm, it was cancelled for some reason, like. Yeah, the flights were cancelled. And I was planning on staying at hers tonight, you know, to feed her cat and stuff, and I wanted to surprise you tomorrow. I wanted to take you out for a munch and stuff. But she called earlier to tell me she was still in London. Then I thought, seeing as I had my ticket booked anyway, why not surprise you? And, ta dah, here I am.'

Charlotte's brow furrowed.

'I was hoping that I could crash for a night or even two . . . until my mate's place is available, or I find somewhere else to stay. It'll only be a couple of nights. Maybe three max . . . uhm, the most four, if my mate doesn't go away. I'm happy to sleep on the couch, like the last time. I'm sure your sis wouldn't mind. What do you say, Charl? Come on . . . help your old school friend out.' My cheeks burned from all the nervous talk.

As I stood there frozen, waiting for an answer, I tried my hardest to well up for extra effect, but the tears weren't coming. They'd dried up years ago.

'Please. I need a place to stay, like.'

'Okay, Bernadette. I guess you better come in from the snow,' she said. 'Taffy's down south visiting her fella. Maybe you can crash in her room for a couple of nights until you can cat-sit or something. Two nights maximum, okay?'

Good old Charlotte. I knew she wouldn't let me down.

'That would be great. Thanks.'

'No problem, Bernie. Just don't get all weird like the last time, okay?'

33

'Okay.'

Picking up my soaked bin liners, I followed her into the warmth of her home. What did she mean by weird? Weird how? I decided not to press and instead kept my mouth shut, in case she changed her mind.

'By the way, my name is Bee now,' I said, closing the front door behind me. 'Bernadette is dead.'

CHAPTER SIX

Back then

I'd only just turned sixteen when a Romani Gypsy named Maria read my palm. It was at the local fair by the seafront in Folkestone. I'd eaten a bag of chips smothered in vinegar when I spotted a sign outside a traditional caravan decorated in red and brilliant gold saying, *Let Maria predict your future. £10 for tarot and £5 for palm reading.* Inside were Indian-style floor cushions, red velvet curtains pulled back with gold-tassel tiebacks, and lanterns and precious stones of various sizes. It looked exotic and unlike anything I'd ever encountered before. The woman who I assumed was Maria was sitting by a small round table covered in a laced tablecloth. Tarot cards were fanned out on the table next to a crystal ball and a bowl of apples. The whole place reeked of burning incense. Maria's black hair parted in the middle and cascaded down her back. She wore a leather jacket, which I thought was pretty cool. She clicked her black-painted fingernails on the cards, gesturing me to come over. I sat and stared at the rotten apple which was spoiling the rest of the fruit and wondered why she hadn't thrown the bad apple away. She took my hand in hers and turned it over, palm facing up, and stared at it for quite some time, not uttering a single word. I was more worried that my fingers smelled of vinegar than what she was going to say next.

'I see your death. Drowning in the sea,' she croaked.

Pulling my hand away from her tight grip, I stared at her, confused. She'd caught me off guard. I thought she was going to tell me about boyfriends and leaving home and being rich and famous and happy. So very happy.

I looked toward the exit and stood up. Maria held her hand out expectedly, wanting payment. I emptied my pockets and spilled £3.26 onto the table. It was all the money I had left. My hands were now shaking. Shaking from her words. Shaking about what Dotty was going to do when she found out I'd spent all her money on crap. Dotty had given me £10 to buy provisions from the shops and I'd wasted it all on a stupid twister ride and a bag of chips because I was starving and hadn't eaten since yesterday. The rest went on the stupid palm reading. Dotty was going to freak.

And she did. She gave me a good hiding for what I'd done. And for days, weeks, months later, Maria's words haunted me.

I was going to drown in the sea.

Maybe that was for the best.

CHAPTER SEVEN

Bee

It was three in the morning on my second night at Charlotte's, and insomnia had hit me hard. Tossing and turning, I'd had enough of lying in Taffy's uncomfortable bed, so I kicked off her stupid Taylor Swift sheets (I thought she was twenty-one, not twelve) and got up. The heating was blasting through the radiators even though it was the middle of the night, and I was hot and thirsty. I crept downstairs and drank some tap water. Snatching Charlotte's house keys, which were hanging on the key rack in the hallway, I put on the warmest jacket I could find and headed out. Needing to tire myself out, I was desperate to walk Mum out of my system. She'd been playing on my mind.

The sharp air hit me as soon as I stepped outside, as though I'd plunged into an icy lake. I was alert, alive and bursting with excitement. For the first time I could remember, I wasn't feeling burdened or bogged down. No longer did I have Dotty breathing down my neck, watching my every move. This was *freedom*.

I skipped along the pavements making virgin footprints in the snow. The streets were empty, and I didn't pass one single person along my travels. The only thing I saw for a while were a couple of rats near an overturned bin with rubbish spilling out.

Weaving in and out of the cars, I peered into people's houses and kicked snow about, pretending to be in a musical. I was still wearing my pyjamas and regretted not changing. At least Taffy's Ugg boots had good grips. It was getting cold, so I picked up the pace.

There was a place I wanted to visit.

At a crossroads, I checked the directions on my phone. My pulse raced when I approached Highbury and Islington tube station. I turned onto the deserted high street, which twinkled with Christmas lights. It was an affluent area, with fancy restaurants and cafés offering every cuisine imaginable: homeware, furniture and interior design shops with ridiculously overpriced items. Even the charity shops had designer shoes in their displays. A homeless man with a bruised face slept in one of the shop doorways with only a dirty duvet and a cardboard box for shelter. I was in a good mood, so I dug around in Taffy's bomber jacket and pulled out the pound coin I'd found under her bed earlier. I dropped the coin on the floor by the guy's head for him to find when he woke up. I wondered if he didn't have a family anymore either.

A few metres further, I passed another homeless man sleeping on a bench outside the town hall, but I didn't stop for him. I couldn't be giving all my money away when I needed it myself. I counted down the shop numbers until I reached my destination, my chest bursting with anticipation when I spotted the gold business signage in a fancy font up ahead.

Pilaga Gym, the intelligent way to exercise

I approached the glass shopfront and fogged it with my breath, careful not to set off any alarms. The soft lights which were set into the wooden floorboards were still on, making it easy to take a look. It was fancy inside with a dominant white curved reception desk at the front and white leather seating opposite with magazines fanned out on the glass coffee table. From what I could make out, the big exercise studio where Frankie worked was towards the back of the gym. I'd seen loads of pictures of the place on her socials, but it was nothing compared to standing outside and being there in the flesh.

I was overcome with emotion and thought I was going to cry for real.

Pulling my phone out, I flicked onto Frankie's Instagram account and scrolled through a ton of photos until I found one of her standing outside the shop. It was an artistic picture that someone had taken from below looking up, so she looked tall and lean and slightly out of proportion, like she was growing out of the ground. *Who took that photo of her?* I patted my hair flat, then switched to camera so I could snap a selfie of me standing outside to see how it would compare. Hating what I saw, I deleted it immediately. I wasn't exactly the ugliest person alive, but I was no way as pretty or as photogenic as Frankie, and I couldn't take a selfie to save my life.

Maybe she could show me one day soon?

The snow was coming down heavy. I tilted my head back, closed my eyes and stuck my tongue out, catching flakes in my mouth. My teeth felt spiky and were chattering, and my tongue and fingers had numbed. An engine rumbled behind me — a truck spraying grit on the roads in preparation for the next day. Daylight was breaking, so I headed back to Charlotte's.

* * *

A few hours later, Charlotte was shaking me awake.

'Bee. Bee. Guess what? Taffy has managed to get VIP tickets to *Blow Your Mind* at Fabric on Saturday. You're coming, right?'

She was dressed smartly, ready to go back to the advertising agency she worked at. Her cold had disappeared, thanks to yours truly running after her making her lots of tea. Selfishly, she pulled the curtains open, allowing all the light from outside in. The backs of my eyes were grainy from the lack of sleep and I squinted from the brightness in the room. I sat up, rubbing them, feeling groggy and irritable. *This had better be worth my while, Charl!*

'What's Fabric?'

'Only the coolest club in London. What ya say?'

'I dunno . . . maybe.' She woke me up for that?

Charlotte paced the small room, fiddling with her fingers. 'Bee? Have you heard back from your ski friend, the one who wants you to cat-sit? Is she going to go away?'

'Uhm. Not yet, no.'

'Oh. Okay. Okay.'

I straightened up. 'What's wrong?'

'Taffy doesn't know that you've been staying in her room.'

'Does she have to know?'

'I guess she doesn't.'

'So, what's the problem?'

'It's just . . . the last time you stayed. Well, Taffy was a little annoyed with you.'

'For fucks sake.' I rolled my eyes.

'It's not me. It's her. She's convinced you stole her top.'

'Are you still going on about that bloody top? Jesus, Charl. Can't you girls get a life or something?'

'But you didn't take it, did you? You promise you didn't steal her top.'

'I promise, okay?'

'Okay. Okay.'

'Look. If it's going to be a problem, just kick me out of the house, like.' I knew she didn't have it in her and was too soft.

'What? I couldn't. No. I wouldn't.'

I smiled knowingly. What a wimp.

'But you did say you had a friend that needed you to cat-sit. Maybe you can . . .' She stammered. 'You know . . . stay at hers very soon?'

A red fog formed around my tired eyes, blurring my vision slightly. Didn't she know I had no family, no money, no job, no permanent place to live? 'Don't worry, Charlotte. I'll have things figured out by Saturday.'

'Oh. Great. That's great,' she said, relieved. 'I'm heading to Zara in Oxford Street after work to find something to wear for Fabric. Fancy coming along?'

'I'll pass, thanks.' I was so mad, I couldn't even look at her.

Charlotte skipped out of the room like she didn't have a care in the world. Spoiled little brat. She'd changed since her dad won the lottery and she'd moved to London. Before then, she was just a regular skank.

I pulled the duvet over my head and lay back down, burrowing myself under the covers. I wanted to scream. My tummy rumbled, reminding me that I hadn't eaten since yesterday lunchtime. I'd been living off a bag of chips a day. The credit card I'd stolen from Reg, Mum's useless partner, had been disabled and I'd only forty pounds in cash left to my name.

This was not how I imagined London to be. The front door slammed, making the window rattle. I was alone. I kicked the duvet off and punched the pillow as hard as I could.

I will not give up.

Jumping out of bed, I rummaged through Taffy's clothes, trying to look for something smart to wear. Then I ransacked her desk, finding a notepad and pen. I ripped a piece of paper out and wrote *GOALS* as a header. Beneath that, I wrote:

Get a job.
Find somewhere new to live.
Stop myself from belting Charlotte in the face.

I stuffed the paper in the pillowcase and pounded the pillow with my fist once again.

CHAPTER EIGHT

Frankie

Hopeless. Totally hopeless.

'Mia? Can you come here, please?' I yell from the exercise studio.

'Yes?' Mia enters holding a notepad and pen.

Her cheeks are flushed and, oh God, I think she's about to cry. I inhale. I'm not in a great mood this morning. All weekend, Lynda has been ghosting my messages, I haven't slept well and to top it all off, I received another creepy message from my admirer, *@ubitch666*, this time saying, *I'm going to expose you for who you really are.*

Tears form in Mia's eyes. Great! I don't want to start off another Monday with her in floods. Lately, she's been one step behind trying to keep up with the work demands. I know we've become busier, but I thought she would have gotten the hang of her role by now.

'I want to show you something,' I say as delicately as I possibly can, pointing to the dirty shoe marks on the studio floor.

'I have a class in fifteen minutes and this floor's not clean. It should have been washed last night. Not your fault, I know. It's down to the cleaner. However, I do expect you, as per your job description, to notice these things before we open. You should be inspecting all the rooms, making sure they are clean and have all the equipment they need before the day starts.'

Mia looks down at her black studded boots. Obsessed with *Star Wars*, she wears her hair in two buns all the time, like Princess Leia.

'What time did you get in this morning?'

'Eight-thirty,' she says with eyes peeled to the ground, avoiding mine.

'So you had time.'

'I'm sorry.'

I glance at my phone to check the time. There are no messages from Lynda, only Stefan. He's clogged it up with WhatsApps, which I haven't read yet. It's making me panic. I know he wants more, but the idea of being in a stable relationship brings me out in hives. I like my independence. I've always liked it. The day I left home at sixteen, I knew I would never rely on anyone else for happiness again.

'We don't have time to discuss the whens, whys and hows. What we need is a solution,' I say.

'Right.' Her eyes widen with fear.

Mia's not understanding. I wish she would stay off the science fiction long enough to concentrate on real life.

'So, we need the floor cleaned before class begins. And the other rooms checked, pronto.'

'Oh right, yes. I see. Yes. Shall I get the mop?'

Hallelujah. I nod, rolling my eyes. 'Yes, get the mop and a bucket. Fill it with liquid. And hurry, for goodness' sake. The floor also needs to dry before class. We don't want a client slipping and suing us, do we? We only have ten minutes now.'

Mia's incompetence is bugging me. Stefan's messages are bugging me. The fact that Lynda has been ghosting me is bugging me.

Even the stupid Instagram troll is bugging me. I let out a huge sigh as Mia rushes from the room.

Two minutes later, I'm mopping the floor myself with the heating jacked up to the max. I've told Mia to keep the clients outside. My phone buzzes in the pocket of my Pilaga tracksuit bottoms. I fish it out. Stefan's name flashes on the screen. I ignore the call and finish up, handing Mia the bucket and mop to put away, as the clients come in.

'We need a new cleaner,' I say to Mia in the reception area. 'And pronto.'

'Right.'

'That means you need to fire our existing one. Call the cleaning agency and make a complaint. See if they can send someone new tonight. The cleaner must arrive before you leave because you have to run through everything with them. Give them the punch code to the front door.'

Mia's eyes well up.

'Maybe put a notice up on the window, Mia. You never know,' I say softer.

Looking out of the large reception window where there's a fresh blanket of white, I notice a girl leaning up against the glass with her head buried in her phone. I hope she doesn't smear the window, I only had them washed on Friday. Just as I'm staring, she whips her head around and holds my gaze for a split second. She's peculiar looking, with jet-black hair, a long nose and piercing blue eyes ringed with heavy black make-up. A client maybe? I appraise her further. She's wearing a jacket clearly wrong for the weather and dirty Ugg boots. She's not a Pilaga client. A passer-by, perhaps from the Marques Council Estate off Essex Road.

I'm happy to see her go. As she does, she smashes into Stefan, who's racing towards the gym at lightning speed. What the hell has gotten into him? He knows the rules. No mixing business with pleasure. The front door swings open. Stefan's standing in front of me, panting and looking very troubled.

'Frankie. It's urgent.'

'I'm about to do a class . . .'

He takes me away from the hustle and bustle of reception, towards the stairs at the back of the building. 'Have you checked your socials?'

'Haven't had a chance. Why?'

After the message from my mystery stalker, I've been avoiding social media.

'It's Lynda! She took an overdose after the show. Heroin. Somehow it went viral last night. I've been messaging you to let you know.'

'You're kidding, right?' I hold onto the stair railing for support.

'Grace raised the alarm. They'd been at an after-show party Sol hosted. Grace left early. Sol said that he put Lynda in a taxi around one. He said she was fine. Drunk but fine.'

'Sol?'

'You know. Sol. The guy you were talking to at the exhibition.'

The mysterious guy with the flat cap and dark eyes.

'Grace came home to their apartment and went to bed. She woke up to get water and found Lynda slumped on the sofa. Vomit on the floor. Eyes rolled to the back of her head.'

'Holy shit. Is she . . .' I hold my breath. I can't say it. *I can't say it.*

'She's alive. In hospital.'

'Oh, thank God. I have to get to her, see if she's okay.'

Stefan puts his hand out, preventing me from moving. 'I think it's best if you stay away for a little bit. Until the hype dies down.'

'What are you saying? She's my friend, she'll need me. Grace will need me, even though she hates me. They have no family, Stefan.'

'Frankie. Think about it. Your work. Your health brand. This whole ghastly business has gone viral. You can't associate yourself with her. You'll get cancelled. People are getting cancelled for the slightest things these days.'

A lump forms in my throat. Could he be right?

'What about you?' I ask.

'I'll be okay. I sold all of her pieces on Saturday. You know what the art world's like. What's another addict, hey?'

'Sure.' I'm numbed. 'Sure.'

With my shaky hand, I check my last Instagram post. The picture of the two of us at her art show. 3,450 likes.

My head's in a spin. Without thinking, I delete the picture. Maybe I'll wait until she leaves the hospital. She won't be in there for long. She'll understand. Grace will too. I'm sure Lynda will be out by tomorrow and all this nasty online business will blow over. She'll be yesterday's news before long.

My body shakes from the shock. Stefan steps in and before I know it, he's embracing me. I melt into his arms.

Oh Lynda, what have you done?

CHAPTER NINE

Frankie

It's the last Pilaga session of the day and I'm exhausted. Stefan suggested I take the day off, but I couldn't bring myself to. I've had to keep working to stop myself from spiralling about Lynda. It's what I do when I'm troubled — I work and I exercise. My day is coming to an end and I don't want to go home. I don't want to be alone with my thoughts.

The last class is waiting for me to take a selfie with them. I promised I'd take one after the session ended. It's their pay-off for working hard. They're looking toned and sweaty and pumped. The picture will help build up fresh content after deleting the picture of Lynda, filling my pages with health and fitness, so people don't question what I did. A wave of guilt pierces through me when I think about us together on Friday. I can't believe we didn't speak during the event. Or afterwards.

I wish I'd taken the time to hear her out instead of dismissing her when she called me before my interview.

What if she doesn't make it? *What if* . . . I shake my head, dismissing my stupid thoughts.

I flick onto Instagram to take the snapshot and notice another message from *@ubitch666*. This is *not* what I need to be dealing with right now. I should block this idiot right away, but something niggles at me. I find myself opening the message.

I know about your past, bitch. I know what you did. And I'm going to expose you.

Adrenaline courses through my body. On high alert, I look around, confused, paranoid. I re-read the line: *I know what you did.* The class are waiting, yet I find myself frozen. *No, no, no. This is not possible.* It's madness to think that there's someone out there who knows about me and my past life.

I'm overreacting and giving more weight to this nasty troll's words than need be. This person's a nobody, a nutjob, an internet loon that's trying to get a rise out of me. They're probably sending the same message to other influencers at the same time. The message is pretty generic. Most people would be able to relate. Haven't the majority of us made mistakes?

Deep in my gut, I worry that it's not just a nobody.

I delete the message. There! It's over. I don't want to interact with them and encourage whoever it is further. They'll soon get bored and move onto the next person. I flip the phone onto camera and force a smile. 'Huddle close and say cheese, everyone.'

Snap. I post the pic with the caption, *No pain, no gain.* The likes come flooding in. As does a fresh message from *@ubitch666.*

What the . . . They're watching my activity live. The thought sends a chill down my spine. With trepidation, I open the next message.

I'm going to show you what pain really is.

'Holy shit,' I mutter under my breath.

I hurry out of the studio before someone stops to ask some question or other. I don't have the headspace for individual chats and dishing out advice tonight.

The reception area is a hive of clients and practitioners. Mia's tapping on the computer, frowning. She looks up to talk to a woman standing next to her desk, who has their back to me. I ignore them both, especially Mia.

Mentally exhausted, I stand by the window and fire out a message to Stefan asking him to come to mine after he finishes at the gallery. Having company will keep my mind off Lynda. It'll also make me feel safer in the house.

I have the strangest sensation that I'm being watched. Looking out onto the high street, my paranoia peaks. What if this lunatic is following me in real life? I stare out of the shopfront to see if I can spot anyone suspicious hanging around. It can't be that hard to find out where I work. In fact, I've only just posted my location. I mean, I'm pretty much inviting this sort of thing. My tummy knots at the thought.

'See you on Wednesday, Frankie,' says Amanda. 'Maybe we can grab that coffee after the session?'

'I'll check my diary,' I say with a weak smile. 'Until then.'

She leaves the gym with a couple of other regulars, yoga mats under their arms. She's holding her mobile in her hand. I look to see if the screen is on Instagram. I shake my head. I'm being ridiculous.

When I glance out of the window again, I think I spot Stefan's ex-girlfriend Vic standing on the opposite side of the road, phone pressed to her ear. What the hell is she doing in this neck of the woods? She lives in South London. I haven't seen her for nearly a year, so I can't be sure it's her. I inch right up to the window and squint. Is it her? There are hordes of passers-by and it's dark outside. Whoever's pacing the pavement resembles Vic. They have the same mousy hair and are the same height and build, only this woman is wearing glasses. Two red buses, one after the after, crawl past. They come to a halt. Frustrated, I move across the window but can't see anything because the buses are obscuring my view. By the time they pull away, the woman is no longer there. I'm convinced I'm seeing things.

My phone buzzes in my hand, which makes me jump. Stefan.

Be there within the hour. Heard from Grace, Lynda still in coma.

My chest tightens.

The lady standing by Mia at the reception desk spins around. She's much younger than I expected. Peculiar looking with bulging blue eyes, badly applied eyeliner, pimply skin and greasy jet-black hair. She's wearing a thick scarf, a bomber jacket and Ugg boots. It's the girl who was leaning against the window earlier. When she untangles the scarf from around her neck, I clock a pretty heart pendant. Mia puts the receiver down and stands up. She spots me by the window. Damn it.

'Frankie, I wanted to introduce you. This is . . . what's your name again?' Mia asks.

'Bee.' Her voice squeaks out of her like she's a mouse.

'Bee? Just Bee?' Mia asks.

The girl nods. I approach them.

'Frankie. The weirdest thing happened. I put a notice up on our window for a new cleaner and in walks Bee about five minutes later enquiring about the job. Is this serendipity or what?' Mia is beaming.

'What a coincidence,' I say, suspicious. 'Have you worked as a cleaner before? Do you have any references? Come from an agency?'

The girl shakes her head. She looks terrified.

'Is that a no? You don't come from an agency?'

She nods her head.

I stare at Mia trying to communicate with my eyes, wishing she hadn't encouraged this random girl off the streets for the job.

'Have you cleaned before?' I ask.

The girl's pupils dilate. Her heavy black eye make-up is smeared. It does nothing for her pale complexion. Her eyes dart to the exit. She pulls the scarf off her neck and then re-wraps it again. She seems young up close. Something about her innocence is endearing and almost familiar. She reminds me of when I first moved to London. At the age of sixteen, with no real guidance, there wasn't a chance in hell I was going to make the right decisions in life. I had to learn the hard way.

The girl, Bee, or whatever her name is, steps back and clears her throat. 'Yes. Yes, I have cleaned before,' she says. 'If you show me where all your cleaning products are, I can get to work right away.'

Finally, some confidence.

Do I have the time to give this matter much thought? At least Mia has found someone. Am I being stupid here? Should I call the cleaning agency myself? But it's after hours. How on earth will I get someone else at such short notice unless I bloody clean the place myself. Oh, Mia, Mia, Mia!

'Okay, why the hell not? We'll give you a trial for one week. See how you get on. Mia, take down Bee's credentials and go through everything with her. She can start tonight.'

I find a quiet corner to check my Instagram messages again. I'm relieved to find that the only message waiting for me is from Kelsey, the yoga teacher from California, asking for a follow-up live interview.

CHAPTER TEN

Bee

It was her. In the flesh. Standing in front of me. The woman I'd been following on Instagram, TikTok and YouTube for the past six months. The woman who'd posted a picture of herself in a headstand, with the caption, *Look at the world this way.* The woman who'd given me new purpose in life while I watched Mum shrivel up and die. The woman who was everything that Bernadette wasn't, but who Bee could become.

She didn't know who I was yet, but she soon would.

Frankie was only inches away from me, real flesh and blood. Tall and beautiful. A goddess in an electric-pink leotard.

She was so perfect it made me want to lick her face.

Not trusting myself, I stepped back and fiddled with my scarf instead. Frankie's eyes followed me down to my boots and back up again. I held my breath while she worked me out. It was hard to tell what she was thinking because she had an expression I couldn't read. At least she didn't have that normal repulsed look I'd get from strangers, the one of judgement and superiority. In fact, she didn't seem pissed off or angry, nor like I was wasting her time, which I kind of was, seeing as I was standing there unable to string a bloody sentence together. She didn't have that look of indifference either, like I was a nothing. A nobody.

She just stared.

Maybe she was looking at me blankly because she'd asked a question and was waiting for a reply? Fuck. Fuck. Fuck. She *was* waiting for me to answer. My legs were about to snap beneath me, and my mouth had dried out. Typical Bernadette. I hadn't paid the slightest bit of attention to what she'd been saying because I was too busy being a complete moron, acting all starstruck and stuff and hoping she wouldn't judge me.

'Have you cleaned before?'

The scarf around my neck was scratchy. I was sweaty under the collar. Unwrapping the scarf, I scrunched it into a ball, reminding myself that I was Bee now, and Bee could do whatever she wanted, get whatever she wanted, say whatever she wanted. Look how far Bee had come! Frankie was standing in front of *Bee*, talking to *Bee*, interacting with *Bee*, waiting for a fucking answer from *Bee*.

Frankie turned to her assistant and rolled her eyes.

Say something!

I looked down at Frankie's pedicured feet and noticed that she had new varnish on. I opened my mouth and words thankfully formed.

'Great. That's all settled,' Frankie said, flinging her arms in the air, mobile in hand. 'Mia, can you show her the ropes?' She turned and strode across the room, one long leg after the other, leaving me with Princess Leia.

I squeezed my legs together not wanting to wet myself from excitement. I'd never been high before, but I knew that no drug in the world could compare to the emotions I was feeling right at that moment. I'd gotten myself a job. And it was a job at one of Frankie's gyms.

The receptionist sent an email, pressed some buttons on the phone, putting it on voicemail, and shut down the desktop. I felt like I was dreaming as I watched the *Star Wars* screensaver fizzle away, disappearing from sight. Mia glanced at the time on her phone and huffed loudly. If there was a type of person that got under my skin, it was the die-hard sci-fi fans. They reminded me of Reg and his love of *Star Trek.* I bit the inside of my cheek hard as she mumbled under her breath for me to follow her down the stairs to the storeroom.

'This is where all the cleaning stuff is kept.' Mia pointed to some products and a vacuum cleaner in a darkened corner.

The storeroom smelled of damp and was full of Pilaga stock. She leaned against the wall and crossed her arms over her body.

'She likes the whole place spick and span. And as a warning to you, she notices everything, like every single little detail, so you can't get away with sloppiness around here. You'll have to work hard to impress her. Really hard.' Now Mia was away from Frankie, she was coming out of her shell. 'The last cleaner we had was a disaster.'

'Okay.'

'I mean, fair enough, she is the boss and a little bit famous or whatever, but honestly, this place isn't *that* special. She treats it as though it were a palace.'

'Can I take what I need?' I said, looking at the bleach and wood polish.

'Yeah, yeah, go ahead, go ahead, take whatever you want.'

'So is Frankie a control freak?'

Mia flung her head back and laughed hard. 'Let's just say she likes things done her way.'

'Her way or the highway, sort of thing?'

'Exactly.'

'Gotcha.'

'*We have a certain image to uphold, don't you know,*' she said mockingly. 'Mustn't say or do anything that jeopardises the business and her precious Pilaga brand. God, wish she'd lighten up a bit. She takes herself so seriously sometimes. It's a bit much.'

What a traitor. I picked up the bleach and imagined squirting it into Mia's eyes.

'How long have you worked here?'

'Too long.' Mia looked around and whispered, 'Don't tell anyone, but I'm thinking of jacking in the job.'

'Really?'

'Yeah, I've had enough of this place. The pretentious clients. Frankie's pretentious posts. Exercise isn't my thing, you know. It's boring as hell. I'd rather be on the sofa bingeing *Star Wars*, eating popcorn.'

I nodded, like I identified.

'Did you see her post from the other morning?' Mia asks, sticking her finger down her throat pretending to vomit.

'No, I . . .'

Was she crazy to think that I hadn't! Of course I'd seen it, along with thousands of other followers. That morning, Frankie got over 15,000 likes.

'I don't follow her,' I lied.

Her post was flawless. She'd taken a selfie in the morning with no make-up on, her platinum hair un-styled, and she was wearing a golden dressing gown with birds on it. She was standing by her bedroom window with the shutters open and the sunlight streaming in, making her face naturally glow.

She'd captioned the picture, *I see you.*

I see you.

It was as though all her online followers had disappeared and she was talking directly to me. I stared at the post for ages, mesmerised by her face, zooming in on her as much as I could, looking into her clear blue eyes to see if I could work out what she was thinking.

I see you.

It reminded me of the day Mum had caught me in her bedroom rummaging through her jewellery box. I was aimlessly looking for goodness knows what, answers to questions I wasn't even sure about. I'd been so preoccupied, I hadn't realised that she'd entered the room and was staring with her arms crossed. 'I see you,' Mum had said to me.

I see you.

'*I see you*,' Mia laughed, bringing me back to reality. 'What the hell is that supposed to mean?'

I shivered.

Mia pulled herself off the wall and pointed. 'Anyway, there's all the stuff you need to clean with. Please check before you enter the rooms, in case there's a class or a treatment happening. People leave the studio around six thirty, so you can get cracking shortly. We pay eighteen pounds an hour. The whole place shouldn't take you longer than two hours to clean and we need it cleaned every night. No muddy footprints for us to find in the morning, okay? I'll take your details down tomorrow, maybe. I can't be bothered now. I have somewhere to be and I'm running late. What else, what else? Oh, and the punch code for the front door is 12-10-89. Frankie has been meaning to change the digits like forever, but never does because she's always busy.'

The room spun around me.

My hand went to the necklace around my neck that I'd stolen from Mum's jewellery box after she'd died. The same necklace I was eyeing up when she'd caught me red handed that time.

The day she died, I'd crept back into Mum's room to steal the necklace from her. A copy of *Hello* magazine was on her bedside table, a towelling dressing gown hanging on the hook on the door, her slippers by the side of the bed. On the dressing table, her hairbrush had her trademark red hair tangled in the spikes. I pulled some out and balled it into a clump. She'd hated losing her hair after chemo. I sprayed her favourite perfume in the air, and it was as though she was still alive and with me in the room. Next to the hairbrush was the jewellery box. I flipped open the lid. There was £70 in notes inside, which went straight into my pocket. The pretty heart-shaped necklace was underneath. I pulled it out and thumbed it; it felt like real gold. I could pawn it for a bit of cash when I left Folkestone.

I turned it over and noticed an engraving with a date on the back. A date which I didn't recognise.

12.10.89.

I clasped it around my neck and left.

CHAPTER ELEVEN

Frankie

On my way home I ring Grace to check on Lynda. The fact that I haven't visited the hospital or even called is playing on my mind. The guilt gnaws my insides. Now that I'm thinking clearer, I question Stefan's advice. I know he means well, but Lynda's my friend and deep down, I know I should be there for her. The phone rings. I'm about to give up when Grace picks up.

'Yep.' She's curt. Understandable, I guess, but still a shock to hear.

'Is everything okay? Is Lynda—'

'No, it's not fucking okay. My girlfriend's in a coma, fighting for her life. Why haven't you called until now?'

Taking a moment, I bite down on my lip to stop myself reacting. Grace and I have never seen eye to eye, but we've always managed to be civil, for Lynda's sake. I put her hostility down to the stress she's under. 'Stefan only told me this morning and I've been working all day, back to back with classes, so I haven't had the chance.'

The phone goes quiet.

'Grace? Are you there?'

'Yes.'

'What can I do? Tell me.'

'Come and visit. She needs to hear familiar voices,' she says shakily.

I take a pause, thinking about Stefan's warning.

'You know what, Frankie, don't worry about it.'

'Hang on. Give me a chance to explain myself. You don't understand—'

'No, *you* don't understand. I've been watching how you operate around Lynda for quite some time now. How you *all* operate around her. And you want to know what I see? Hmmm? I see parasites. That's what I see, Frankie. You're all users. She may not realise it, but I certainly do.'

I swallow down a lump in my throat. 'That's not fair.'

'You take and take from her and then discard the real person inside,' she says, cutting me off. 'Just as long as she can give you fame, fortune, make you all look good on your socials, give you more followers, status, then that's okay. But when she needs you, you abandon her. You. Stefan. The rest of them.'

Her comments catch me off guard. I don't know what to say to make things right for her. I need to get to the hospital. I've been selfish. I see it now. Stefan's wrong. Grace is right.

'Why did you take Lynda's picture down on your Instagram page? Why? WHY?' she shouts, making my ear ring. 'Why did you replace it with more fucking self-obsessed shit. Pictures of yourself looking happy in your gym gear with your fucking class, looking like you don't have a care in the world. When my girlfriend, your so-called best mate, is lying in a hospital bed about to die.'

'Grace, I promise I didn't mean to upset you . . . I swear, Lynda has been in my thoughts all along.'

'Oh really? So if she's been in your thoughts, why haven't you dropped everything to visit us? Instead, you take down a picture of the two of you together, carry on working like nothing's happened and flaunt it all on social media. Now, if that isn't two fingers up, I don't know what is.'

'I don't know what to say. It's complicated. I haven't been thinking straight. I can see how it looks . . .'

'It's not complicated to me, Frankie. In fact, it's crystal clear.'

'What do you mean?'

'Don't you dare think about visiting. Not now. We don't want you here. We don't need the negative energy. You're toxic.'

'What?'

'We only need true friends. Don't call again. We don't need you. We don't need any of you.'

She drops the call without even a goodbye.

I stare at the dead phone wanting to throw up. I contemplate calling back. I think about jumping into a cab and going straight to the hospital. But what if it makes matters worse for Lynda? Grace is upset and I don't want to make a scene. I'll have to wait until tomorrow. That's what I'll do. I'll wait until the morning when she returns home.

As I near my house, a car honks a couple of times. Stefan gets out of his black BMW. Still shaken by the call, I jog towards him. My jog turns into a run. He runs towards me, and we meet in an embrace. Stefan hugs me tightly and I burrow into his chest, breathing him in, holding back unexpected tears. I pull away and look into his grey eyes. I can't bring myself to tell him what Grace said. It's not his fault. It's my fault for agreeing with him. He was just protecting me. But I should have known better.

'Let's get you inside,' he says.

I fumble with the door key, unlock the door and step inside. Stefan follows. My hands are shaking. My legs are shaking. I'm broken. Grace. Her words have cut me up. She's right. I do use Lynda in some ways. We all do to a certain extent. It's only natural for us to cling onto those that make us feel and look good. We cling on for the good times. Cling on for the likes and follows, letting go of the friendships that become too complicated or problematic, when people become a burden. We say it's because we want to protect our own space and mental health, and sometimes this is true. Sometimes we need to let go of that toxicity for our own sanity. I know this more than most. But is it true all of the time? Lynda doesn't deserve a shitty friend like me.

In the hallway, I turn to look at Stefan and there's instant heat between us. A palpable yearning in his eyes. Without saying a word, Stefan pushes me up against the wall and kisses me urgently. We both fumble with our jackets, taking them off. The intensity in our kiss grows. My hands glide over his chest. He runs his hands over my body and I'm burning from his touch. I want him here and now. He pulls my top off. Huddled together, we make our way to the stairs. I kick my trainers off and wrestle with my clothes. I sit on the step in front of him and unzip his jeans. I pull him down on top of me. With his mouth agape, moaning out loud, his hand travels up my thigh. I'm aching from his touch. He holds my gaze and his eyes flicker mischievously.

'Oh Frankie. Frankie. What are you doing to me?'

He thrusts himself inside of me and my mind empties, melting into the moment. I close my eyes. I'm light-headed, turning to liquid. My hands are under his t-shirt as I tear at the skin on his back. He groans with pleasure.

'Oh, Frankie. I'm going to—'

'Don't stop.'

'But—'

'I don't care.'

He explodes inside of me, making me climax at the same time. Our bodies shudder in unison. I grip onto him tightly, not wanting to let go. He pulls himself out and lies besides me on the steps, pulling his pants and trousers back on, zipping himself up.

He's quiet. I'm quiet. We stare at the ceiling. This is the second time this has happened in the last month. He takes my hand in his and squeezes, like he's reading my thoughts.

'Franks. It'll be fine. It'll all be fine.'

I unhook my hand from his and stand, pulling my clothes back on. I'm being so careless.

'Can I stay the night?' he asks.

I think about Lynda lying on the hospital bed. Grace sitting beside her, holding her hand. I think about being alone in this house with only my thoughts for company. I stare at him sitting on the step. He looks so unsure of himself, so vulnerable.

'I'd like that,' I say, smiling warmly at him.

'Great. That's great,' Stefan says, sitting upright, looking more secure in himself. 'Oh, I forgot to mention . . .'

'Yes?'

'I told Vic about us. It's about time she knew.'

My smile dries up.

CHAPTER TWELVE

Frankie

Stefan's lying next to me in bed, snoring lightly. I've had a fitful night, managing around three hours' sleep, and even that was plagued by my nightmare of drowning. A headache has been creeping in too. Twisting my body around, I stare at Stefan's exposed chest, watching it rise and fall as he sleeps. I look at his soft boyish features and feel his breath on my face. He looks peaceful, handsome. It's weird having him stay overnight; I've never let him before. Am I softening to the idea of being in a relationship?

Blood thumps inside my temples. A twinge of annoyance spreads through me when I think about what happened between us. The unprotected sex. I'm always reckless when I'm most vulnerable.

Daylight's piercing through the shutters. I rub the sleep from my eyes and slip out of bed hoping not to stir him. I take a shower in the main bathroom, not the en-suite. As the cold jets startle me awake, my mind strays to the new message I received in the early hours. *You can't run away from your past forever.* It makes me think about Kelsey and the second interview I have with her this evening. I've got to remain private this time.

God only knows who's watching.

I turn the shower off, sit on the toilet seat and do something I haven't done in a very long time. I check Victoria's Instagram account. Her content is colourful and vibrant, filled with recipes, nutritional tips and detox advice. Her follower count has grown too. I scroll through her posts, like *I'm* the stalker. There's nothing personal, nothing suspicious, nothing jarring, just run-of-the-mill stuff. I realise that I'm being stupid. Paranoid for no reason. Why would Victoria be the one behind my messages? Surely she's over Stefan. Surely she's too busy with her own life to worry about mine. And how would she know about my past, anyway?

I creep back into my bedroom and find Stefan still sleeping, the duvet wrapped around his torso. I pull fresh clothes out of my wardrobe and change in the spare bedroom, deciding to go to the gym. I need to clear my head. Two paracetamol and one black coffee later, my migraine is finally subsiding.

Outside, the winter sun is out and burns the backs of my eyes. I check both ends of the street before I leave. A smartly dressed woman is bundling two kids into the back of her SUV, a couple are powerwalking towards the high street away from me and a man with a French bulldog is crossing the road, heading my way. My body stiffens. The man stops by the lamppost so his dog can wee up against it. He smiles warmly.

I flash a smile back and check my phone to see whether the troll has sent another message. Nothing. My shoulders relax. I need to stop obsessing about this whole stalking business.

* * *

It's nearly the end of the day and my classes have passed in a busy flash. When I enter the reception, I find Mia standing behind her desk, eyes watering and Amanda yelling, arms by her side, clenched fists. There's a small huddle of clients watching their row erupt. I hurry over.

'What's happening?' I look to one woman and then the next, perplexed.

'My bracelet. It's gone. Someone must have taken it,' Amanda snaps. 'And she's trying to tell me I'm mistaken.' She points accusingly.

'Mia?' I turn to her.

'Amanda says that she left her bracelet in the treatment room after her massage last night. But there was nothing there this morning and no one has handed it in.'

'Are you calling me a liar?' Amanda's nostrils flare.

'Amanda, no one is doubting you,' I say.

'Well . . . Actually, I am,' Mia jumps in.

'Mia?'

'Hold on a minute. What happened to "the client's always right"?' Amanda says.

'What happened to "the client is obsessed with Frankie and will find any excuse to get her attention"?' Mia whispers under her breath.

'Excuse me?' Amanda growls.

Someone in the communal area fishes out a phone and points it in our direction. I pray they're not filming the dispute to post online.

'Mia! Please. Stop this. Amanda, I do apologise. It's been a long day and Mia doesn't know what she's saying. Mia, I think you should go home and calm down. I will deal with you in the morning.'

A tearful Mia takes her jacket from the back of the chair and with her head bowed, shuffles past us all. Embarrassed, she mumbles a goodbye and leaves.

'I'm sorry, Amanda. She didn't mean it. She sometimes acts out when she's under pressure.'

'She should be sacked! How dare she question me.'

Inhaling, I say, 'Let me ask the cleaner when she gets in later.'

'Don't you have internal cameras? We can have a look now.'

'I'm afraid I don't.'

Amanda has a point. I should get a better surveillance system at work. A temperamental external camera isn't enough. Come to think about it, I should get a surveillance camera at the house too. I'm too nonchalant about security.

'I don't feel like you're handling the situation appropriately, Frankie. I'm a long-standing customer. I should be your priority. You should have sacked Mia on the spot. You should be compensating me. You should stick to your word when you say something.'

I pull my breath deep into my belly and hold it for a few seconds. Why does she have to be so difficult?

'You're right, Amanda.'

'Of course I am.'

'Can I offer you a complimentary treatment as a way of saying sorry?'

The crowd watching disperse, and the angry energy evaporates. The Chillout Lounge album can now be heard through the speakers.

'And that coffee date?' she pushes.

'Of course. Sure. Coffee next week, I promise.'

Amanda's eyes light up. 'Thanks, Frankie.'

She almost skips out of the gym.

I finish up Mia's last jobs of the day. One by one everyone leaves the gym and I'm alone. My headache's back with a vengeance. There's so much going on in my life, I don't know whether to laugh or cry. After I shut down the desktop, I spin on the office chair, away from the computer, and face the files stacked up on the shelves. I close my eyes and rub my temples with my fingers. I still haven't summoned the courage to call Grace back. I'll call her after my interview but right now I need to focus on Kelsey.

A sudden hand on my shoulder jolts me back in my chair. My eyes spring open, and I swivel around to see the peculiar looking cleaner, Bee, all wide-eyed and awkward, standing by the desk, biting her lip.

'Sorry I scared you,' she says mouse-like.

'That's okay.'

'I've come in a little early because I wanted to drop this bracelet off.'

What a saviour. I can't believe my luck.

'I found it under the reception desk last night when I was washing the floor.'

'Oh, that's strange.'

She hands over the charm bracelet. I stare at the gold charms — a cherub, a horseshoe, the letter A. How did it end up under Mia's desk?

'Thank you so much for bringing it in. That's very decent of you.' Mia had sworn she hadn't taken the bracelet from the treatment room.

'Shall I clean now, or should I wait?'

I place the bracelet on the desk and check my phone for the time. Stefan has sent me a message. I ignore it, swiping it away.

'Yes, of course, that's fine. I have an interview in ten minutes. I'll use the smallest exercise room this time, so you can get cracking.'

'Okay. Thank you.'

Bee scuttles across the room, head bowed, her black hair covering her face.

'How are you finding it?'

'Hey?' She turns to face me, blowing her hair.

'The job. I must say, I found it spotless this morning when I came in. It made for a nice change.'

'Oh, wow, thanks so much. Yeah, it's fine. I mean, yeah, it's great, actually. I love the job. I love being here, like.'

'Oh, good.' I glance at my phone to see another message from Stefan. I hope he doesn't become clingy after his sleepover. It's my fault for encouraging him.

'This place is so cool. It's like . . . I can't describe it. It's like nowhere I've been before. It's all calming and stuff. Makes me relaxed, almost like I don't have any thoughts.'

I can't help but smile. 'Thank you for saying that. You've put me in a more positive frame of mind for the interview. I've been feeling gloomy.'

She smiles back, and I notice a chip in her tooth. I take a moment to look at her properly. Bee takes off her jacket and hangs it over her arm, looks around, avoiding eye contact. Her collarbones are protruding, and her bad clothes are hanging off her. She's skinny as hell. I notice the pretty heart necklace around her neck.

Where does she live and who does she live with? Is she getting enough nutrition in her diet? Her complexion is waxy pale, she has blemishes on her face and dark circles under her eyes. The goth-like make-up makes her look drawn. Her black hair is greasy, and the colour isn't doing her justice. It's draining. She'd be pretty if she put a bit of weight on, ate the right food and got some sunlight on her skin. Perhaps dying her hair a lighter colour would lift her features.

'So, why were you gloomy?' she says. 'If you don't mind me asking.'

'Oh . . .' I sit back into my chair. Bee's quite direct for a person that's painfully shy. I consider my words. 'Someone I've known a while is not in great shape. They're very ill and I'm concerned about them.'

'That's harsh.'

'Yes, it is. I feel like I could do more for them. Be there more.'

'Yeah well, we always feel like we could be doing more.'

Wise words coming from such a young, awkward thing.

'Where are you from, Bee? I can tell you're not from London.'

Her brow furrows. 'Kent.'

I bolt upright and brush my hands down my legs. 'Well, it was nice to chat.'

'You know Kent?'

'No. Not really.'

'I've just moved to London,' she says gingerly.

'Why London?'

'It's complicated.'

This makes me chuckle. When is life not complicated?

'Right, well, I have that interview now. I'll be in exercise room three. Make sure you don't vacuum outside until I finish. And thanks again for handing in the bracelet.'

CHAPTER THIRTEEN

Frankie

I'm not sure whether it's my extreme fatigue or the guilt I'm feeling because I've yet to make contact with Grace, but the interview with Kelsey is the last thing I want to be doing right now. However, it's too late to cancel. I've got one minute left on the clock until we go live.

Turning my camera onto selfie mode, I check my reflection, noting new stress lines on my brow. My palms and pits are sweaty. I roll my shoulders out and say my mantra out loud for what it's worth: *You got to fake it to make it.* I'm not prepared in the slightest. She's already warned me that she'll probe into my past again. Why this fascination, I do not know. However, this time, I'm going to make sure I don't give any personal information away. Especially now I have my very own stalker. It was stupid of me the first time. I'll keep the conversation light and hollow, focus on exercise and lifestyle, like I usually do.

I'm gripping my phone as I count down the seconds. Three. Two. One. And we're live.

'Frankie Fitz. How are you?'

I smile, mirroring her Californian grin, and stare into my phone and beyond. A vulnerability I've not felt before washes over me as a dark thought flits into my mind: *Is my secret troll watching?*

'Frankie?'

'Sorry, yes. I'm a space cadet today. I've been good. Busy as usual. Just finished an excellent class. My students worked extra hard today and I'm very proud of them.'

'Yes, I saw the new post. However, I've noticed that you haven't created much content since we last spoke. Is there a reason?' She maintains a wide grin, teeth gleaming white. She's sitting cross-legged on a beach and the sun is beating down on her.

I hesitate, searching my memory for all the posts I've made recently. There have been a few exercise-related ones. Perhaps Kelsey means that I haven't been spotted out and about.

'Work has been full-on, so my social life has taken a back seat.' The words feel sticky in my mouth.

'Frankie, you know how much we adore your social posts. The last one was at the Lynda Smyth exhibition. How was the event?'

The picture I deleted.

Bee's vacuuming in the distance. Kelsey looks at me expectedly. The phones connecting us disappear and it's as though she's sitting opposite, boring into me. I shake my head. My mind draws blanks. The viewer count stays as it is while she waits for an answer. The people beyond the screen, floating in the ether, wait for an answer.

'What were you wearing at the show? It was a fabulous dress.'

'Umm. It was a Stella number.'

'It looked incredible on you,' she says.

'Thank you.'

'Tell me something. I've heard rumours that Lynda's in hospital. Is this true? All her posts on Instagram have been taken down today. Are you aware? What's the scoop?'

'What? No. I wasn't aware they'd been deleted.'

What the hell?

'You've known Lynda for some time, haven't you? Before either of you were in the public eye. Has she always been into narcs? Even back then? Or is this a new thing? What are your thoughts on heroin? Have you ever seen her get high? Have you ever gotten high yourself?' She broadens her smile.

I swallow a few times, trying to generate saliva, but it's no use, my mouth is desert dry.

'Frankie?' Her expression contorts to exaggerate her confusion. 'Are you okay?'

'What was the question again?' I see a kaleidoscope of colours in front of me as my vision blurs.

'Is there something else going on that we should know about, Frankie? You don't seem yourself today.' She beams. 'Are you *feeling* okay?'

I want to hang up. Screw the views and likes and followers.

'Frankie?'

Images flash in my mind of Lynda lying in the hospital bed, in a coma. How have I not visited her yet? I'm such a coward for not even calling Grace back. The guilt tears me up. I think about how all the bad decisions Lynda's made have led her to this exact point in time — fighting for her life.

I think about heroin. I think about it trickling through my veins.

'Frankie?'

I push my cascading thoughts aside. 'It's terrible what's happened to Lynda. My heart goes out to all her family and friends and I wish her a very speedy recovery.'

She shoots me a stern look. 'Are you two not close?'

It feels like I'm being interrogated by the police rather than a playful yogic guru from California. My jaw tightens.

'Are you trying to distance yourself from her? Is that why you took your last post down?'

Kelsey's getting under my skin. The silent assassin always comes with a smile. Kelsey may look innocent, but I'm quickly realising that she's far from it.

'Lynda and I aren't close.' I swallow.

'I assumed—'

'You assumed wrong,' I jump in. 'I went to her show because I love art and I love her artwork specifically. She is a very talented individual. However, I want to make it clear to all the viewers out there that I do not condone her lifestyle and I do not condone any sort of drug use. I am all about fitness and well-being. Healthy body, healthy mind, healthy spirit.'

'Well, this is a relief to hear.'

Right in front of Kelsey's face, a text message pops up on my screen from Stefan. This time, I don't swipe it away because this time, I can't ignore the message if I tried. The words appear in caps and are screaming at me.

SHE DIDN'T MAKE IT. LYNDA DIED.

'So, Frankie. Let's take some questions from our online viewers. There's lots coming in. Here's one from Joanna in Texas. What's your favourite yoga pose and why?'

She didn't make it. She didn't fucking make it.

My world tips upside down.

'I'm sorry, I have to . . . I need to . . . Please stop. I have to go.'

I cut the interview short and stare at the black screen in my shaky hand. Sandalwood essential oil pumps through the electric burner in the corner of the room. It's supposed to reduce stress and anxiety, rejuvenate the senses. But all I'm experiencing is an icy numbness spreading throughout my body.

I hear the creak of the door. When I look up, I find Bee standing over me. She crouches down. Her perfume is dizzying, floral and cheap. It overrides the sandalwood and scratches the back of my throat. It's so overwhelming, I think I'm about to vomit.

'Are you okay?' Her eyes are soft and kind.

'I don't know. I don't know . . .'

Lynda didn't make it. *She didn't make it.*

I want to be held. Comforted. I want . . . I want . . .

And just like that, Bee cradles me in her arms. I collapse into her and sob.

CHAPTER FOURTEEN

Bee

The situation I was in was blowing my mind.

I'd been watching Frankie's interview through the glass door, when she suddenly dropped her phone and looked shocked. Without thinking, I stepped inside the studio. I headed over to her, crouched down and took her into my arms as she cried. It was a mechanical reaction and felt like the right thing to do. I hadn't a clue how to deal with all that gooey emotional stuff.

Kneeling down beside her, I'd developed pins and needles in both legs, but was too chicken to move. Frankie's head rested on my chest and her spikey hair tickled my neck. Her tears had wet through my t-shirt and I felt a strong heat coming from her body. The whole thing was uncomfortable. The ugly crying, the closeness, the weirdness of it all. I tried my best to hold in my nervous laughter.

Growing up, Mum was never affectionate towards me. I don't know if she knew how to love without wanting something back. There was always a condition to her love. I could count on one hand the amount of times Dotty cuddled and comforted me, like how I'd imagined a real mother would have. She'd give me a few scraps here and there, like rewarding a chained-up dog with a treat.

She never allowed me to express myself either, not in a normal, healthy way; she'd shut me down as soon as she sensed emotion. One time, Dotty found me crying in my room when I was ten.

'What's wrong with you?' she'd asked.

'If Reg wasn't around maybe you'd love me more,' I'd said in between wails. 'Why is he always around? He's not even my dad.'

Dotty sat down on the bed and put her arm around my shoulders, which seemed to immediately calm my hysteria. I looked up and wiped my snotty face. Then I heard the front door slam. Reg was home! She jumped up from the bed; her pretty skirt swished as she stood. I noticed that she had extra make-up on, and her hair was in an up style, not in rollers like it normally was, and she was doused in stinking perfume. She was going out and leaving me alone. The thought brought fresh tears to my eyes.

'Pull yourself together, Bernie Bee. Don't be so wet all the time.' Snot and tears ran down my face. 'Me and Reg are off out. It's date night,' she'd said as an afterthought.

'But what about my dinner?' I'd asked, but she'd already left the room.

In some ways, she was right to tell me to pull myself together. What use was crying? It didn't get you anywhere. It only made you more hopeless, more alone, feeling even more dumb and stupid.

But the Frankie incident was like no other. She mattered to me. She mattered a hell of a lot more than Dotty ever did. I had to somehow make her okay again, and if that meant kneeling on my aching knees and losing the sensation in my legs, then so be it.

She stopped balling and pulled away. 'I'm sorry.' She dried her puffy eyes with the sleeve of her workout top. 'I'm so overwhelmed.'

'What's happened?'

She turned to look at me, eyes bloodshot. 'Lynda . . . umm . . . my friend . . . my very best friend.' Her voice broke. 'She . . .

she died. Lynda, my friend, died. And I wasn't there for her. I wasn't there. *I wasn't there!*'

I placed my hand on her shoulder like how Dotty did that time and patted it a few times to console her. The move felt cringy. I slipped it away and sat on my bum, crossing my dead legs. 'You shouldn't blame yourself for your friend dying, you know.'

'Why do you say that?'

'Well, people die, don't they? They die all the time. Nothing we can do about it, like.'

She sniffed. 'This is true.'

'One minute they're here and the next, gone. It's life. We all gotta go sometime.'

Frankie pulled her legs into her arms and rested her head on her knee. She looked beautiful. 'How does someone so young know so much about death?'

'I'm going through my own stuff right now. Losing someone can be hard. But you get through it. You have no choice. You just gotta.'

'I can't believe I'm never going to see her face again. Hear her voice.'

Sometimes that's not a bad thing. 'Yeah, I guess that's the hardest part. But I promise you, it does get easier. It always gets easier. And one day, your friend will be replaced by a new friend and you'll forget and—'

'I'm not sure I can ever replace Lynda.'

'Oh, I didn't mean it like that. I mean, like . . . you know . . . one day you'll stop thinking about her so much and you'll be surrounded by other friends.'

'It's okay. I know you didn't mean anything negative by it. And of course, you're right.'

She went quiet and stared into my eyes. I'd seen her face a thousand times online before, but up close, she looked different. Softer, less machine-like.

'There's pain in your eyes, Bee. Who's hurt you?'

My lungs felt tight, like I'd been winded. I took a deep breath. 'My mum. She died.'

'I'm so sorry to hear. What was she like?'

I shook my head, no.

'It's okay. You can open up. There'll be no judgement here,' she said.

'I don't know if I can explain. It's complicated.'

'Complicated how?'

'She was sometimes very mean.'

Frankie chuckled under her breath. Her reaction surprised me. Hurt me, even.

'I'm so sorry, Bee. I don't know what's come over me. Your words. You. Something about what you've said reminds me of a certain someone in my past. I don't mean any disrespect by it. Maybe I'm in shock about . . . Lynda . . . and well . . .'

'Who does it remind you of?'

She cleared her throat. 'My own mother. The only person in the world I know that can ruin my day without even being in it.'

Frankie laughed and cried at the same time.

CHAPTER FIFTEEN

Frankie

The conversation comes to a natural end. Bee stands and clutches herself. I don't know what it is about this girl, but she makes me feel comfortable. She's quiet, gentle and non-judgemental. Lynda has the same effect on me. Lynda *had* the same effect.

Guilt and grief forces its way to the forefront of my mind. I could have done more as a friend. I *should* have done more. Lynda was always there for me.

Leaving Bee to finish cleaning, I step out into the crisp evening. There's fresh snow on the ground and the air is icy on my exposed skin. A stiff wind comes in and the cold numbs my brain. I walk the high street and back peering into all the shops. I stare at passers-by Christmas shopping, wondering what their stories are.

Outside the town hall I sit on the bench and open Instagram. My news feed is flooded with pictures of the hottest reality TV couple, Jordano and Angela, who won *Love Conquers All*. I notice my messages on Insta are flagged. Dozens of people have tagged me in their posts and my name is a trending hashtag. Flicking onto the pages that have attached my handle, I read comments from strangers about the interview I cut short with Kelsey and my 'alleged' friendship with Lynda, questioning how well I knew her.

Why did Frankie turn silent during the interview? Is she on drugs? What is she hiding? Did she do heroin with Lynda? Why did she delete the picture of them together? Why did she stop the interview? Was she high?

The posts go on, slagging me off, asking questions, making assumptions and wild accusations. These people don't know me. They understand nothing about me and nothing about the true nature of my friendship with Lynda and what she meant to me. I switch to see whether Kelsey has come to my defence. Her logo is highlighted blue which means she has a new story up. I press to view. Her story says, '*People are strange.*' My stomach muscles clench. She's stoking the fire. I'm sure of it.

Scrolling, searching, reading. Refresh. Refresh. Refresh. There's one particular comment in a long thread which catches me off guard. It's from *@ubitch666*. Somehow, my stalker has managed to screen-grab the shot I took of Lynda and me at the show the night of her overdose before it got deleted and has posted it into a thread. Not only that, they've managed to accumulate thousands of likes within minutes and a wave of nasty comments following.

@FrankiePilaga is a liar. Here's proof of her close friendship with @LyndaSmythArtist.

It makes me want to weep when I look at the picture of the two of us together, the very last time I saw her. On instinct, I check Lynda's page. Kelsey's right. All her pictures have been taken down. Grace must have done that after she passed. Using the hashtag #LyndaSmyth, I check to see what's been said about her. The posts are mostly tributes coming in from the art world with a few comments about her drug addiction. At least that's something.

I flip back onto my page to search for any pictures I have of us together and find a recent one. My finger brushes over a shot of us at her art show in Ilfracombe in the summer. I was her plus-one because Grace was working. We booked our adjoining hotel rooms by the seafront and celebrated with fish and chips on the beach. There's a fresh lump in my throat. I dial Lynda's number and it goes straight to voicemail. Her husky voice plays in my ear.

Hey, thanks for calling, but you know how much I hate chatting. Try a text instead.

I play it over again. Fresh tears appear. I flip back to my messages on Instagram and notice a new message from my troll *@ubitch666.*

Distancing yourself from Lynda proves that you're a nasty piece of work. I know the truth about you and who you really are. Soon enough, the world will know too.

My blood comes to the boil. Before I can stop myself, I fire out a response, my fingers tapping hard against the screen, my pulse thumping in my temples.

You're a sad little nobody. Get a life.

My message goes unread. Coward. In a foul mood, I stomp home, scanning everyone around me. It's dark, and it's hard to take in facial expressions, hard to see who's across the street from me, hard to tell one dodgy looking person from the next. It could be anyone sending the messages. Anyone.

As I head home, memories of Lynda flood my mind. When I first moved to London, we were neighbours, living in a huge house that had been converted into bedsits in King's Cross. It wasn't long before we became close friends, attached to one another like Velcro. A struggling artist, she liked to invite me over when she finished a painting to celebrate.

'What do you think, Franks?'

Lynda propped up the piece, which was almost as tall as her, against the wall. Two women entwined in a naked embrace, fire burning at their feet, crawling up their legs. The painting was vibrant and exotic, bursting with reds, oranges and yellows.

'Wow. You're so expressive. I love the way you have the freedom to let yourself go like that, splattering your soul on a canvas.'

'The painting isn't quite there yet. Another week and it'll be finished. It hasn't got a name. Can you think of one?'

'*Passion and Fire*,' I said.

'*Passion and Fire. Passion and Fire*,' she mulled. 'I like it. Actually, I fucking love it.'

There were three hard knocks on her door. Lynda answered. Standing in the doorway was a man dressed head to toe in Adidas, a cap covering his face. Without saying a word, she stepped back into the room allowing him to enter. He sat on the bed, opened a small wooden box and pulled out a baggie with a brown substance inside. He shook it at me and smiled, revealing crooked yellow teeth.

'Lynda?' I turned to her. She sat down on the bed next to him. 'Lynda? You're scaring me.'

'It's all good. Heroin helps with the creativity. It's not like I'm injecting. It's clean. I smoke it through a pipe.'

The Adidas guy had taken out foil from his wooden box and folded it in half and then half again, making a square.

'Come,' he said, looking up so I got a flash of his eyes. 'Come sit with us and smoke a little ting. Let loose. Set your mind free.'

He emptied a small amount of powder onto the foil and lit beneath it. The powder congealed. It had no odour to it. Lynda leaned over and used a straw to inhale it. She fell back onto the bed and groaned. Her eyes rolled to the back of her head and she rubbed her hands up and down the bedsheets.

I turn onto my road, burying the thorny memory. The streetlights are off and no house lights are on. The whole street is plunged into darkness and is pitch black. There must be a power cut. Feeling unsafe, I hurry along the pavement towards my home. But then, I stop in my tracks when I see a silhouette of someone up ahead. Whoever it is, is coming straight for me.

It's too dark to see properly. I curse under my breath and inch towards them, unsure of myself, unsure of them. The person races towards me. There's no time to think. I want to scream, but my voice gets stuck in my throat. I want to call the police but I'm all fingers and thumbs and can't yank my phone out of my pocket in time. They're so close, now. My hands shake. My heart slams against my chest.

The stranger's standing in front of me. I squeeze my eyes shut, put my hands up to protect my face.

'STOP!' I yell.

'Frankie?'

I flinch.

'Franks, it's me.' Stefan stares back at me. 'Are you okay?'

'I think I'm being stalked,' I say, meeting his gaze.

His face falls. He doesn't ask questions. He doesn't offer reassurance. All he does is take me by the arm to escort me back to my house.

Something about his reaction isn't right.

CHAPTER SIXTEEN

Frankie

We're at the same Italian restaurant we went to on our first official date after Stefan split with Vic. He thought it would be a good idea to get out of the house and go for food to take my mind off Lynda — and the stalker, of course, which he believes is nothing to worry about. He thinks he's helping me. Stefan leads the conversation while I half listen and play with my food. He's chit-chatting about a young artist that popped into his gallery that he's excited about and sees huge potential in. He believes this artist is going to hit the big time and says it's a great opportunity to invest in some of his pieces.

It makes me think back to when Lynda first met him. She was twenty-eight at the time. After her meeting, she came bouncing into the gym, bursting with excitement and fresh promise. She had a new energy about her and looked different too. Lynda didn't waste any time, and got straight to work, even managing to stay clean for a couple of years after that. I always knew she'd shine from that moment onwards.

The restaurant is nice enough with good food and soft, flickering candlelight, giving off a romantic, intimate vibe, but it's not where I want to be. All I want to do is curl up in bed and wish everything away. Stefan's trying his best to keep the mood light. I sip my wine, pushing my porcini risotto around my plate, making little piles with it, feeling more numbed by the second. Nodding at him every so often, while memories of Lynda bombard my brain.

I'm trying not to cry and am annoyed at myself for not insisting on staying home. But I didn't have the energy to fight my case. Stefan had pulled a dress out for me to wear and helped me into the shower, after which, he poured me a large glass of wine while he watched me getting changed and applying make-up. Half an hour later, we were in his car on our way.

The waiter clears the table. Stefan's plate is empty, as though it's been licked clean. My bowl is at least partially empty thanks to him leaning over and eating some of mine. Stefan tops me up with wine, then fishes his reading glasses out of his blazer to read the dessert menu. I'm beat and feeling the fuzzy effects of the Barolo. I want to go home.

'The tiramisu looks great,' he says, lowering the menu and looking at me over his reading glasses. 'Will you have dessert?'

My head is filled with cotton wool and my vision is blurred. I'm not used to drinking, but tonight, I couldn't see any other way to take the edge off things.

'I'll have some of yours,' I say.

'That's nice. I like the idea of sharing, don't you?'

'What do you mean?'

'Sharing our desserts. Our lives . . . We're good together, Franks. You and I. Made for one another.'

I swallow hard. 'Can I ask you something?'

'Anything.'

'Why did you tell Vic about us?'

'Isn't it obvious?'

The quiet murmurings of the diners are becoming a cacophony. Guests are getting more raucous and drunk by the minute.

'I don't want us to be a secret anymore. I don't want to hide anymore.'

'How did she take it?'

'Exactly how I expected. She freaked out. She cried. She said she wanted me back.'

The restaurant spins as I stand. 'I'm going to the bathroom,' I slur.

Swaying unsteadily on my way to the bathroom, I bump into tables in the tightly packed space. In the ladies, I stare at my reflection. I find it hard to focus as I'm now seeing double of everything. The woman next to me applying red lipstick smiles through the mirror. She's wearing a black-and-white chequered shirt, just like Lynda's. I lock myself inside a cubicle, sit on the loo with the lid down and cry.

When I stumble back to my seat, I'm surprised to see someone other than Stefan sitting at our table. Stefan's seat is vacant. I look around to make sure that I haven't got the wrong table, but I find that it's correct. The round table by the window with one tiramisu and two spoons on it.

With caution, I approach. The man stands up and takes off his flat cap to reveal a smooth bald head. Dark, almost black, penetrative eyes. He extends his hand out to me.

'Stefan said you wouldn't mind. He spotted me outside. My apartment's close by.'

I take his hand and my hand fizzes. *What are the chances?*

Sol. The guy from the gallery. The guy who had the party after Lynda's show. The guy who may have been the last person to see Lynda alive.

'Hi. Nice to meet you again,' I say.

I pull my hand away and feel myself change from being fluidly drunk to stiff and alert. We take our seats.

'Where's . . . ?'

'He's gone to the gents.'

Sol's eyes never leave mine. I drain my glass of wine. He's having a weird effect on me. I sense a danger surrounding him, but I can't quite put my finger on it.

Sol looks away, bowing his head. 'Tragic news about Lynda.'

'It is.' I look out of the window at the passers-by. It's snowing.

He places his hand on mine. 'She'll be missed.'

Startled, I turn to look at him, leaving my hand where it is. There's a heat exchanged between us. Instant familiarity somehow. He pulls away and pushes his chair back, crossing one leg over the other.

'Sorry, Sol. Have we met before?'

Remaining silent, he smiles, but it feels fake.

'How do you know Lynda? Weren't you with her the night she—'

'I've known her a very long time.'

'From the art world or from Sheffield, her hometown? How long ago are we talking here? She never mentioned you to me before.'

'I'm surprised you have to ask . . .' he whispers so I hardly hear him.

'Sorry?'

'Why do you want to play this game with me?'

Right at that moment, Stefan appears at the table, smiling like a Cheshire cat.

'Excuse me?' I say, my gut twisting. 'What did you say?'

Sol puts his cap back on. Ignoring my question, he stands, placing both hands in his trouser pockets.

'There he is.' He turns to Stefan. 'Stef, mate. I have to dash. It was lovely to see you. Let's catch up before the funeral.' He looks at me, the intensity in his eyes gone, like nothing's been amiss. 'Frankie, it was a pleasure.' He nods and leaves.

My cheeks flush from the odd encounter. I'm not quite sure if I heard him right. I'm drunk and disorientated, and it's so, so noisy here.

The people sat near us are getting louder. Four women on a night out, very drunk, sharing crude stories about their exes.

Stefan sits. 'Oh, look. The tiramisu has arrived. Yum.'

He takes the spoon and digs into the dessert, taking a huge chunk out of it and stuffing it into his mouth.

'Where do you know him from?'

'Who?' he mumbles, mouth full.

'Sol. That guy. He creeps me out. Who is he?'

He laughs. 'Just a friend. More associate than anything. Visited the gallery one day and we got chatting. We know some of the same people. Seems nice. He's an art collector. Great taste. Money at his disposal, ready to invest in some pieces. A huge fan of Lynda's work.'

'But how did he know Lynda? Were they close?'

'Not sure.'

'Did he not say?'

'Maybe. I can't remember. You know what the art world is like. Aloof. Vague. You want some before I finish it?' He points at the already half-eaten dessert.

'No. I've lost my appetite.'

I grab my bag and stand, feeling unsteady. My hands grip the red-and-white chequered tablecloth.

'Franks, you okay? You've gone pale.'

'I'm sorry. I don't feel well. I need to go home.'

'Waiter? The bill, please.'

'Stefan, I can get an Uber.'

'Nonsense. I don't want you to be on your own right now. We're a team, remember? You and I. We can get through anything if we stick together.'

The word 'together' vibrates in my mushy drunken head.

Are we officially together now?

CHAPTER SEVENTEEN

Back then

It was a scorching Saturday and we'd gone to the beach in Folkestone. It was packed, noisy, full of semi-naked pink bodies caked in thick sun cream. The seagulls were out in droves looking for scraps. That day, I was giddy from the sun, and looking back, I think I may have had heatstroke. We'd had no food apart from a few bags of crisps, which Reg had scoffed pretty much to himself, and one small bottle of warm water to share. The thought of drinking his backwash made my tongue curl. With no siblings or proper sand to play with (stupid beach had annoying pebbles), and with only Reg and Mum for company, it wasn't much fun for a ten-year-old.

Dotty sat on a deckchair wearing an oversized straw hat and a red polka-dot bikini, basking in the attention. She sucked on one cigarette after another using the holder, blowing the smoke into the airless atmosphere. I swear she thought she was living her life in a movie. Reg had passed out on his Manchester United beach towel and was snoring after one too many beers, his skin shining beetroot red. I was getting hotter and hungrier and dizzier by the second. I looked up to the sky into the blinding sun to work out what time it was, like I'd been shown at school. My eyes watered and yellow and orange splotches danced in front of me for a while, which was kind of cool. 'Think of the sun as a clock,' Mrs Fairfax had said. I liked her; she was kind and patient. I'd been watching it all day, creeping from one side of me, then above my head, and finally making its way around to the other side. My eyes stung every time I checked. I thought maybe it was around three o'clock. Surely it was time to pack up and go home?

Reg stirred awake, grumbling under his breath. He rolled over onto his front, squashing a beer can beneath him. I cringed. God, I hated him so much. The number of hours I'd spent daydreaming about ways Reg could drop off the face of the planet. Car crash, being run over by a bus, alien abduction. He pulled himself up to sitting, rubbed his greasy hair, combing it over his bald patch.

He knee-walked towards Dotty. 'Gis a kiss, gorgeous.'

She leaned into him and they had a full-blown kiss in front of everyone. I hoped people didn't think that he was my real dad. Not that I knew who my real dad was. Surely, my real dad *had* to be better than Reg.

'Yuk,' I said as loudly as possible to catch their attention.

They carried on licking each other's mouths, ignoring me like I wasn't alive. I turned away and threw a pebble, watching it land next to a girl across from me. She looked my age. Huddled under a blue-and-white umbrella with her parents and older sister, she was eating a delicious ice cream with sprinkles, her face all pink and happy. My mouth salivated. My tummy rumbled. The girl didn't acknowledge me so I threw another one, trying to catch her attention, but she was too interested in the ice cream now dripping down her arm to notice. How come she had a sister and I didn't?

I looked at Reg and Dotty, who were still at it. Gross. I followed Reg's hand as it crept up my mum's thigh. She giggled and placed her hand on top of his, slapping it playfully. My anger rose into my mouth. Yes, I desperately wanted a sister to play with, but I hoped Mum and Reg didn't make one for me tonight. An imaginary sister would have to do.

'I'm hungry.' I stood, throwing my arms down by my side in defiance. 'I want to go home.'

Dotty turned, judgemental eyes peering from under the hat. She didn't need to say much because her eyes said it all. She could make me go cold from one look. 'Stop acting like a spoiled cow. Look where we've brought you. Now go and play in the sea like a normal child.'

'But I can't swim . . . I hate the water . . .'

'Dotty, you should let me throw her in. Kids learn quicker that way. That's how I learned. That's how all my brothers learned. Our dad threw us in the deep end and let us figure it out.'

'Oh, Reg.' Mum laughed, like he was telling a joke.

I checked Reg to see if he was joking, but he looked normal — cross and mean — and, oh God, I hated him so much, I wanted to punch him in the face.

The boiling pebbles scalded my feet as I ran, zigzagging past crowds, deckchairs, umbrellas and windbreakers, towards the sea. I stood on the edge of the water, as far as I could go, letting the foamy waves crash onto my toes, feeling a little seasick, even though I wasn't on a boat.

In the sea, people swam and splashed about, some kids had armbands and rings around their waists to help them swim. I looked past the bathers, beyond to where the colour had changed from light blue to dark.

Were there monsters under the sea? What would it be like to fall to the bottom and never come back up? What would happen if I drowned and was never found? Would anyone care if I was gone?

Would Mum and Reg even notice?

I closed my eyes and squeezed them tightly. *Take me away. Take me away. TAKE ME AWAY.* The noise around me quietened down as I transported myself to an imaginary place where everything was perfect.

My imaginary sister and I were sitting side by side on the school bus, sporting the same long plait, the same uniform, the same satchel, the same black patent shoes with pretty bows. People always thought we were twins, even though we were two years apart, her being the older one. On the bus, we held hands and spoke in code, adding 'vo' or 've' onto vowels in the middle of words, so 'going to the beach' would become 'govoing tove theve beavech'. Nobody could understand us. My sister and I were best friends and nothing or no one would ever come in between us.

A spray of water on my face shocked me back to reality. I opened my eyes.

Everyone on the beach was staring. Some people laughed. A few kids pointed in my direction. One kid screamed.

I could feel a damp heat spreading between my legs. Dripping down. A pool of yellow by my feet.

I'd wet myself.

CHAPTER EIGHTEEN

Bee

The three of us bypassed the huge queue outside Fabric. I was cursing under my breath as I wobbled along the pavement, trying not to topple over because of my heeled boots. I'd found the pair stuffed under Taffy's bed, right at the back, covered in thick dust. It was a gamble, but I figured that she'd forgotten about them, seeing how they'd been thrown away in such a way. And she obviously had because she didn't even mention them to me.

London life had been good to me. I'd been busy with work and Frankie, and also busy kissing Charlotte's arse so I could keep a roof over my head. In fact, I was so preoccupied, I'd stopped thinking about Mum and my old life in Folkestone all together. But sometimes, she'd slip into my thoughts late at night when I least expected it. It was her way of getting me back, I think. *How dare you have a life of your own without me*, she'd be saying from wherever she was. Probably Hell.

Unlike Mum, Frankie was sweet and considerate. She wasn't even embarrassed about breaking down on me the other day. It was a godsend that Lynda had died and I was there to pick up the pieces just at the right time. Frankie seemed to enjoy my company and I got the impression that she was staying late after work just for our little chats. She'd mainly stuck to the topic of work, sometimes complaining about Mia not doing something right. I'd been itching to mention the bracelet incident, but she never brought it up. She never brought up Lynda either, which was a shame because I wanted the opportunity to practise what I'd read about the best ways to display empathy. Listening without interruption was number one. Good eye contact was number two.

However, yesterday caught me by surprise when out of the blue, Frankie disclosed something personal. This time she told me about her recurring nightmare of drowning, water being a genuine fear of hers. I couldn't quite believe my ears. How could she have the same phobia as me? *Could it be fate?* I was too scared to say anything to her, worried that she'd think I was lying, so I kept my mouth shut and listened, forcing myself to maintain eye contact while she talked.

Life was so good that I'd almost forgotten Taffy was coming home to ruin everything.

'I think you should move out tonight so my sis doesn't find out about the sleeping arrangements,' Charlotte said as soon as she got off the phone to her. 'Do you think you can get your stuff out of her room? Maybe out of the house too? Oh, and while you're at it, do you mind washing her sheets?' Cheeky cow. I wasn't her bloody maid. She was lucky I didn't leave a shit on the bed as a welcome home present.

So, the Taylor Swift sheets were washed and my clothes were repacked in two bin bags, taken out of the house and hidden at the gym, tucked inside two empty cardboard boxes which were labelled 'Pilaga Leotards' (alongside a few extra items from Taffy's wardrobe).

We approached the two bouncers by the ropes, hands clasped in front of them. They looked straight out of *Men in Black*. It was cringy watching Taffy flirt with one of them, fanning the VIP tickets like a slut. Charlotte moaned about the freezing cold, and my teeth were chattering so much they felt like they were about to fall out. One of the bouncers stamped our hands and unhooked the rope to open the barrier. Taffy linked her arm through her sister and entered the club, leaving me two steps behind.

'Come on, Bee,' Charl said as an afterthought.

Instantly, the smell of sweat and beer hit me. The contrast from the cold outside and the heat inside made my skin sting with pain. The club was heaving, the dance music pumped hard and the strobe lights made my vision flicker. People were drinking, snogging in corners, taking selfies and screaming at one another so they could be heard over the irritating music. The girls knew their way round the club, and it was a real hassle keeping up. The floor was sticky, and my heels were already killing me. We dumped our jackets in the cloakroom and headed straight to the toilets. The queue for the ladies snaked outside.

'Do you want some?' Taffy asked.

'What?'

'A line of coke,' she shouted over the rumble of the music.

The thought of losing control made me nervous. I had to remain sober so I could secure a place to sleep. 'I'll get us some drinks first,' I yelled, not sure if I had enough money to buy a round.

'Suit yourself.' Taffy fished a lipstick out of her bag, applying it.

'Get us two vodkas and Red Bull. Make them doubles, Bee. Meet you at the bar on this level,' Charlotte shouted. Not even a please or thank you.

I pushed my way to the rammed bar. People were shoving one another with no idea of personal space, scrambling to be served. I hated every second of being there and wanted to go back to Charlotte's. Problem was, I hadn't figured that part out yet. I ordered two singles — because let's face it, they wouldn't be able to tell the difference — and the cheapest bottled beer for me. They could get drunk on their own stinking money. It didn't take long before they were out of it, heading for the bathroom every so often to top up, while I nursed one beer. At some point, Taffy found her gaggling girlfriends, which made me feel even more pushed out of their clique.

'Taffy, what's going on with . . . you-know-who . . .' One of the slutty girls gestured to me, speaking so loudly that even the people at the other end of the dancefloor could hear.

The more Taffy laughed, the more I tensed.

'Oh, she's my sister's mate from back home.'

'But what's going on with her, though?'

'No, don't . . . I know, I know. What can I do?'

The bitches may have thought they were talking in code, with their quick-fire cocaine sentences, giggling away like a pack of hyenas, but I wasn't a fucking idiot. I got the message loud and clear. *I was the loser no one wanted to hang out with.*

'Charlotte, are you gonna stand there while they all take the piss out of me?' I spat.

'I mean . . .' She shrugged her shoulders, looking at her fucking sister for support.

'I thought you were my friend.'

'I am . . . I was . . . I mean, we haven't been proper friends since I moved to London.' She bunny-eared the word *proper*. 'And now that Taff's back . . .'

My mood had reddened. The angry mist was back. 'Oh, fuck off, then. You and your sister. Fuck off.'

Charlotte was going to pay.

With fists for hands, I stomped to the cloakroom to get my coat before something bad happened. I handed in my ticket to the girl behind the counter. My coat was on the same hanger as Taffy's. I persuaded the girl to give me both jackets. Outside, I rummaged through her pockets hoping to find a key to the house, but no such luck. Annoyed, I threw my old tattered jacket into the bins at the back of the club and wore Taffy's cosy one instead. I left the club in a stinking mood with no idea what I was going to do next.

A plan began to formulate.

It was 2 a.m. when the bus arrived. The queue of people behind me were getting rowdy and impatient as I delayed the bus driver, pretending to be too drunk to find my oyster card. I searched my handbag and swayed for effect. After a while, he took pity, waving me on and allowing me to ride for free along City Road towards Islington.

* * *

Arriving at the gym, I punched in the code and unlocked the door, slipping inside like a cat in the night. My breath fogged inside. The heating was off. My feet were frozen and stung. I slumped on the sofa, unzipped the boots and rubbed my feet, circulating blood back to them.

It wasn't a bulletproof plan, but it was all I had. A guaranteed roof over my head. The gym was closed the next day, as it was Sunday, so I knew I wouldn't be disturbed. I'd be out of there early Monday before anyone would even realise. As far as I was aware, they never checked the external camera unless the alarm triggered.

A treatment bench to sleep on, showers and a toilet, it would have to do.

I took a Pilaga towel and hopped in the shower to warm myself up, after which I made myself a herbal tea and pulled my bin liners out of the storage cupboard into the largest treatment room to settle in for the night. I climbed into my polar bear onesie and polar bear socks and then checked the boiler to see if I could give the radiators a blast, but the thing was too high-tech and complicated to work out.

After I brushed my teeth, I sat on the treatment bench, checking Frankie's socials to see if she'd posted anything new. There was nothing since the interview with Kelsey. However, her name was continuing to trend. Following the hashtag, I read the gossip. The posts were getting more brutal, and she was coming under attack. The cancel mob were out in full force. That fucking Kelsey woman had been piggybacking on all the negative comments. Frankie was being made out to be a drug user. I'd seen it happen to other influencers before — they could be the online darlings one minute and torn apart the next.

Frankie would need a good friend to get through all the turmoil.

I read every single comment, then read them again, until I tired.

Switching off my phone off, I lay on the bench and drifted. It was the best night's sleep I'd had since Mum died.

CHAPTER NINETEEN

Bee

I heard a voice. A woman's voice.

'What's going on?' she asked, her feathery tone echoing in my mind.

I knew that voice. I knew it well.

It was her.

She'd come to me in my sleep. Deeper and deeper I slipped into my dream. She was standing in front of me, her blue eyes sparkling like the sea. She was so beautiful.

I always knew that one day we'd be reunited. I always knew she was out there somewhere. I always knew that I'd find her.

My sister.

The sister I longed to have. The sister I always imagined I'd find.

The woman spoke again, plucking me from the depths of my heaviness. I was lost, somewhere in between waking and sleeping.

'I SAID, WHAT THE FUCK IS GOING ON?'

Why was she angry? It was a dream, I told myself, and dreams were meant to be weird. I fell back into the void, ignoring her.

'Get up!'

Hands were on me, shaking me awake.

The fog in my brain cleared as I started to recall. I remembered the night before. I remembered the club. I remembered that Charlotte and Taffy were bitches. Their friends too. I remembered the cold night. I remembered the smelly night bus. I remembered punching in the code for the gym, my fingertips and feet frozen. I remembered taking my boots off. I remembered lying down and falling asleep on the treatment bench. At the gym!

At Frankie's gym. Holy shit.

'WAKE UP!'

My eyes sprang open. It took a while for my blurry vision to come back.

I wasn't dreaming anymore; I was in full-blown reality and Frankie was standing over me with her hands on her hips. She looked pissed. Totally pissed.

'Well? What do you have to say for yourself?' She tapped her trainer on the floor.

My brain was still half asleep and I couldn't come up with an excuse quick enough. I kicked off the scratchy blankets and sat on the edge of the treatment bed, rubbing my eyes and kicking my legs.

'Well?' Her eyes followed me up and down, then looked around the room. She was piecing the clues together. My clothes were scattered all over the floor. My toothbrush was in the sink. I was wearing frigging pyjamas with polar bear motifs on them, for God's sake.

'I, umm . . .'

'I'm waiting, Bee. What are you doing sleeping at my gym?'

Frankie said she never worked on Sundays.

'Answer me!'

'I'm homeless.' I was so embarrassed, so ashamed; I couldn't even look at her.

'Excuse me?' Her voice broke. 'But I thought you said you had a friend who was away skiing, and you were cat-sitting and that you had things lined up.'

'I know. But . . .'

'So that wasn't the truth?'

'I'm sorry. I'm not cat-sitting.'

'You lied to me.'

'Not exactly. I do have a friend in London, but she turned out to be spineless and I got kicked out of her house because her slutty sister who hates me turned up. I had nowhere else to go. And I didn't want to go back to Folkestone, because you see, Mum, she died and that, and my stepdad, well, he hates my guts.'

'Haven't you got any other friends in London? Any other family members?'

I shrugged my shoulders as I focused on a long black hair on the floor.

'How long have you been sleeping at—.'

'I promise it was only last night. One night, that's all. Before then, I was staying at my friend's house, that bit's true, and she did chuck me out last night. It was so late. We'd been out clubbing. And I was hoping they'd let me stay another night. But they didn't even ask me. It was either stay here or sleep in the freezing cold.'

She paced the room, scratching her head.

'It was just for one night. I swear, like.'

'Bee, I'm sorry . . .'

My toes curled.

'I'm sorry, Bee . . . I am.'

'Fine. Whatever. Just give me some space so I can get changed and get my stuff together. Don't worry, I'll be out of your way before you know it.'

'I mean . . . surely you can find a better place to stay. Can you not go back home?'

I scoffed. 'Did you want to move back home after you ran away?'

Frankie's hand went to her neck. 'How do you know about my past?'

Think fast. 'Mia.'

'Mia?'

'She told me about what you'd said in your interview with Kelsey the other day.'

'I see.' Frankie crossed her arms over her chest.

'Well, since you're gonna send me packing, I might as well let you know that Mia doesn't have many nice things to say about you. In fact, she slags you off all the time, like. And I'm the one sticking up for you. Me. I've also got proof that she lies and is a thief.'

'What do you mean?'

'The day I handed in the bracelet, I saw her take it from the treatment room and stuff it into her desk drawer. She was going to steal it, but I took it before she had a chance and gave it to you. I didn't find it under the desk, like I said, it was actually in the drawer. I didn't tell you because I didn't want her getting the sack.'

Frankie's mouth opened.

'Can't you see that you've got the wrong people surrounding you? Can you trust her? I know I fucked up here, like, but you've got to believe me, I had nowhere else to stay. That's the honest truth. It was only going to be for one night, I swear. I'd swear on my mum's life if she were alive.'

She rubbed her forehead.

'You know you can trust me, because I handed in the bracelet, not Mia. Me.'

'Bee, I'm sorry your situation is so terrible.' Her voice had softened.

If she cared, she'd give me a break. If she was different from Dotty, she'd give me a chance. She paced the room, looking lost in thought.

She had to forgive me. She had to. We were the same, after all. Me and her.

Sisters.

'I'm afraid this isn't my problem. You're not my responsibility. I can't help you, Bee.'

And just like that, I'd gone from being a somebody to becoming a nobody.

CHAPTER TWENTY

Frankie

I fire up the computer for something to do while I wait for Bee to pack her things and go. I can't believe what's happened. If it wasn't for my insomnia and my worries, I would have stayed at home. But I came to the gym to do a hard workout. So much for the stress release. I stare at the bookings system on the screen, conflicted. In some ways, I wished I hadn't caught her. Ignorance can sometimes be bliss.

Ten minutes later she's dragging two filled bin liners across the reception floor, heading for the exit.

'I guess this is goodbye,' she says, hesitant.

Bee's greasy hair falls in front of her face. Her stomach growls.

'It was nice knowing you, Frankie.' She opens the door.

'For fuck's sake,' I mutter under my breath. 'Wait, Bee. Wait.'

She looks my way, blowing hair from her eyes. Yesterday's make-up has run down her face. She's been crying.

'I can't let you leave. You're so young. You don't know the nasty side of London. There are so many dangers out there. People who prey on vulnerable women.'

'I'm a big girl. I can take care of myself.' She opens the door wider but doesn't move.

'Look . . .' I stand, running my hands down my leggings. 'What?'

'I know this is a crazy idea. I'd like to help you out, just for a couple of days until you find your feet again. Everyone deserves a second chance no matter who they are and what they've done.'

I'm not sure if the outpouring of guilt I'm feeling stems from Lynda's death and somehow by giving Bee a chance, I can redeem myself for all my wrong doings, or if there's something about Bee that reminds me of when I was younger.

'What are you saying?' she asks.

I draw in a breath. 'You can stay at mine. Two nights max, okay? You have to promise me that you'll use the time wisely and find a place to live. You can keep your job here as well, so you have some money coming in. But I'm warning you, one more mess-up and you're out on your own.'

Her mouth drops open and she's nodding. Her reaction makes me smile and fills me with hope.

'Don't let me down.'

'I . . . I don't know what to say.'

'Say that you won't let me down.'

'I promise I won't let you down.'

'I guess I better take you home, maybe get you something to eat on the way. But first, why don't you take a Pilaga gym bag from the shop and fill it with the essentials you need for two days. Leave the rest of your stuff in the storage room.'

'Sure. Okay. Wow. Thank you. God, thank you so much. I don't know what to say, or how I'll ever repay you, like.'

'Remember: actions speak louder than words, Bee. All you have to do is prove to me that you'll make the most of this opportunity.'

'Oh, I will. Don't you worry about that. I definitely will.'

* * *

We head to my favourite café so she can get something to eat. She's two paces behind, struggling to keep up with my strides. When we arrive, Bee takes her coat off and looks skin and bone underneath, like she hasn't eaten a decent meal in weeks. At the counter, she's hesitant about ordering. I guess she doesn't know what half the stuff they're serving up is. It's endearing. I remember being in the same predicament, baffled when I first went to a fancy restaurant, not understanding half the ingredients on the posh menu. She chooses a plain cheese baguette and we head back to mine. She's nervous and chats non-stop while she munches on her food. With every mumbled sentence there's either a 'thank you' or a 'sorry' or 'I'm so grateful' at the end. I pray she'll run out of steam soon and isn't this talkative at home because she'll drive me insane.

'I'm going to make a call,' I say, pulling my phone out. That'll shut her up.

I ring Grace for the umpteenth time. There's no doubt she's ghosting me now. The phone rings out and I leave another voicemail. She'll have to face me sooner or later. The funeral is next week.

I need to squash this whole Lynda saga and put a statement out denouncing drug use, but I've yet to summon the courage. Deep down, I was hoping the story would fade away, but it hasn't. In fact, it's picked up momentum. I worry that if I put something out online, someone from my past will come out of the woodwork.

It makes me think about my stalker's latest message. *I'm coming for you.* Yesterday, I blocked *@ubitch666*, something I should have done a long time ago.

'This is us, up ahead,' I say, turning onto my street.

'Wow. What a beautiful neighbourhood.'

'Thank you.'

'Have you been living here long?'

'About six years.'

'Are you sure it's okay for me to crash at yours?' she presses.

'Yes. Yes. For the millionth time, yes. Now, don't ask me again unless you want me to change my mind.'

'Sorry.'

'And for goodness' sake, stop saying sorry.'

'Okay, sorry.' Bee looks at me apologetically. 'I mean, sorry about saying sorry. And thanks again for taking me in.'

'Stop thanking me. It's driving me nuts.'

'Okay. Sorry.'

A smile creeps across my face, I can't help it. The girl is hopeless for sure.

The snow is melting. My neighbour's cat Pickle prowls across the street, taking her time. Black and elegant, I watch her as she springs up on a wall and walks across it, like she's expertly treading a tight rope. My eyes follow the road ahead and I notice a figure climbing the steps to my house. I scrape my hand through my hair. It's hard to tell who it is. All I can see is a man smartly dressed from behind. He's too smart to be a delivery guy and there's no van in sight. He rings the doorbell. As I slow down I almost bump into Bee behind me.

'Everything okay?'

'Ssssh.' I linger outside number 23.

Stefan answers my door. I check the time on my phone: 11.20 a.m. What's he still doing at mine?

As we approach, unfamiliar smells waft from my house. Cooking smells my home isn't used to. Comfort smells like onions and garlic. Now it's my stomach's turn to grumble. The mystery man standing on my doorstep has his back to me and Stefan hasn't spotted me yet. The pair are in deep conversation. Bee hovers behind me.

'Stefan?' I ask, climbing the steps to my front door.

'Oh. Hi, babe.'

Babe? Since when was I his babe? I try to supress my mounting irritation. The smart man whips round so we're facing one another. A pulse of adrenaline rushes through me.

First the gallery. Then the restaurant. And now my home!

Sol.

A darkness creeps from his eyes as he glares in my direction, unsmiling. A chill runs down my spine.

Who is this guy?

CHAPTER TWENTY-ONE

Frankie

'Frankie, you remember Sol?'

'Umm. Yes, I . . .'

'I hope you don't mind but I've invited him round to take a look at Lynda's *Passion and Fire* painting on your wall. He's keen to collect some of her earlier pieces.'

Stefan's left me speechless. Is making money off dead artists the only thing he cares about? I stare at him, giving him my widest eyes to quietly demonstrate how furious I am. How dare he assume I'd want to sell Lynda's artwork. And how dare he invite this man, this stranger, into my home when I'm not around.

'Stefan, she's only just—'

'I understand,' he butts in, head bowed. 'But Sol wanted to take a look and I thought it was worth exploring, just in case.'

I try my best to reign in my anger.

'I did try to call you,' he says breezily.

Glancing at my phone, I do notice three missed calls, but they were made in the last five minutes. My jaw tightens.

'I'm afraid I'm not in the market for selling anything of Lynda's. It's all I have left of hers and I can't imagine parting with it.' A lump appears in my throat at the thought.

Sol stands back and puts his hands inside his jacket pockets. 'That's a shame,' he says, holding my gaze, producing what I can only describe as a fake smile.

His insensitivity rubs me up the wrong way. I can't tell whether he's being genuine or sarcastic, whether he's deliberately trying to press my buttons.

I'm so mad at the pair of them, I find myself barging past them to get inside my house, making a point. Once in my hallway, I turn around to face everyone. All three are staring back at me. Bee looks mortified. Stefan's frowning. Sol, whose expression I can't quite read, catches my eye again and holds me there. My body has a mind of its own and reacts, fizzing as though a bolt of electricity is passing through it. I breathe deeply to steady my nerves.

'Sorry, Sol, but have we met before?'

'Lynda's show,' he says with another sly smile. 'Oh, and the restaurant,' he adds.

He's trying to be cute. 'No, I mean in another life?'

He laughs. 'I'm not too hot on my past lives, I'm afraid.'

'A bit of a coincidence that you've come onto the scene just as Lynda passed away, don't you think?'

Stefan shoots me a look, but I ignore him.

'An unfortunate accident, you could say,' Sol says.

'Is it?'

'Is it, what?'

'An accident.'

'Excuse me?'

'And now you want to buy her painting?'

Stefan approaches, resting his hand on my shoulder. He leans in and whispers, 'What's going on?'

He pulls back. I chew my lip as the silence envelopes around us.

My instincts are haywire. I've no idea what I'm insinuating. Why would he have something to do with Lynda passing? Just because he hosted the party the night she overdosed. I assess Sol's smooth features. He looks as confused as I feel. Bee's in my periphery, shrinking into herself, looking like a frightened mouse.

I'm suddenly aware that I'm standing in my doorway with tight fists for hands not saying a word, wondering if Sol's going to volunteer any information about himself to me.

'Franks, everything okay?' Stefan says.

'Yes, fine,' I exhale. 'I wished you'd warned me that Sol was coming over, that's all,' I say quietly.

'I didn't think it would be an issue, and I did try to call.'

'Next time, please check in with me before arranging.'

Stefan nods. He's doing what he does best — trying to sell art. My anger towards Stefan subsides, but I'm still wary of Sol and what his true intentions are. I haven't quite worked him out yet.

Bee is stiff and awkward. Poor girl's probably regretting coming along with me. I feel bad for dragging her to my home and creating a situation.

'Where are my manners? Stefan, Sol, this is Bee. She works for me. She's my cleaner. She's going to be staying here for a couple of days.'

It's Stefan's turn to look bemused. Sol turns to Bee and offers his hand out to her. He's gentlemanly and polite, which puts me more at ease. Stefan says hi, then turns to me, looking for answers. I keep him hanging; I'm not obliged to explain to him or anyone else what I do. It's my life. My home. Bee squeaks hello to them both.

A strong wind sweeps past, making me shiver. It's freezing standing in the doorway. I want to go into the warmth of my home. The comfort smells are drawing me inside.

'Well, I guess you should all come in from the cold. Sol, I'm not selling the art piece, but do come in and take a look. It's striking.'

What do they say, keep your friends close and your enemies closer? I need to work this guy out.

They follow me into the basement kitchen, which is filled with aromas of home cooking and where Lynda's early artwork takes centre stage next to the dining table.

All of us can't help but stop and stare at it. It's haunting and I feel her essence all around me. I'd never part with it.

* * *

I've no idea how this has come about, but all four of us are sat around my large dining table, which hardly gets used, about to tuck into the roast Stefan has been cooking since the morning. That's what the smells permeating from my house have been. A relaxing jazz album plays from my Bluetooth speakers, Sol uncorks the second bottle of red, while Stefan talks about the gravy he's made using a whole bottle of Burgundy. It isn't technically a gravy, he informs us, but a jus. He picks up the gravy boat and pours the glistening sauce over my beef. The smell is an intense mixture of wine, herbs and rich stock, and hits my empty stomach. I move my hands onto my lap, licking my lips as he pours. I'm not sure whether he's trying to gain brownie points because he invited Sol to join us for lunch, putting me on the spot, or whether he's always been this charming and I've never noticed, but whatever Stefan's doing, he's certainly winning me over.

The more I ease into the afternoon, the more my suspicions about Sol disappear and my other worries evaporate. Earlier on, when we were all talking about Lynda's painting, I slipped out to the bathroom to google him and couldn't find anything incriminating. Sol's just intense, a philosopher of sorts, choosing his words carefully. He's thoughtful and serious.

It's been soothing to watch Stefan work the kitchen and seeing all four hobs on my range being used, pans bubbling away, and witnessing my spotless oven being used for the first time. It makes a change from the sound of the doorbell going as my Uber Eats arrives. My home feels full for the first time. It makes me think of the upcoming Christmas period. I consider putting up decorations, something I don't normally do, seeing as I'm usually alone during the holiday season.

I smile to myself, thinking I should be more spontaneous. I've been controlled in many areas of my life and maybe I've been missing out on all the fun.

I savour my surroundings. The table is the perfect setting for an Instagram shot. The appetising plates of food, the over-sized lit candles which were gifted to me two years ago and have never been used, and the empty crystal decanter with remnants of sediment at the bottom. Even though I'm tempted to snap a photo and post, I stop myself. That would only fuel my online haters. It would also upset Grace. Stefan pulls up his chair and sits down next to me. Perhaps I can take one for myself? I want to remember this moment. When I pick my phone back up, I sense the intensity of Bee's stare. I catch her gaze and she recoils into her seat, her hair falls in front of her face. Even though she's relaxed a little, she doesn't like to talk much in a group, unless she's asked a question. I don't want to make her uncomfortable, so I put my phone away, out of sight.

'It is beautiful,' says Sol.

We all turn to him. Sol's admiring Lynda's painting on the wall to his left. 'It captures the essence of her, don't you think, Frankie?' My name sounds silky on his tongue.

'Lynda painted this piece when we first met. She gave it to me as a present to congratulate me on the opening of my first studio in Islington.'

'I can't lure you with a ridiculous amount of hard cash for it, can I?'

'I'm afraid not.'

He pushes his plate away, even though it's pretty full. With his elbows on the table, he folds his hands together pensively. 'Tell me about your life with Lynda when you first met. I'm intrigued.'

'Do you really want to hear boring stories about our youth?'

'I would!' Stefan butts in eagerly.

I pick up my wine glass and take a sip. 'I'm not sure there's much to disclose,' I say as casually as possible.

'You lived in King's Cross together, didn't you?' Sol says, winking at me.

What the . . . Did Lynda tell him we lived together? I drain my glass.

'Steady on, Franks,' Stefan says.

'It was King's Cross, wasn't it?' Sol presses.

An overwhelming sensation of being trapped with nowhere to run overtakes me and my survival mode kicks in. I can't tell whether the danger I'm feeling is real or imagined. I force my shoulders down.

'I, umm . . . Well, yes. I lived there for a while. We were . . .' I grumble under my breath, looking anywhere but him.

All eyes are on me. They're watching. Assessing. Waiting for me to continue.

Just act normal, Frankie. He's only asking about where I lived! Nothing more. *Nothing more.*

'We were neighbours,' I finally say. 'Stefan, can you pour me some more?'

'Do you remember the tiny corridors? The carpets were shitty and there was rising damp on the walls . . .'

My shoulders rise back up.

Who the fuck is this guy?

'. . . and the tenants were either playing awful house music or were having noisy sex. It was such a dive.' He belly-laughs.

116

'Honestly, each time I came I felt like I was in a horror movie. Not a nice place at all. How long did you live there for?'

A whimper escapes from my mouth.

'Good grief. I had no idea it was *that* bad. Frankie never talks about her past with Lynda. Sounds horrendous. Poor Franks. And poor Lynda,' Stefan says, pouring more wine.

My heart's beating like a drum. I place my napkin on the table. Voices muffle. Faces blur.

'If you'll excuse me, I need to go to the bathroom. I'm a little nauseous.'

'Too much wine?' Stefan asks.

I stumble out of the kitchen and lock myself in my en-suite bathroom. I vomit up all the food and wine.

Good God, is Sol from my past?

The thought makes my head spin. I throw up again.

CHAPTER TWENTY-TWO

Bee

The playlist had ended and there was a tense quiet in the room, pressing down from the ceiling. Frankie was taking her time in the bathroom upstairs. After a painful ten minutes spent with Stefan and Sol making small talk, I offered to check in on her to make sure she was alright, but Stefan put his hand out, physically stopping me. He said that he should be the one to see if she was okay, not her 'cleaner'. He spat the word out like it was dirty. It made me burn with fury. Before I could tell him that I was more than just a cleaner to Frankie and slap his pretty-boy face, he'd left the room, leaving me alone with Sol — another creep. I sat back down and prayed that Frankie would hurry the fuck up.

The afternoon was going from bad to worse. Creepy Sol tapped his fingers on the table, not hiding the fact that he was fed up, bored, irritated — exactly the way I felt. What set my mood off from the beginning was the whole Frankie–Stefan thing, which took me by surprise, and if there was one thing I hated most in life, it was surprises. How was I supposed to know that she was in a relationship with someone and that someone happened to be a complete and utter arse-licker. She hadn't posted any pictures of them together on her socials. Frankie could have at least warned me about him on the way to hers. I thought we were supposed to be good friends now. All day, I was forced to watch him slobbering all over her like some desperate puppy stealing her attention away. It made me sick to the core. I wanted to strangle him with his brown crocodile belt.

R&B music played out of nowhere. Sol stood, fishing his phone out of his pocket. *That was his ringtone?* He approached the patio overlooking the courtyard and flung the glass doors apart. A cold breeze swept through the room. Standing half in, half out, he answered.

'Yes, bruv . . . Nice . . . Nice . . . Where she from? . . . Cool . . . And the gear? Did dat thing come through? . . . Cool, cool . . . Listen, bruv,' he said, turning to me, noticing I was listening, 'can't chat now. Catch ya laters, yeah?'

Sol terminated the call.

He was a fake. A total, utter fake. No self-respecting middle-class art dealer would ever use language like that. Was he even an art collector? Beneath the gentleman's get-up, posh accent and expensive watch, he was like me, common as fuck. I wondered what his connection with Lynda was — more importantly, his connection to Frankie. She seemed rattled when he talked about King's Cross. Her place sounded like a real dive.

He may have had Stefan and Frankie fooled, but not me. All that talk of girls and gear. Sol didn't sound like he belonged in the art world to me. I'd been watching him all afternoon, seeing the way he manipulated the room. The way he asked questions, too many questions, like he already knew the answers and was just waiting for someone to trip up. All afternoon he'd been snooping around me, hovering like a fly over shit. 'How long have you been working with Frankie for?' 'Have you always been a cleaner?' 'What did you do before this job?' 'Where are you from?' I'd been returning his questions with one-word answers. Eventually, he got the hint.

Now that we were alone, I decided it was my turn to ask a few questions of my own.

'So, you're an art dealer, huh?'

He huffed. 'Yes, among other things,' he said deadpan, his fake posh accent back.

'Other things such as?'

'You ask a lot of questions.'

'So do you.'

'Touché.'

Sol pulled a cigarette packet out from the inside of his blazer.

'Can you keep a secret?' He winked, making me cringe inside.

'I can.'

He lit up, blowing the smoke out into the paved garden. 'Would you like one?'

'No, thanks. I gave up a while ago.'

'A while ago?' He laughed hard. 'Were you fifteen when you gave up?'

I ignored his question. 'So why do you want that painting so bad? What's so special about it? Doesn't look that good to me.'

'Wouldn't you like to know?'

'That's why I'm asking, like.'

'You're an inquisitive little so and so, aren't you?'

'Are you gonna answer the question or what?'

He dragged on the cigarette and blew the smoke outside. 'Let's just say, it's something I believe should be mine.' He winked again. 'Now tell me, how has a cleaner landed herself a place to stay in one of London's finest neighbourhoods? What did you do to convince her? Maybe I need to take some tips from you. You're clearly gifted in the art of persuasion.'

I pursed my lips shut.

Raised voices from upstairs changed the focus in the room. Stefan and Frankie were rowing. Sol flicked his cigarette onto the spotless grey tiles in the courtyard and closed the patio. I stared at the burning tip, straining to listen to the escalating argument upstairs.

'Oh dear. Trouble in paradise.' Sol sat back down, crossing one leg over the other.

He smiled like he was enjoying himself and I got busy with the huge clear-up for something to do. I sensed his eyes on me while I loaded the dishwasher. He drummed his fingers on the table again.

'Wonder what they're quarrelling about?' he said.

It was hard to hear what the two of them were saying. Without turning around, I shrugged my shoulders, deciding not to engage with Sol anymore. I could tell that he was baiting me to say something off about Frankie and I didn't want to ruin my chances now I was in her home.

Sol continued to drum his fingers on the table while I tidied. I stared at my distorted face that reflected back from the aluminium splashback while I took a Brillo to one of the trays, scouring it clean. A sharp memory of Reg and Dotty arguing sprang to mind. I hated their rows because they always seemed to blame me for them. One time, when I was washing dishes, I could hear them shouting at each other from their bedroom.

'You're smothering her,' Reg had said.

'Don't be daft,' she'd said in defence.

'It's not normal, Dotty. She should want to leave home. Get a life of her own. She's in the way. The flat isn't big enough for the three of us now she's all grown up. Bernie's at your beck n' call, all the time, chained to your apron strings. She's old enough to fend for herself. Let her go.'

'Well, it's useful having her around.'

'Dotty, it's not normal. Ever since you made us keep—'

'Don't you ever question my decision again. The choice was made,' she'd bitten back.

I'd no idea what she was referencing.

Their arguments always ended the same way. She'd rile him up, he'd storm off to the pub, and she'd come gunning for me, blaming me for everything wrong in her life. 'Selfish little bitch, look what you've gone and done. He's left.'

Stefan and Frankie's argument died down. Sol was now humming to keep himself entertained. Stefan entered the kitchen alone, eyes glued to the floor, looking defeated. Frankie had a migraine apparently and had taken herself to bed, he said, speaking only to Sol, ignoring me. I carried on clearing the mess, pretending to be invisible.

'She turned pale when I asked about Lynda.'

'It's not you, Sol, it's her migraine. I know what they're like. I suffer from ocular ones where I lose my sight.'

'Perhaps,' Sol said.

'I didn't realise you and Lynda went that far back.'

'Oh, yes. Yes, we did. Poor Lynda.'

'So tragic.'

'The funeral is end of next week. Are you going?'

'Yes, I'll be there.'

'And Frankie? Do you think she'll come?'

'I hope so.'

'Jolly good,' Sol said, sounding nothing like the person on the phone earlier. 'Do speak to Frankie about the artwork again. And I apologise if I caused any offence. Some people can be touchy about their pasts.'

A hand landed on my shoulder. I whipped around, soap suds dripping from my hands.

'Nice to meet you, Bee.' He squeezed hard enough for me to know that he wasn't being friendly.

Two minutes after Sol left, Stefan tried to coax Frankie out of her bedroom again. He came back downstairs looking more deflated than before, hands in pockets, cheeks bright red.

'Right, well. I should be off too. Will you be okay on your own? Been here before, I presume. Know where everything is?' He kicked his foot.

I nodded. God, couldn't he just fuck off? What an idiot, of course I hadn't been in the house before. We stared at each for a few seconds, like we were playing a game of chicken.

'I should leave,' he said, breaking first.

'Okay.'

'Right, then.'

My nostrils flared. He was utterly head over heels in love with Frankie, wasn't he? The thought of them together and me being flung out in the cold made my mind race. No. No. NO. Their relationship couldn't develop any further. The fact that they'd been arguing was a good sign. A great sign, in fact. Luckily, I was in the house now, so I could fix Frankie's problems.

I flicked the kettle on, turning my back. 'I'll make a cup of tea and take it up to her.'

'Please ask her to call me if she resurfaces.'

'I'm sure she'll just want to sleep off that alcohol. She's not used to drinking.'

He looked at me confused. Yes, that's right, Stefan, you total arse-licker, I know more about her than you think. He left without saying goodbye, slamming the front door hard to make a point. What a loser.

My hand reached inside the cupboard for a mug. The one I picked had the caption 'Queen of Islington' as its slogan and had deep tea stains inside the rim. It was obvious from the staining that it got used a lot and maybe was one of her favourites. Could it have been a gift from someone special?

I pictured Frankie in the morning, reading her socials, drinking from her favourite cup, thinking of the person who'd bought it for her and the fun times they'd had together and all of the fun times they were going to have.

Before I could stop myself, I let the mug slip from my fingers. It smashed into pieces on the floor.

CHAPTER TWENTY-THREE

Bee

Frankie hid in her room after everyone had left and I spent the evening tiptoeing around like an unwanted house guest. It was rude of her, and I was raging. She could have at least made an effort to check in on me to see if I was okay and ask if I needed anything. I wanted to give her the benefit of the doubt, so tried my hardest not to stay mad for too long. Something had clearly upset her earlier in the day, and I knew it wasn't me, because I was on my best behaviour. I'd have to wait to see what the morning would bring.

She lived in a massive four-storey townhouse with everything decorated in white. White walls, white furniture, white floor-boards and even white carpets, the only pop of colour being Lynda's painting in the basement and the odd cactus plant placed here and there. It was nothing like I'd ever seen in real life, maybe only glimpsed in magazines and fancy home makeover shows on TV, with rich people complaining about unpronounceable paint colours and scatter cushions and lamps. Frankie's house had three spare bedrooms to choose from — two at the very top of the house with a Jack and Jill bathroom and another on the first floor, next to hers. They were all decorated the same, a double bed with a white headboard, a white wardrobe and a cactus plant on a white chest of drawers. The crisp white bedsheets smelled fresh and the pillows were soft and squishy. Naturally, I took the one next to hers because I wanted to be close. The main bathroom had lovely smelling soap, hand wash in a white dispenser and luxurious hand cream by the basin. The toilet paper was velvety. Inside the mirrored cabinet above the double sinks was every single toiletry that you could imagine, still sealed in its packaging. I brushed my teeth and used the bar of soap to have a quick wash, taking a fresh white fluffy towel from the long cupboard to dry off.

I felt like I'd won the lottery.

Before I turned in, I tapped on Frankie's door to check in on her. There was no sound coming from inside. The door was ajar, so I pushed it open. Her room was pitch black; the only light source came from the chandelier downstairs in the hallway. I stood in the doorway, squinted my eyes and watched her sleep. She must have been having a bad dream because she was breathing heavily, and stressful sounds were coming out of her mouth. She turned over on her side, facing the window, away from me. I crept inside, peering over her shoulder to take a closer look. It was hard to hear what she was mumbling about. I was sure she'd wake up and scream, seeing me over her like some lunatic. On her bedside, her mobile flashed a message, illuminating the room briefly. I picked it up, shaking the phone awake to see who was messaging her in the middle of the night.

Stefan! Blood rushed to my brain and an angry red fog circled. I turned the phone over and forced myself to leave.

In bed, I plugged my phone in to charge and lay down, head melting into the softest pillow I'd ever rested on. I went online to see what I could find on creepy Sol. After digging around and coming up with dead ends, I realised that he didn't have an online footprint. No results showed for 'Soliman art dealer in London'.

I'd need to get more details. I checked on Frankie's socials and hashtags to see if there was anything new posted. Nothing.

Before lights out, I fished the letter that Mum had given me out from my new Pilaga gym bag, which I was determined to keep. The note had an address in London scribbled at the bottom.

The same address I was now staying at.

Butterflies flitted inside my stomach. I smiled to myself as I stuffed the letter into the pillowcase so Frankie wouldn't find it.

I closed my eyes and fantasised about what our new life together would be like. My dream was becoming a reality.

Oh, Frankie, if only you knew the truth.

CHAPTER TWENTY-FOUR

Bee

The following morning, I set my alarm early and dressed with Frankie in mind, choosing something smart. A pair of black trousers I wore at Mum's funeral and a high-collar white blouse from H&M, thanks to Taffy. My hair was washed and tied in a ponytail, away from my face for once. I knew it was silly of me to even bother, and that Frankie wouldn't care what I looked like or how I dressed, but I wanted to impress her in any way I could.

I was in the kitchen, trying to work out her complicated DeLonghi coffee machine. As I pressed lots of buttons to see what function they had, I felt a tap on my shoulder. It made me jump. *Frankie.* She'd slipped into the kitchen without me noticing. She was wearing black-and-gold pyjamas which looked expensive and silky. Frankie looked like she hadn't even slept, even though I knew she had.

She gave me a tight smile. Something was off.

'How are you feeling?' I asked her, biting my bottom lip.

Frankie eyes flashed. 'Not great.'

'Oh.'

128

'Headache hasn't gone yet, so I'm going to take the morning off. I need to get someone to cover my classes, so I'll be making a few phone calls.'

'Okay.'

'In private.'

'Oh. I'll just make myself a drink and then get out of your hair.'

I picked up a mug and thought about her smashed 'Queen of Islington' cup, which was now in pieces in the bin outside. She approached the cupboard next to where I was standing and fished around with her hand. I held my breath, hoping she wouldn't notice it gone, focusing my attention on the coffee machine. Frankie pulled a plain mug out and slammed it on the worktop. She turned around to face me. Nervously, I looked up. She crossed one leg over the other as she leaned against the counter, her lips pursed together.

I turned away, back to the machine. 'I can't work out how—'

'Look, stop pressing random buttons. Stop, before you break it. Let me help you with the damn machine.'

Up close, she smelled musky and oily.

'What would you like to drink?' she asked.

'A coffee, please.'

'Yes,' she huffed. 'But what type?'

'Oh, with milk, you mean?'

She rolled her eyes and placed her mug beneath the spout, pressing a couple of buttons. The machine burst into life. The loud grinder crushed the coffee beans inside, and the kitchen filled with the aroma of chocolaty coffee. Years back, I'd watched a travel programme where the presenter said that the streets of Rome smelled of coffee. I'd never been abroad before. If only I could click my heels and be transported away someplace exotic like Italy, right now. I didn't know what I was doing that was so wrong.

'Flat white, cappuccino, espresso?'

'Oh. Cappuccino, please?' I was unsure if that was the right choice.

She made us both a cappuccino using the frother to make the milk foam. She sat down and pulled her phone out of her pyjama pocket. I wasn't sure what to do, so I perched on a chair opposite her, looking around the room, sipping a little at a time.

'Are you hungry?' she asked while staring at her phone. 'I never eat breakfast, so you have to say if you want a slice of toast or something before you go out.'

'I . . . I can grab something from that nice café.' My face was blazing hot. I took a big gulp and burned my tongue. 'Mmmm. The coffee is delicious. Better than Starbucks.'

'That's not hard.'

'What?'

'Starbucks make terrible coffee.'

'Oh.'

She cleared her throat. 'So, did you sleep okay?'

'Oh yes, thank you. Yes. So comfortable.'

'Which room?'

'The one next to yours. I hope you don't mind.'

'Right, I see. That wasn't the one I wanted to give you. Never mind, you weren't to know.'

'It's okay. You had a bad headache and I didn't want to disturb you.'

She looked around. 'Was it you?'

'Excuse me?' My heart jumped into my mouth. How was she going to finish the sentence? *Was it you who crept in my room late last night? Was it you that . . .*

'Was it you who cleared the dishes from yesterday?'

'Yes, I—'

'Thank you.' Her voice softened. 'Stefan made quite the mess, didn't he?'

I fake-laughed, clutching onto my cup of coffee with both hands.

'What time did they leave?'

'Pretty soon after you went upstairs.'

'Good. Good.'

'You seemed upset.'

She stared at me, not responding. The silence lingered, dense and unbearable. Why was she being so cold? She turned to her phone, which had returned to a black screen and used her facial recognition to unlock it. Frankie had a pained expression on her face as she read something.

'Goddamn it!' She slammed it on the table and buried her head in her hands.

'I'm sorry. I shouldn't have said anything about last night. It's not my place. I should leave you in peace. I'll come back later. I'm sorry. Shall I—'

'Stop fucking apologising.'

'Sorry.'

She took a moment, breathing heavily, like she had the world's problems on her shoulders. 'It should be me apologising. I'm aware that I'm being a terrible host.'

'It's okay.'

'No, it's not okay. None of this is okay.'

'I don't mind.'

'I'm not used to having someone in my space. There's a hell of a lot going on in my life at the moment and I'm feeling the strain.'

'I'm sorry.'

She shot me a look. I held my breath. *What was wrong with me?*

'For heaven's sake, it's not you, Bee. I'm *not* angry at *you*. It's everything else.'

My shoulders eased. Of course she couldn't be angry at me! I hadn't given her anything to be upset about. I was hoping it was Stefan who'd pissed her off.

'You can tell me your worries, if you want. I mean, I know that I'm only your cleaner, like. But sometimes opening up helps. It seemed to help the other day, didn't it?'

Her head was back in her hands.

'Is it Lynda's death?'

She shook her head, no.

'Stefan?'

'Yes and no.'

'Work? Mia? That guy Sol? Because you know he—'

'Take a look at this,' she said, cutting me off. She handed me her phone.

I stared at a message from *@Imcomingforyoubitch666*.

You think you can block me and I'll go away. Think again. I'm coming for you, bitch. I'm coming for what is rightfully mine.

'Oh my God. That's awful.' I handed it back. 'Who's it from?'

'That's the thing. I don't know. I've been getting these messages for a while now. I blocked the original account, but of course they just created a new one.'

I paused for a moment, chewing the inside of my mouth.

'Can I tell you something?' It was a gamble.

She searched my eyes. 'Of course.'

'There's something about that Sol dude, something he said on the phone to his friend, when you were upstairs, that didn't sound right to me.'

'What was it?'

'He mentioned gear. "Have you got the gear?"'

'But that could mean anything, Bee,' she said.

'There's more.'

'Go on.'

'After he finished the call, I asked him some questions.'

'And?'

'No. Never mind, it's stupid. Just ignore me. I could be making a big mistake.'

She placed her hand on mine. My skin tingled with excitement. How could I even imagine she would be angry at me. I was sent into her life to help her.

'Bee, for goodness' sake, just spit it out.'

'Last night, after you'd gone to bed and Stefan went to check on you, Sol took a call from his friend. He sounded weird, like, not how he normally talks. He was more street, if you know what I mean. He cut the phone call short because he realised I was listening in. After that, I was suspicious, so I asked him why he was so interested in Lynda's painting.'

'What did he say? What did he say?'

'He said he wanted it because he believed it belonged to him. His words were, "This painting's rightfully mine."'

CHAPTER TWENTY-FIVE

Frankie

My stomach lurches. 'Excuse me?'

'Sol said the painting's "rightfully" his.'

I take my phone and re-read the troll's message.

> *You think you can block me and I'll go away. Think again.*
> *I'm coming for you, bitch. I'm coming for what is rightfully*
> *mine.*

A chill runs down my spine.

I feel unsafe in my own home. I feel stalked. Vulnerable. The walls in the kitchen close in. The stalker's messages echo in my mind. This new piece of information has me questioning everything. Could my mystery troll be Sol?

Bee's heart-shaped necklace dazzles as I zone out, thinking about the first time I met Sol at Lynda's show. It was his impenetrable eyes that I recognised. They were from another place, another lifetime. My thoughts linger on the conversation we had yesterday, where Sol described in meticulous detail the corridors to the bedsits in King's Cross. It was as though I'd left my body and transported myself there, back to the squalor, reliving every moment and sensation. The smell of urine and rising damp, the noises from the flats, the peeling wallpaper. *The dark endless days spent in a smacked-out haze.*

There was a period in my life where I spent three months blacked out on heroin. Back then, many people came and went in my life, but I was so out of it, I wouldn't have been able to recall their names or even their faces if I were to encounter them today. Could I have met him then?

I want to throw up.

Making a quick dash into the basement loo, I vomit my coffee into the toilet bowl. I'm sweaty, a shivering mess, and my whole system feels like it's shutting down. At the sink, I splash my face with cold water and then sit on the toilet lid with my head in my hands, rocking backwards and forwards, sieving through murky memories from my past, trying to place Sol. He's locked inside my brain somewhere, I know he is. I'm scraping the memory with my fingernails trying to get at it.

Then, my first time springs to mind.

* * *

There was an aggressive knock on the door. Lynda opened it and allowed the young skinny man in the Adidas tracksuit with a cap covering his face to pass. Even though he was straggly, he strutted in with an air of confidence like he owned the place. He sat down on the bed, patted it for Lynda to sit next to him, opened a box and pulled out a small baggy with a brown substance in it. 'Relax, Franks. It's all good,' said Lynda. She took the straw and inhaled the substance from the foil, after which, she lay on the bed.

'Come, pretty ting,' he said, patting the empty space on the bed beside him on the other side. I don't know why I didn't leave. I don't know why I sat down next to him and stared at his hands transfixed as he emptied a small amount of powder onto a piece of foil, lighting it up. I don't understand any of my actions that day. I watched as the powder congealed. It had no odour to it, which I thought was odd. Weird the things you remember.

'What will this do?' I asked.

'Help you escape,' he said, clearing his throat. 'Do you need to escape, pretty ting?'

'Yes. Yes, I do.'

'What are you escaping from?'

'My past. I need to escape my past.'

He lifted his head and flashed me a quick look. We locked eyes.

The intensity of his stare drew me in and I vanished into their blackness.

Sol.

He's the guy who first gave me heroin. The guy who got Lynda hooked. His name has changed. He went by the name Laurence back then. And he looks different now — he's heavier, is bald and has good teeth. He's cleaned himself up and appears smart.

Sol is Laurence. Laurence, the young drug dealer from King's Cross, is Sol, the art dealer.

Now I know who he is.

He's Laurence Soliman, the guy who can destroy my career. Destroy my life. I throw up in my hands. This time, it's bile.

* * *

When I re-enter the kitchen, I'm surprised to find Bee on my phone, talking to someone.

'Yes. Yes. Is there anything else I should know before I go in?' she's saying. 'Right. Okay. And the passwords are . . . Hang on . . . Let me find a pen.' She looks up and spots me. 'Frankie, do you have a pen and paper?'

Bemused, I open the drawer with all the odd bits and pieces inside like Sellotape, batteries and menus. I take a notebook, rip a piece of paper out and give it to her along with a pen. I watch as she writes a set of passwords. Access to the gym computer.

'Yes, I'll tell her. She's just walked in. Do you want to speak to her now? Okay. No problem. I'll let her know. Get better.' Bee terminates the call and hands the phone over to me.

I sit down and turn the phone in my hand, waiting for Bee's explanation.

'Mia kept calling, and after the fourth missed call, I thought maybe it was important, so I answered it for you. I'm sorry, like. You were taking so long and I didn't know what else to do.'

'It's fine. It's fine. What did she say, Bee?'

'She's ill. She has a tummy bug. She can't come in today.'

'Great. That's all I need right now. I'm stretched as it is.'

I pace, unsure what to do. I'm annoyed that Mia has added more stress to my already stressful day. Annoyed that she'd rather avoid me than have a chat about the bracelet incident. 'I've got a temp covering Lyndsay in Primrose Hill and Shannon in Highgate is coming in late today because she has a doctor's appointment. There's no way I can get cover at such short notice. I'm going to have to go in, fill in for reception where I can.'

I want to cry.

'That's why I'm stepping in. I told Mia I can cover for her and she seemed okay with that.'

I nod my head, mulling it over, impressed and bewildered.

'I've watched how she works,' she continues. 'I've heard what she says to clients. I have the passwords for the computer and bookings system. If you show me how to book and cancel an appointment, I'm sure I can muddle through with the rest, like. Oh, and I've already asked Mia to call another Pilaga practitioner to cover your class this morning. She's calling someone called Martha. I know you said you weren't feeling well and needed a day off. Is that alright?'

Bee says this with an air of quiet confidence that I haven't seen before. She's ambitious, solution oriented. I like that. I like that a lot. Maybe this is the break she needs to help her excel.

It's a no-brainer. 'Okay, great. Let me get my laptop for you so I can show you how the bookings system works.' I'm sure Pilaga will be safe in her hands.

With no time to waste, I fish the laptop out of my gym bag and fire it up. For the time being, I dismiss all my pressing worries and focus on work, which gives me some respite. I talk through the basics with Bee, how to book a client onto a class or a therapy appointment, how to cancel, how to swap from one practitioner's page to the next and how to create multiple bookings. Bee's not super-fast on the keyboard, typing with her index fingers, and now that she's on the laptop she seems more nervous than I anticipated, but I have faith that she'll pull it off.

I text Mia and ask her to keep an eye on things remotely from home, as she has access, and tell her that I expect her in at 8.30 a.m. tomorrow without fail. No excuses. By 9.15 a.m., Bee is on her way to Pilaga to cover reception in Islington, my busiest gym.

When I'm alone and the house falls quiet, I send a message to Laurence, or Sol, or whatever he calls himself these days.

How much are you willing to pay for Lynda's artwork?

I'll be damned if I'm going to allow this son of a bitch to hold me to ransom. I've come too far in my life for that. I've come too far for some scumbag drug dealer masquerading as an art dealer to destroy it all. I switch onto Instagram and reply to *@Imcomingforyoubitch666.*

And what is rightfully yours?

Waiting for both replies, I pace once more, biting down on my already bitten down nails.

Two can play his dirty game.

CHAPTER TWENTY-SIX

Back then

The day I met him was one of those uncomfortably hot days. My home was stuffy and the heat from the tower block had risen to the top floor and was trapped inside our tiny flat, making the space feel smaller. Tempers flared and it wasn't long before Mum and Reg were at it again, bickering. It became a competition of who could shout the loudest, who was in the right, who was the one out of order. Of course, it was all Mum's fault, it always was, and of course Mum would always win the battle, being the more resilient and stubborn of the two. Reg would have to back down, if he knew what was good for him; he had no choice. Her threats of running away with another man and leaving him (and me) behind was enough to scare the pants off him.

During that particular row, Dotty had sent me to my room like I was ten, despite the fact I was turning sixteen. She still didn't allow me to do anything unless I was running errands for her. She liked it that way. That day, I was feeling boxed in and my hormones were raging like an uncontrollable fire. The shouting, the heat, the tense atmosphere. I was a bomb about to explode. By late afternoon, the temperature had cooled and Reg had been reduced to tears. Only then did she forgive him. They'd decided to celebrate down the local pub, leaving me behind.

Finally, I had the place to myself. Padding around the flat, I opened and closed drawers and cupboards and searched for food. There was nothing to eat as per usual. Flopping on the sofa, my feet dangling off the edge, I flicked the button on the remote control to see what was on the box. Nothing.

Something in me stirred. I jumped up and made my way to their bedroom. I'd be damned if I was going to spend another night hungry, another night alone, another night so angry I would be unable to sleep. Reg was a runner for a local drug dealer, selling weed for everyone in our tower block. I knew for a fact that he had a small stash of cash and weed in a shoebox somewhere. He wasn't very original, and my guess was it was hidden under the bed. The problem with Reg was, he was hopeless. Having smoked most of his supply, he now owed the dealer more money than he had made and so had to take a second job at the bookies to pay the dealer back. What a plonker. He repulsed me with his bald patch and sideburns and his annoying nervous tic in his left eye, which got going when he was lying. Rummaging under the bed, I pulled the Converse shoebox out. There wasn't a lot inside, a few bags of skunk, which I wasn't interested in, and £68 in cash. I took a clean twenty and made a break for the great outdoors.

It was dark outside, and the air was electrically charged from all the heat during the day. I headed straight to the seafront where the funfair was, enjoying my first ever taste of freedom. The fair was full of kids my age and buzzing with loud music and flashing neon lights. The air was laced with the weird smell of the smoke machine as well as fried onions and candyfloss. The entertainment stalls were packed with people shooting stuff, throwing hoops over objects and rolling balls into holes to make horses go faster in races, in order to win oversized useless prizes.

I'd been missing out on loads of fun. *I hated Dotty so much.*

After I'd stuffed myself with chips smothered with vinegar, I stood by the dodgem cars. The bell had rung and there was a rush of people grabbing dodgems. Taking centre stage, in a red-and-blue-striped car, was a stocky guy with long hair past his shoulders, who I later found out was called Daniel. There was something about the way he carried himself, like he was a rock star, which caught my eye. The bumper cars started. He stood up while his vehicle moved around and around in circles. He held onto the pole that was attached to the electric fishnet ceiling and laughed, flicking his hair out of his eyes every so often. He nodded his head in time to the music and was revelling in the attention. That boy did not give a shit. One of the workers waved at him, telling him to sit down, but Daniel ignored them and carried on. He was king of the fairground in my eyes.

It wasn't long before he got kicked off, right by where I was standing, and in a twist of fate, he bumped straight into me as he was leaving. Wearing black jeans, white trainers and a Joy Division t-shirt, not only did he act differently from the locals, he dressed differently too.

'I like your t-shirt. Love the band,' I said, my stomach in knots. Not that I knew any of Joy Division's songs.

'Thanks. They were pretty amazing. Shame about Ian Curtis. Such a talent. New Order aren't so bad though.'

'Yeah,' I mumbled, not having a clue who Ian Curtis was either.

'You local?' he asked.

'Yeah. You?'

'Nah. Visiting my dad, he's just got relocated to this dump. Got a new council flat. Thought I'd come and check it out for myself.'

I laughed. 'Yeah, this area is a dump. One day, one day soon, I'm gonna get the hell out of here and move to London.'

'London, hey? Me and Mum don't live far from there. We're in Milton Keynes.'

'Oh, cool.'

'Yeah. It's a dump there too.'

He made me laugh.

'So? You gonna show me around, local girl?'

'Yeah, sure.'

And that was it. That was all it took. I was smitten for the first time in my life.

We strolled towards the beach and slipped down the pebbled dunes and sat by the shore. He put his arm around me. I was so nervous, sweat had collected in the small of my back and I was sure that he could feel me trembling. I prayed he had more experience than I did.

At school, there was a stigma surrounding me, being the poorest pupil. The kids would often tease me, calling me a 'flea bag'. I didn't blame them. My uniform was tatty, and my shoes were from the charity shop. I wished Dotty had sent me to the one around the corner from where I lived instead, maybe I would have fitted in better with the local scallywags. Or even letting me hang out with them after school would have helped. But she didn't. And so, I had no friends at all, zero, and definitely no chance at getting a boyfriend. My imaginary sister was the only friend I had to keep me company, which was tragic.

Daniel held my face in his hands. 'Can I kiss you now?'

'Yeah, go on then.'

I parted my lips and waited. He slipped his tongue inside and flicked it around. It felt nice and I could tell he was getting aroused because there was a bulge in his trousers. The thought made me sticky. He laid me down and clambered on top. Squeezing my eyes, I felt the impression of his hot breath and hands manoeuvring around me. My skin sizzled from all the new sensations it was being exposed to and my body's chemistry was altering, like I had a fever. He pulled down my knickers. After a few moments of him fumbling around, there was a hot burning sensation deep inside of me. He was panting quickly. I tried to relax even though it hurt.

The sea sprayed my face and I could taste the minerals in my mouth. Wet sand stuck to my hair and the waves crashed onto my feet, soaking my trainers.

The proximity to the water got me panicked.

My mind shut down and travelled to my imaginary sister, like it always did when I was stressed. What she would make of the situation. In the depths of my imagination, she had more experience than I had. *Well, you wanted adventure and now you got it!* she'd say.

One minute later, he groaned and collapsed on top of me. It was over. He pulled himself out, adjusted his trousers and lay by my side. He tried to take my hand, but I bolted upright, pulling my knickers and jeans up. I stood and looked up to the sky.

Heavy droplets of rain landed on my face. I heard a clap of thunder as the night sky lit up.

'Where are you going?'

'I've got to go home. Dotty. She's gonna kill me if she finds out.'

The heavens opened and rain poured down hard. Using my hands, I climbed the dunes and ran all the way to the flat.

I never saw Daniel again.

CHAPTER TWENTY-SEVEN

Bee

When I arrived at the gym, I was greeted by an angry mob waving yoga mats at me, wanting to be let in. I opened the doors and the clients took to stampeding inside, like they were at the Boxing Day sales. *Why was there no one at reception? Where was Frankie? Where was Mia? Wasn't I aware they had work, another class, shopping, nursery-school pick-up, a very important meeting? Blah, blah, blah.* It was Frankie's 9.30 a.m. class and they were a fucking nightmare. I explained that Frankie wasn't well and that the class would begin later than usual with someone named Martha, but that didn't satisfy them.

Ten minutes after the gym had opened, there was still no sign of Martha. I had sweat patches under my arms. I'd never encountered work-related stress before, having only worked at a fish shop and then as a cleaner. Had Mia even called Martha? Reception was full of angry yogis demanding their money back.

I was drowning.

I didn't know how to work a refund. I didn't have Martha's number. I didn't want to call Frankie, proving that I'd failed right from the get-go. I didn't even have the time to get my revenge on Mia for setting me up. *She'd have to wait until later.* It was obvious that she hadn't contacted Martha — a deliberate move to ruin my first day. I sensed that she had a nasty streak to her. No one could be that boring and *meh*. Thank God another practitioner saved the day, giving me Martha's number and showing me how to work the card machine for the refunds.

I didn't catch a break until late afternoon when the gym cleared of people and the phones died down. Everything turned calm and for the first time, I felt I had things under control. Two workout classes were happening at the same time, the massage therapist in the basement was halfway through a free session with Amanda, with another session booked afterwards, and all previous clients had been refunded and dealt with. Putting my feet up on the reception desk, I was proud of what I'd accomplished. I wrapped my hands around the back of my neck while I listened to the mellow music pumping out.

Just as I was relaxing, Mum sprang to mind, ruining my mood. *Bernie Bee, don't get too comfortable. You know that the local chippie is as good as it gets for you.*

Huh. That's what she'd expect from me, but I was proving her wrong. I was more than someone with no prospects, stinking of fish and with chip grease in my hair. What did Dotty expect to happen after I read the letter with Frankie's address at the bottom? Did she think I would bury my head in the sand and ignore it? Did she think I was too gutless to search for answers?

Nothing was going to stop me now.

I thought about Mia sabotaging my first day. She was a traitor and untrustworthy. I kicked my legs off the desk and fired up the desktop. Now that it was quiet, I wanted to search her internet history, dig around to see if I could find some dirt. Moonpig, Amazon, Instagram, a *Star Wars* fanpage and a job site. Interesting. Very interesting. My legs bounced up and down from excitement. Before I knew it, I found myself going onto her Instagram page.

Her social media account would reveal more about her than any-thing else. On Instagram, I used the dropdown key on the login box, praying it would provide me with Mia's actual username and password so I could log onto her account. Her username popped up. Underneath that, eight asterisk stars concealing a password. I pressed return, crossed my fingers and hoped for the best.

Bingo. I had complete access to her account.

A quick glance up to make sure I was alone, then I began to rummage through her profile. It was all so dull. Her feed was swamped with pictures of her stupid rat-like dog named Vader and countless images of her and her nerdy friends at various sci-fi conventions and nerdy dress-up gaming parties. The work phone rang, breaking my concentration. I picked up the receiver and put it straight back down. I flicked my eyes around the gym to make sure no one caught me in the act. One more call from a client wanting to book an appointment would melt my eyes. Fuck them.

I carried on with what I was doing. Mia was such a geek and, unfortunately for me, angelic. There was nothing out of place on her Instagram account that made my hairs stand on end. Somehow, this made me dislike her even more. How can anyone be that squeaky clean?

Amanda appeared in reception out of nowhere and was head-ing straight for me. *Go away*, I begged, *go away*. I flicked onto Mia's Insta messages. Things were getting interesting . . .

'I'd like to book a follow-up appointment. Tristan worked the knots in my neck and shoulders, but I still need more body work,' Amanda said.

For fuck's sake. I minimised the screen and looked up, forcing a smile on my face. 'I'm on my break. Can I phone you later to arrange?' I said in my most 'professional' tone.

She smelled of essential oils from the massage she'd just had, and the scent filled the room.

'Listen here, what's your name?'

'Bee.'

'Bee, I don't have time to take your calls and deal with this later. Do you understand how busy I am? I have three kids and two dogs to look after.' Her hands rested on her protruding hips.

Just before my blood was about to boil, I clocked the expensive Tiffany's charm bracelet on her wrist. It was the one that I'd given Frankie. I settled into my chair.

'Of course. When would you like to come in?' I opened the booking system.

'Great.'

I went into Tristan the massage therapist's booking page to see when he was next available. 'What about Friday?'

'No can do.'

I chewed hard on my lip. She was lucky I didn't sell her damned bracelet in one of the pawn shops on Chapel Market, the more run-down area of Islington. I scanned for further appointments. 'How about next Tuesday at twelve?'

'Perfect.' Amanda was about to leave.

'I'm so glad I found your bracelet,' I jumped in.

'Sorry?'

'Your pretty bracelet,' I said. 'It was a good job I found it and handed it in, you know, before it "disappeared".'

Her hand traced the bracelet on her wrist. 'What do you mean? It was in the therapy room where I left it. That's what Frankie said.'

'Oh no it wasn't. Frankie was covering up for "you-know-who".'

'No. I don't know who.'

'Mia.'

Amanda took a step back. 'Okay, spill the beans.'

'Well, I was cleaning the other day and I found it stashed inside the desk drawer,' I whispered. 'I mean, how did it make its way inside her drawer? Was she planning on handing it in the next day, or was she thinking about stealing it?'

'You are kidding, right?'

'I'm not.' I nodded and kept eye contact.

Truth was, I found it in the therapy room, where Amanda, the dopey cow, had left it.

'I don't understand. Why on earth would Frankie keep her on? That's outrageous, to be honest with you. What else has gone missing over the years? How can Mia be trusted? If it were me, I'd have her fired. Immediately. The way *that girl* spoke to me.'

'I know, I know. But hey, I can't say anything to Frankie. I'm only a worker.'

'Well, I can mention it. I'll mention it when we have that coffee. She owes me. Thank you for being so honest. You're a real gem and Frankie's lucky to have you.'

'No problem.' I smiled, that time for real.

Today was the best day ever!

After Amanda left, there was an afternoon rush, pretty much in the same vein as the morning, and I found myself swept off my feet again. I had to pause my Mia investigation, but I felt far more in control of work this time around.

And far more in control of my life too.

CHAPTER TWENTY-EIGHT

Frankie

By the time I flick the kettle on to make tea, Sol replies. With nervous anticipation, I open the message.

> *My offer is very competitive. May I pop over with my art valuer, so we can talk numbers?*

Blood thumps inside my temples. Why is he acting like we don't know one other? He's pretending that we don't have a history together, pretending that it's all about the painting. My hands are shaking as I check my Instagram account to see if there's been a reply there. Radio silence from my mystery stalker. Hmmm.

Could it really be about the painting or am I falling into a dangerous trap? My grip tightens around my phone. I want to call his bluff, tell Sol that I know who he is, that I think it's him trolling me, blackmailing me about my past, but the thought of resurrecting the bad times fills me with dread.

The past is in the past for a reason.

Taking my emotions out of the equation, I force myself to think logically. Maybe I'm putting two and two together and coming up with five. The fact that he's carrying on with this facade, and even mentions an art valuer, means that he may legitimately want to buy the painting. If this valuer is accompanying him, it also means I won't be alone with him.

I'll be safe from harm.

Turning my phone in my hand, I know I must come to a decision and stick by it. My compulsion to get to the bottom of why he's appeared in my life outweighs the paranoia I have nestling in the back of my mind. I sit and inhale, trying to get my thoughts in order before I reply.

There's only one way to find out if he's a changed man. There's only one way to find out if he's the one behind the messages.

Come now. I'm home.

As soon as I press send, I'm regretful. Sol was a mystery back when I knew him, always keeping his cards close to his chest, and he's a puzzle now.

I race upstairs to get ready. Scenarios flash in my mind as I take a shower. Sol arrives early while I'm showering. I see him breaking into my home. I picture him bounding up the stairs, two at a time. I envisage him smashing in the locked bathroom door, shouting, 'The painting is rightfully mine!' I see it all unfolding. Reaching through the broken door like Jack Torrence in *The Shining*, twisting the handle from the inside and pushing the door open using his full body weight, toppling the chair that I've wedged up against it. He's coming at me while I'm showering; this time he mimics *Psycho*, a kitchen knife in his smooth hand. He stabs and slices, tearing me to shreds.

I see him, the younger version of him, with a bag of brown. Unwrapping the substance onto foil, taking a lighter to it, he tells me to sit down next to him . . .

Stop. STOP. Fucking stop this.

As these awful scenes rotate in my mind, growing into a horror show, I realise that I've left my phone downstairs. Panicked, I turn the shower off without rinsing and dry myself, choosing something conservative to wear. Leggings, a shapeless jumper and a pair of thick winter socks. Once dressed, I rush back down and take my phone, checking Instagram. Still nothing.

I pace the kitchen, bite down on my non-existent nails, make another cup of tea and await his arrival. My brain is in overload. He must be a different person now. *He has to be.* He looks different, acts differently, even goes by a different name. I mean, I'm a different person from my past. Being in recovery does that to you. You dissociate yourself from anything that reminds you of your addiction. Lynda's overdose could be a coincidence. There's nothing tying him to her death. If there was, the police would have found something. But as soon as I dismiss my paranoia, I think about what Bee said. The weird phone call she overheard. What he said about the painting being rightfully his.

The doorbell chimes.

The hairs on my arms stand on end. I take in a lungful of air, convincing myself I'm being suspicious over nothing. All he wants is to buy Lynda's painting and leave me alone. Since she passed her artwork has increased in value.

I'm standing in my hallway, my hands pressed against the door. I feel his presence on the other side. I unbolt the front door and open it.

It takes me a couple of moments to soak him in. He's wearing a flat cap, tweed jacket and brown Hunter boots.

And he's alone.

Sol's face breaks into a smile. 'Hello, Frankie.'

My heart's racing. I'm transported back in time.

It *is* him. It's really him. *Laurence.*

He's much heavier than he used to be. The nose ring has gone and so has all the hair and boyish stubble. Also gone are the dodgy tracksuits he used to love wearing so much. But the eyes remain the same; they freak me out the most. Now I know who he is, his sheer presence is evoking the same feelings I used to have each time we encountered one another. The same electric energy he used to bring with him when he'd arrive at the bedsits delivering drugs is flooding my system now. The combination of fear and excitement combined.

My mind relives the rush I used to get from the opioids travelling through my bloodstream. The warm tingle on my skin. The heaviness in my limbs. The blissed-out coma, helping me forget . . .

I hated myself so much back then; I was so ashamed. All I wanted to do was slip in between the cracks of life.

'Are you okay? You look like you've seen a ghost.'

CHAPTER TWENTY-NINE

Frankie

We stand on the doorstep in silence. He's staring intently; his eyes are black and cold, radiating danger. He moves his gaze to my 'welcome to my home' doormat, which has a fresh scattering of snow on it.

Sol taps his foot. 'So?'

I realise I've been holding my breath all this time. A guttural sound comes out of my mouth as I release the air. I straighten up. I will *not* be intimidated by ghosts from my past. I'm not a scared little girl anymore. I'm a woman. A grown woman who appears to have her shit together.

'You're alone,' I say stoically, my arms crossing over my chest.

'My business partner will be here any moment. May I come in?' His breath fogs as he speaks. 'It's freezing.' He rubs his hands together for effect.

I hug myself, looking up and down the road to see if I can spot the art valuer on the street or if a car is pulling up, but there's no one about. The road is desolate. The arctic breeze runs through my damp hair, making me shiver. I don't want to be standing in the doorway any more than he does.

But he's alone.

Against my better judgement, I find myself brushing off the negativity and allowing politeness to take over. 'Come in,' I say. 'I'll put the kettle on.'

He closes the door behind him and shakes his boots clean of snow onto my runner. I head to the kitchen. He's so close, I sense his icy breath tickling the back of my neck.

In the kitchen, I switch on the kettle and feel his eyes boring into the back of me.

'Would you like some tea? Does your colleague like tea? Perhaps coffee? I can get drinks for us while we wait for him. It's a him, I presume. Or perhaps a woman. Of course. It could also be a woman.'

As I throw two teabags into a pot, his hand lands on my shoulder, making me jump. He squeezes tightly.

'Frankie, why are we acting?'

My heart's in my mouth as I spin to face him. His hand drops to his side. He's standing inches away from me. The aftershave he's wearing is sharp, laden with spice. He takes his cap off and flings it across the worktop and steps further in, closing the gap between us, so our noses are almost touching. I smell coffee on his breath. His eyes are haunting, and I'm desperate to say something, tell him to back off, ask him to leave, but my voice is stuck in my throat. I'm young again. Vulnerable. It's as though the heroin he once sold me is lingering in my veins.

'Laurence,' I whimper.

'It's Soliman now. Please call me Sol.'

I swallow hard. He's got me tongue-tied.

'You're shaking. You seem to be in a delicate state of mind.'

'Lynda . . .' That's all I can manage to say.

'Yes. About her.'

'Why do you want the painting so much?' My voice wobbles.

'The water's boiled. Here, let me help you.' He leans over me so our shoulders touch momentarily. He resumes the tea making, pouring water into the pot. 'I assume Stefan doesn't know about your past and about us.'

I shake my head. 'No one does,' I whisper.

'Apart from me, and of course Lynda. But she's . . . well, you know . . .' He steps back, puts his hand in his trouser pocket and smiles. 'Dead.'

I come over giddy. I steady myself, holding onto the countertop.

'Are you okay?'

'Yes, I . . .' My brow is sweaty. I head to the sink, thinking I may spew up.

'Why are you so nervous around me these days?' he asks.

I splash water over my face.

'You never used to be this shy.'

'What do you want from me?' I turn to look at him, pleading with my eyes.

'I think you know the answer.'

'No, I don't know the answer. Why don't you explain what you're doing in my life. What you were doing in Lynda's.'

He reaches into a cupboard and takes two mugs out, then pours the weakly brewed tea into them. My eyes dart across the counter to where my mobile is sitting. It's within my reach. I take my chance when he retrieves the oat milk from the fridge. My phone is slippery in my sweaty palm. I place it in my back pocket for insurance. I'll dial the police if things turn bad.

'Oh, sweet ting.'

I shudder. He always called me that. 'Why did you come back into Lynda's life?'

'Quite simple. She called me.'

'Did you have anything to do with her death?'

'Now, why would you say a nasty thing like that?'

'Because you were with her the night she died. Because I know who you are, Sol.'

He eyeballs me. 'And who am I, Frankie?'

My cheeks are burning. 'The new name changes nothing. You're still a drug pusher and a snake and I should never have allowed you to influence me when I was younger. You almost destroyed me.'

'You almost destroyed yourself.' He hands me a mug.

I don't take it. Sol places it on the worktop, takes his own and goes to the dining table to where Lynda's painting is.

'She thanked me when she finished it, you know,' he says, referring to the oil on the wall.

'Thanked you?'

'Yep.' He slurps noisily. 'Lynda said that the H helped her unlock her creativity. Or some shit like that. It helped open her mind. That gal was fucking nuts.' He turns around. '*Passion and Fire* is what made her famous. It's what started her career. And it's now worth a fortune.'

'Hang on a minute. Let me get this straight. You think this painting belongs to you because you sold her a bag of brown once and she was high on your supply when she painted it?' I laugh, not quite believing the guts he has. 'That's the most ridiculous thing I've ever heard.'

'Is it?'

'When is your valuer coming? I want this over and done with.'

'There's no valuer. I lied. Whoops. Sorry, sweet ting.'

My hand slips into my back pocket. I take my phone out and tap 999, showing him.

He steps towards me, grinning. 'Am I supposed to be scared?'

'Don't come any closer. My finger is on the dial button. I'll call the police if I have to.'

'Why would you want to do that?'

'I want you out of my house. I don't feel safe anymore.'

'Come on . . . we're old pals.'

'No, we're not. Stop right where you are. I mean it. Don't come any closer.' I steady my mounting nerves. 'Now, I'm going to tell you how it's going to go down. I'm going to walk towards the courtyard and you're going to head out of my kitchen and then out the front door. You'll ring Stefan to tell him that you're not interested in the painting anymore. And then, we will never see you again. You got that?'

He laughs hard, his bellows echoing around the room. 'Frankie. Relax, sweet ting.'

Shivers run down my spine.

'Your threats are empty. Pathetic. You have no say in the matter. None at all. Now, *I'm* going to tell *you* how it's going to go down.'

I'm shaking.

'You owe me your life, or have you forgotten?'

'I . . .'

'I'm the one who saved you.'

'It was you who supplied me—'

He doesn't let me finish my sentence. 'It was me who rushed you to the hospital when you overdosed, and it was me who waited for you to be discharged. I could have left you there, on the floor, foaming at the mouth. But I didn't.'

My breath hitches.

The overdose was what made me change paths in life. It was the shock I needed. I never saw him again after that. I got myself clean and got out of that bedsit as fast as I could. I never asked Lynda about him. I never dared. I just buried him and my addiction in the back of my mind.

'Do you remember what you said to me when I brought you home?'

I shake my head, no.

'Of course you don't. Most smackheads can't remember when they last took a dump. Let me refresh your memory, gal. You said, "I owe you. I owe you my life." And now I'm here to collect my debt.'

'You can't . . . You don't know . . . I mean, what proof do you have?'

He pulls out a crumpled sheet of paper from inside his tweed jacket. 'The hospital report. Right here. In black and white.' He taps on it with his finger.

Sol folds the paper and places it back in his pocket. 'So, you see, my sweet ting, I can't leave. Not yet, anyway. I haven't mentioned the terms of the exchange of the painting yet.'

'Lynda's artwork is not for sale,' I spit, knowing that my words are meaningless. He's set his sights on it.

'I'm not buying the painting off you.'

I'm trembling.

'Let's call it a gift.'

'No. You can't. You can't do this to me. It's all I have of hers.'

'You're giving me the painting and I'm promising you my silence. What will your followers think when they find out you were a junkie? Your career will be over.'

'Are you threatening me?'

'I'll give you until the funeral to think about it.'

I'm seeing life through a tinted lens. I face Lynda's painting on the wall, my eyes welling up. The bright reds and oranges are moving, bleeding into one another on the canvas. The images are blurring into a bloody mess.

There's no doubt in my mind now that he's responsible for the messages on Instagram. He's been playing me all along. Perhaps used poor Lynda to get to me and to the painting.

The phone in my hand pings. My heart jumps into my mouth. Earlier, while I was waiting for him to arrive, I set up a bell sound to notify me when I received something new from my troll.

But I must be mistaken because he's standing in front of me and hasn't once reached for his mobile.

A smile creeps across his face, like he knows what's going on. I glance at my screen. A message from my stalker *has* come through.

Sol slams his mug on the dining table. 'Thanks for the tea. I'll show myself out. You have until the funeral to decide. See you Friday.' He brushes past me.

He leaves. A moment later, the door slams. His threat hangs in the air, thick, unbearable, choking me.

My hands tremble as my gaze rests on the notification on my phone. I open Instagram. Another message from *@Imcomingforyoubitch666* is awaiting me. It's in direct response to my earlier question, what's rightfully yours?

Your life.

That's all it says. *Your life.*

Am I being threatened by two people? Could karma be catching up with me?

CHAPTER THIRTY

Bee

I placed my phone on the desk and looked at the time: 6.15 p.m. There were no more classes or therapy sessions scheduled, which meant I could leave work. I shut down the computer, put the phone on voicemail and left for Frankie's. Even though it was late, Upper Street was buzzing with Christmas shoppers. Cars honked, buses blocked roads and buskers sang carols. My feet ached and my brain was tired, but I felt good inside, like a grown-up with responsibility and life prospects for the first time, entertaining endless possibilities for my future.

Skipping across the road, I zigzagged between traffic and snaked past people on the pavements. Butterflies flapped in my tummy when I thought about the holiday season. There was never anything to get giddy about with Dotty and Reg; a dry shrivelled-up turkey, served up late while Reg and Dotty drank themselves into oblivion, was as good as it got. Christmas would be different with Frankie. I knew it would. We'd decorate the tree in reds and golds, and sit together in our matching Santa pyjamas, drinking our morning coffee. Carols would play in the background and there'd be plenty of gifts wrapped with pretty ribbons. I'd have been working a few weeks by then, so would have saved a bit of cash to buy her a special present. A gold heart necklace, like the one I was wearing, so we'd match. I'd get an engraving on the pendant.

Sisters forever.

I wanted to surprise Frankie with a meal to celebrate my first day, so I popped into the local organic store to get some groceries. Inside, I cruised the aisles confused about what to buy. So many vegetables I hadn't a clue how to cook, like swede and turnip. In the end, I decided on a ready-made lasagne meal for two, some lettuce and the cheapest bottle of red I could find, which wasn't bloody cheap at all. The whole thing came to a staggering £32! Luckily for me, Amanda had paid cash up front for her next massage appointment and I logged it on the system as unpaid, pocketing the money. I saw it as an advance for the day's work I'd done. I'd every intention of putting it back.

My chest warmed as I picked up the pace to get home. *Home.* I said the word out loud, trying it for size. It felt right. Sounded right. It was the perfect fit. For the first time in my life, I belonged. My phone rang. I fished it out of my pocket, thinking it was Frankie checking up on me. Charlotte! It had been a couple of days since I'd seen her at the club.

'Hey, how's it going?' I said, breathless because of my pace.

'Don't you "how's it going" me. Where's all the stuff?'

'What stuff?'

'Taffy's belongings. Her jumpers, blouses. The bloody jacket from the club, for God's sake. A pair of boots. Are you kidding me?! How can I ever trust you again after this?'

'Tell her I don't know what she's talking about,' I said, smiling to myself, wearing Taffy's coat and blouse.

Charlotte turned quiet and I didn't feel the need to say any more. The way I saw it, it wasn't up to me to prove my innocence. It was up to them to prove my guilt. And how were they going to do that? They didn't even know where I lived or what I was doing. Not that they cared about my whereabouts or well-being. I could have been killed that night after the club for all they cared. Hacked to pieces and thrown into the dumpster by some maniac next to my old coat. Charlotte didn't even bother checking on me the next day. Some friend she turned out to be.

I hardened at the thought.

'Taffy's pissed, Bernie. She said that if you don't return her stuff by Friday, she's gonna hunt you down, grab you by the hair and take all of her things back herself. Her words, not mine. I'm ringing you as a warning.'

Charlotte ranted about her trust being broken and how she'd been kind to me by offering a place to stay. Blah, blah, bloody blah. I soon got bored of the moaning and cut her off mid-sentence. Fuck Charlotte and her sister. I didn't need them anymore.

I had Frankie and that was all that mattered.

I turned onto her road. There was a van parked outside her house — Highbury Security Systems — and the front door was wide open. One man, all tooled up, walked inside; another was propped up on a high ladder installing what looked like a security camera just below Frankie's bedroom window.

Inside, our home had been invaded by technicians, fitting sensors, cameras and alarms, fortifying the place.

'I'm home,' I said, ducking under another ladder, bypassing a workman.

No reply.

In the basement kitchen, I placed the bag of shopping onto the counter and made my way into the snug area where the sofa faced the large mounted TV. There I spotted Frankie and Stefan sitting, chatting quietly. Her head resting on his shoulder. His arm around her. They were too engrossed in whatever they were saying to notice me come in. The TV was on a lifestyle channel.

It was some rerun of a reality show with posh kids drinking cocktails in a swanky bar. A red haze clouded my vision. Couldn't pretty-boy Stefan leave her alone? Having people work at the property was an annoyance in itself, but Stefan being at the house as well? I thought it would just be us tonight. I'd bought us food.

I pulled back into the shadows so I wouldn't disturb them and listened in.

'I don't understand where your anxiety's coming from.'

'I want to feel safe in my own home.'

'But you are.'

'Stefan, how long have you known Sol for?'

Stefan shuffled in his seat. 'Not that long. About five months or so, I'd say. Great chap. Great connections. He seems to know quite a few up-and-coming street artists. We were talking about opening a modern art gallery together in King's Cross.'

'Hmmm.'

'Why don't you like him?'

'I think he's shady, Stefan. You must be careful. I don't believe what he says.'

My ears pricked.

He pulled his arm off her. 'Why is that?'

'Because I know him from my past.'

'Well, this is the thing. You've never mentioned your connection before.'

Frankie lifted her head off his shoulder and stared at him. 'I didn't know who he was at the time. But I do now. I remember who he is. I'm sorry, I can't explain further.' Her voice was unsteady.

'Well, maybe I should ask him.'

'No, Stefan. Don't.'

'I can't figure you out sometimes.' He shook his head.

'Forget what I said. It's Lynda. The funeral. My head's a jumbled mess. I'll deal with it.'

'Deal with what?'

'Nothing. It's nothing.'

'You just don't like the guy for some reason. Maybe we should go for a drink after the funeral to clear the air.'

'No!'

'I don't understand.'

'Have you spoken to Grace about him? To see what she thinks?'

'No. Should I?' Stefan asked.

'He was one of the last people to see Lynda alive. Don't you think that's a little odd?'

'What? No. Why would it be? That's insane. Franks, you're clutching at straws.' He snorted. 'Is this why you don't like him? Because he was there when Lynda died? You know no one could help her. She was constantly battling with her addictions. No one is to blame for her dying, apart from her.'

'Forget it.'

'You're the one that brought it up,' Stefan said. 'Speaking of Grace, have *you* contacted her yet?'

'She won't take my calls. She's grieving and I don't want to stress her, so I've stopped trying.'

There was a pause.

'I'm sorry that Sol gives you the heebie-jeebies, Franks. But I promise you, he's a solid guy once you get to know him. You mustn't blame him for Lynda's death.'

Frankie looked towards the TV, where the posh kids were now in a café drinking coffee. Her shoulders hunched up to her ears. The couple remained silent, their conversation thankfully over.

I stepped into the light. 'Hi, Frankie, I'm home.'

She whipped round. 'Oh my God, you gave me a fright.'

Stefan turned with a look of disgust plastered on his face. My irritation grew. Frankie rubbed her sore-looking eyes.

'I bought us dinner, Frankie. I didn't realise we'd have company.'

'That was kind of you, Bee,' she sniffed. 'But we've eaten already, haven't we, Stefan? Just sort yourself out.'

'Why didn't you tell me he was going to be here?' The temperature in my body was rising. The red mist circled around my torso.

'Excuse me?' she said.

'Charming,' Stefan added, rolling his eyes and laughing.

'I, err . . .' I had to rein it in. 'I'm surprised, that's all. If you'd called me to warn me, I could have organised dinner for three.'

I was stung. Stung bad.

'Like I said, we've eaten already.' Frankie turned to Stefan. 'Shall we go upstairs to the lounge? Leave Bee to eat in peace.'

'Sure.' He stood up and brushed himself down on his tailored navy trousers.

Stefan was so polished and slick and slippery, good looking in a typical public schoolboy kind of way, I hated him so much. I hated everything that he stood for. Rich and privileged, not a clue about what it was like to go to bed hungry.

'No, don't bother,' I snapped, unable to control my reddening mood. 'It's fine. Stay where you are. I'll go to my room.'

'What about your dinner?'

I shrugged my shoulders.

'Bee? Don't be like this.'

'By the way, if you want to know how my first day went, it was brilliant. No thanks to Mia, of course. She didn't even call Martha to cover for you. She's a real fucking bitch!'

'She didn't?' Frankie straightened herself up. A look of shock on her face. *Good.*

'Mia's not the saint you thought she was.'

I stomped off, stopping at the foot of the kitchen. 'Oh, and I think you should also know Mia's looking for a new job. Found all her online searches on her browser. She wouldn't answer her phone today when I called her, so I'm guessing she lied about being sick as well, so she could go for an interview.'

'Right, well . . .' Frankie played with the silver ring on her index finger.

I stormed out, leaving the shopping on the counter. All that money spent on nothing. In my room, I sat on the bed, with only the sound of drilling for company. My body was rigid, and my brain was erupting.

A loneliness I hadn't felt for a while washed over me — sharp needles, like a million wasp stings at once.

Here I was again, unloved and unwanted, banished to my room.

The red fog scrambled my thoughts. I tried to fight it, but it was impossible to control. Tears of rage streamed down my face. I hadn't cried in years. I pulled Mum's letter out of the pillowcase and scrunched it into a ball.

I was mad. I was so, so, mad. And when I was mad, bad things happened.

CHAPTER THIRTY-ONE

Bee

It was the second night I went to bed filled with rage. Come daybreak, I couldn't tell whether I'd actually slept or not. Mum's laughter had mocked me all night. One thing was becoming crystal clear — Stefan was a distraction for Frankie. And I didn't like it. I didn't like it one bit.

The two days Frankie had given me to crash at hers were up and I hadn't had the chance to schmooze her properly so I could stay permanently, thanks to slimy Stefan. I'd no intention of going anywhere now that I'd moved in. He was lucky that he'd left the house so early because I was so full of red mist come the morning, I wanted to gouge his eyes out with a fucking fork. Whatever her issue was with that dodgy Sol character, one thing was for certain, she couldn't rely on Mr Chelsea Boy to help her. He was too much of a wimp.

It was 7.45 a.m. when I'd calmed down enough to brave it into the kitchen. Frankie was in bed. I was still rejected and bruised, but at least the fog had passed. I'd dressed smart again, just in case I was sent to work. I secretly hoped I'd revealed enough about Princess Leia to send her packing. I wanted to make a coffee for Frankie, giving me an excuse to knock on her bedroom door.

When I opened the fridge to get the oat milk, I saw the lasagne meal for two on the top shelf. My tummy knotted at the sight of it and my anger flared once more. I reminded myself that going to bed hungry wasn't a new thing and that last night was a glitch.

Frankie wasn't Dotty. And I wasn't Bernadette. I was Bee.

It was quiet as I stood outside her room. I suspected that she was still asleep. I knew she had a class in under an hour because I had to print the work schedule out for the next day and attach it to the clipboard. Frankie had to get up otherwise she'd be late. I rapped on the door confidently.

'Come in.'

Pushing the door open, I paused at the doorway, taking her in, sensing the imprint I'd made in the room the night before when I watched her having a fitful night's sleep. Frankie was sitting up in bed, wearing a black silk pyjama set, looking stressed and tired, like she hadn't slept at all. She was turning her mobile in her hand. The window was open and it was cold, but she didn't notice.

'I've brought you coffee.'

'Thank you, Bee. That's so kind of you.' Her face softened. 'I'm sorry about last night, leaving you alone like that. I shouldn't have.'

I was so starved of affection, her comment made me teary. I swallowed down the hard lump in my throat. 'You have a lot on your mind.'

She turned to look me straight in the eye, with an expression I couldn't work out. 'Yes. Yes, I do. How do you know so much all the time?'

'I dunno. I just do, I guess.'

She looked at me curiously and hugged her knees into her chest.

'Where have you come from, Bee?'

I froze. *Did she know? Had she seen the letter?*

'You seem to have this incredible instinct about you.' She smiled. 'Come and sit down next to me. Don't look so panicked. Come. It's okay.' She patted the bed. 'Sit down.'

Placing the coffee on the bedside, I sat next to her and watched as she tapped the code into her phone to unlock it. 121089. The same punch code for the gym. The same numerals that were engraved on the back of my necklace. She handed her phone over to me.

'Have a read and tell me what you think. Stefan hasn't read any of these yet and I want to keep it that way for now until I figure out what to do.'

I was looking at text exchanges between Frankie and Sol from the day before.

Don't ever threaten me again.

Threaten you? Frankie, I explained how things were going to go down.

I'll call the police. I'm warning you.

And say what? I'm an old pal interested in a piece of artwork from a dead skag-head.

After Lynda's funeral, I want you out of my life. Gone. Do you hear?

Frankie, sweet ting', give me what belongs to me and I promise, I'll be long gone. Tell Stefan or anyone else and your secret will come out. Go to the police and you're over. Remember what I'm telling

*you, gal. Remember who you used to be. Remember
that I know everything. Remember, you owe me.*

> *What did I ever do to you for you to come after
> me like this?*

*You have until the funeral,
Laurence Soliman.*

I re-read the messages a couple more times, pondering the
words, overcome with a sense of protection. I wanted to help
Frankie in any way I could. I looked at the name displayed on the
message. It all clicked into place. I'd wasted loads of time searching
under the incorrect name, Sol and Soliman, no wonder I couldn't
find any dirt. Laurence Soliman was his actual name. With this
new piece of information, I was bound to find something.

'What do you think, Bee?' She looked desperate.

'I think you need to do whatever it takes to get this dodgy
guy out of your life,' I said.

'You're right.'

'Call the police.'

'I can't.' She stared intently, like she was secretly communi-
cating something to me.

Was she giving me the green light?

I handed Frankie the phone. What did he have over her that
was so bad she couldn't go to the police? She turned away. Her
shoulders shook up and down as she cried.

'Why is he threatening you?'

'I met Lynda when I moved to London. We lived next door to
each other. The whole place was filled with drug users and down-
and-outs. But hey, I couldn't afford anything else and was grateful
for a roof over my head. I was young. A runaway, only sixteen.

Lynda looked after me, being a good few years older than I was. She was protective and sweet, made all the degenerates stay away. She was a good friend.'

Frankie sniffed loudly.

'But then, the inevitable happened. She got in with the wrong crowd, that being Laurence Soliman and his crew, and he got her hooked on drugs. And I mean, heavy drugs. It didn't take long before I got involved as well.' Her voice quivered.

She turned to me, eyes pleading. 'Don't judge me. Please don't judge.'

'I would never,' I whispered.

'The problem was heroin helped me escape my troubled past . . .'

Her troubled past?

'It helped blot things out. For the short term, anyway. But I soon found out that it wouldn't solve my problems. It made things worse. So, I got myself clean after an incident. Unfortunately, I couldn't help Lynda get clean. I tried my best, but she was too far gone. I couldn't save her.'

She looked pensive.

'Sol came back into her life and look what's happened. She's dead. Dead. And now he's threatening me with exposure. He destroyed her and now he wants to do the same to me. He's evil and twisted. A bad, bad man.'

The room turned silent.

* * *

I waited in the kitchen, processing what she'd said while she took a shower. I was overjoyed that she'd shared so much with me, choosing me over Stefan. I was determined to help her. What *made* her run away from home in the first place? That part of her story was unclear. One thing was for certain — Sol was a scumbag and needed removing from her life. Frankie said she couldn't go to the police, *but what if I did?*

Half an hour later, she entered the kitchen. Her platinum hair was wet and slicked from her face. She sat next to me by the table and looked at the painting Sol wanted, her fingers tying themselves in knots. I placed my hand over hers to reassure her. It felt like the right thing to do. We stayed like that for a few moments, in silence. No distractions for once.

She slipped her hand from mine. 'Bee, I'm sorry to have to do this to you again, but can you cover reception? In fact, do you mind covering for the rest of the week? Mia sent me a message earlier this morning saying she's still unwell. After what you told me about her, I'm reluctant to believe anything she says now. I've asked her to come in for a meeting tomorrow morning to discuss her job going forwards. If you can cover this week, I'd be ever so grateful.'

I held in the smile that was forcing its way across my face and stood up. I looked to the floor and kicked my foot.

'I can't, I'm sorry,' I said, taking a gamble.

'Why? What's wrong?'

'I was going to spend the day looking for somewhere to live. You said I could stay at yours two nights only. I'm so sorry, but . . . I can't. I haven't had a chance to look for a new place because I was covering reception. Where will I sleep tonight if I work during the day? I mean, I could do with the money, like.'

She sighed thoughtfully. 'Look, stay at mine for the rest of the week and cover Mia's job. You can earn extra cash and I'll help you find a place over the weekend, okay?'

'Are . . . are you certain?'

'You're doing me a favour, to be honest with you.'

My heart skipped a beat. *Bingo.*

'Thank you. Thank you so much. I should get going, then. I don't want to be late for work. Oh, you have a class in fifteen minutes. Shall I call Martha?'

'No, don't worry. I've called her myself. But thanks for thinking of me. She'll be covering my classes. I've decided to take a leave of absence myself. I've been feeling a little queasy recently. Maybe I have some sort of tummy bug. And what with Lynda's death, my troubles with Sol and not to mention the other messages . . .'

Frankie stopped herself saying more.

'I'll be back at work after the funeral. I need time off.' She smiled tightly, shutting down the conversation.

I crossed the kitchen.

'Oh, by the way, I won't be seeing Stefan later, so we can have that lasagne meal tonight if you like.'

I turned and smiled broadly at her.

It was the best day ever.

CHAPTER THIRTY-TWO

Back then

Dotty liked to play games. She'd go days neglecting my needs and ignoring me as if I didn't exist, and then when she sensed that I couldn't take it anymore, when she could see how broken and worthless I felt, or when she needed me for something, she'd shower me with the attention and fake love. She'd kick me down only to drag me back up by a single hair. I was so desperate for her love, for her approval, I lapped up anything I could get.

I was a slave to her abuse.

But something snapped inside of me the night I escaped from the flat and found myself at the funfair with Daniel. I'd had a taste of freedom and I wanted more. From that moment onwards, I rebelled. I mean, what was the worst she could do? Mentally abuse me? Punish me? Try to lock me up? Dotty couldn't touch me anymore; she'd lost all her power. There wasn't any part of me that could be more damaged than it had been.

I'd hardened up and was dead inside.

Obviously, Dotty hated my new-found confidence. Her dominance had slipped. Her power, diminished. Of course, Reg didn't care about my rebellious streak. In fact, I think he preferred it because it meant I was out of the flat and out of the few hairs he had left on his head altogether. For Reg, it meant he had her all to himself. The crazy drunken loved-up fool.

There were huge benefits to not loving myself. I didn't give a shit what anyone said or thought or did to me anymore and it gave me the sense of freedom to do as I pleased. It also blurred the lines between safety and danger, and I became reckless and out of control. I ached for adventure. I'd even stopped going to school. There was no point, as I was going to fail my GCSEs anyway. The way I saw it, my existence was a joke.

From the day I was born, I was a mistake. My conception, an accident. When Reg found out Dotty was pregnant by another man, he was so besotted he forgave her straight away and convinced her to move into his council flat, promising to help her with the baby.

I found myself hanging out with the wrong crowd, the kids who lived on the estate, the ones I should have been hanging out with in the first place. I was comfortable being around them, the rougher types. We experimented with weed and acid and took copious amounts of speed, which was the cheapest of all the drugs at the time, and drank cheap booze during the day, taking turns stealing bottles from the local off licence. We'd terrorise the younger ones on the playground and hang out in the parks late at night.

I was drowning from my everlasting bender. I didn't want to come up for air.

Four frenzied months of living as a degenerate, trying to catch up with a life that I'd missed out on, all those years back when I was held captive by my narcissistic mother.

But one day, it all came to an abrupt end. It was the day I realised I was just like my mum, Dotty. *We were the same.*

Of course we were the same. How stupid of me to believe otherwise.

Her DNA was running through my veins, like poison.

How could I ever think I would be lucky enough to escape that?

CHAPTER THIRTY-THREE

Bee

We ate the lasagne meal for two and it was amazing. Afterwards, we sat on the sofa in the snug, where she'd sat with Stefan only the night before, and watched *Love Conquers All: The Reunion*. We didn't speak, just watched the telly, making comments here and there. After her revelations in the morning, I sensed she didn't want to be left by herself. Frankie needed company.

She needed *my* company.

When she fell asleep on the sofa, I looked at her for a while, studying her face. Her lips were perfectly shaped, natural looking with just the right amount of plump, not too overdone and not like most women who had swollen lips injected with goodness knows what into them. Her cheeks were chiselled and looked like they'd been contoured by a make-up artist. Frankie's skin was clear, milky white. She wore no make-up. Her brown brows were bushy, perfectly shaped. She had one silver hoop earring on the left lobe with two silver studs in the inside cartilage and another silver hoop on the right. The roots were coming through her hair, at the base of the platinum blonde.

Carefully, without taking a breath, I leaned in. She smelled good too. A mixture of lavender and thick earthy tones, like trees in a wet forest. It must have come from the Pilaga essential oils she liked to use around the house. I smiled to myself, thinking of Mum. *Who's laughing now, Dotty?* I'd be damned if I was going anywhere now that I was embedded in Frankie's life.

The problem was, I still didn't feel a hundred percent secure about staying at the house and needed a guarantee. I did have the letter stuffed in my pillowcase. That was my backup plan. I'd use it only if I had to.

Timing was everything with that letter.

She was lightly snoring now, in a deeper sleep. Clocking Frankie's phone on the coffee table, I picked it up and used the punch code 121089 to unlock it. I flicked my eyes up to make sure she was asleep and then turned to her messages on her mobile. Stefan and Sol were the last two people to make contact with her. Before that, she'd sent a message to Grace which was left unread. Even though I wanted to read what Stefan had to say for himself, I couldn't waste any more time on that loser. I needed to take down a number. A plan was formulating in my head.

I picked up my phone, switched it on silent and snapped a photo of the contact I needed, then snapped a photo of Frankie asleep, as a keepsake, which I hearted as a favourite. I carefully placed her phone back down and woke her so she could go to bed.

* * *

The next morning, we walked to work together, stopping at the local coffee shop on Essex Road, ordering two flat whites for the journey. Frankie was coming in for a meeting with Mia, hopefully to fire her. Even though there was fresh snow on the ground and the winds were bitter, I was warm inside. I loved my new job, my new home, my new life.

At work, I was on the phone when Mia slipped in, looking smarter than usual, wearing normal clothes and shoes for once.

Her Princess Leia hair was down, covering her shoulders, and she had a middle parting. She slumped on the sofa without saying hello and didn't even look my way, which I thought was rude seeing as I was covering her job. But I secretly didn't care. I was content to ignore her back, making a point to talk extra loud on the phone for effect while I organised a multiple booking. Mia shot me daggers when she thought I wasn't looking. I couldn't have been happier.

When Frankie greeted her, it was like they were strangers, and I knew then that her fate was sealed. Mia looked tearful as she followed Frankie into an empty room, the one that I'd slept in only a few nights before. How our luck had changed.

Twenty minutes later, Mia reappeared, alone. Wiping her puffy eyes, she approached me, her stupid glare hardening with each step. Earlier that morning, I'd gathered up her pathetic belongings in a pile for her to take home — a *Star Trek* pencil case, vitamin C supplements and a framed picture of her rat-dog, Vader. When she approached, I minimised the screen I was using and brought up the bookings system to show that I'd been working.

'I know you're behind all of this.'

'Sorry, Mia. I'm busy.' It was all her own doing — *her* fault, not mine.

'I've no idea about the bracelet,' she said.

'What bracelet?'

'The one you gave to Frankie. Amanda's bracelet. Where did you really find it?'

'In your drawer.' I stared without blinking. 'Is there anything else?'

'Don't think I'll just disappear, Bee. I know you set me up.'

'You can't prove a thing. Now, if you don't mind, I've got work to do.'

'There's something fishy about you and I'm going to find out what it is.'

She couldn't harm me. No one could. I was invincible.

Mia snatched her belongings and turned on her stupid court shoes, storming out of the gym. Frankie left a few minutes after that.

When the gym had quietened down, I pulled up the searches on Laurence Soliman I'd been doing online. Things were heating up. I'd discovered through the Company House website that he was the registered owner of a business named Karma Massage. It had an address in King's Cross attached to it. When I looked at Karma's website, at first glance it appeared normal, like any other spa-like business that offered various back and bone treatments. Nothing suspicious about it at all. But when I checked under the header 'Services We Offer', I found myself staring at provocative-looking women, heavily made up, wearing short white lab coats and fishnet tights, offering personalised massages. *Call now to have all your needs met.*

Feeling like a detective, I rubbed my hands together and opened up Maps on another tab to check out the location of Sol's business. I didn't know London at all, and I wanted to be prepared. Opposite the address was a café called Kafeneo, which looked Greek, with its blue-and-white-striped bunting on the exterior. It was the perfect spot for a stakeout.

Switching screens again, I noted down his business number and address, after which I googled the easiest and most pain-free way to give yourself a black eye. Apparently, if you tapped a hammer lightly around the eye socket for a few minutes, it would bruise within a day.

Satisfied with my day's work, I shut down all my searches and found the contact number I'd snapped from Frankie's phone the night before and smiled to myself. There was no guarantee that my plan would work, but it was worth a try. *For Frankie.*

Now where did she keep that hammer?

CHAPTER THIRTY-FOUR

Bee

After I left work, I messaged Frankie to tell her that I'd be home late so she wouldn't worry. I caught the bus to King's Cross and sat in Kafeneo by the window, opposite Karma Massage, a run-down, brown-bricked building on Britannia Street, sipping my hot chocolate — a real treat, something I was never allowed growing up. I staked the premises opposite.

It was late. The owner, or who I assumed to be the owner, was outside chatting animatedly to two blokes in a foreign language. It sounded guttural and raw and more like shouts than a conversation. But I knew it couldn't be serious because they were smiling at one another. Traffic had built in the area and people rushed around like lunatics, getting home. Every time the owner passed me, he jogged my chair, making me spill my drink. He was getting on my nerves, but I didn't say anything because he was a bulky man, taking up space, and looked like he could handle himself.

As time passed, the street quietened and the café emptied. I was the only customer left. My right eye felt swollen and sore to touch. I flicked my phone onto camera and checked my reflection. There was purple bruising on the lid. Not as much as I'd hoped, but noticeable enough. It was 7.35 p.m. I couldn't help but feel hurt and annoyed that Frankie hadn't replied to my message. I wasn't sat in a café wasting my time for nothing; I was there because of her. She could have at least asked what time I'd be home and if I needed dinner. Pretend to be concerned.

With no one coming in or out of the building opposite for nearly half an hour, I surfed my phone, checking Frankie's socials to see if she'd updated them. She'd been quiet since she suffered a backlash about her friendship with Lynda and I'd been checking Kelsey's pages too, to see whether she was fuelling the gossip, which she had been. In a way, I was glad to see that Frankie hadn't posted anything new. Now that I was in her life, I didn't think she needed to post so much. She had to protect her privacy, especially from the likes of Kelsey and others that had been slagging her off, claiming she was in hiding and couldn't face squashing the rumours about her and Lynda and the drugs.

Frankie couldn't trust anyone apart from me.

The owner began stacking chairs, making a point that he was closing shop. I checked the time, agitated and fed up. I was hungry and my eye was killing me.

But then, everything happened all at once.

A black cab pulled up outside Karma Massage. Coming out of the taxi was Sol. And he wasn't alone — oh no, he wasn't. With him were two women, model-like, wearing black coats, slutty shoes and heavy make-up. Adrenaline coursed through my body as I snapped as many pictures as I could before they disappeared behind the door. A few moments later, a stretched black Mercedes with blacked-out windows pulled up on the kerb outside the café. The chauffeur got out and opened the passenger door in the back. Out stepped a short, sharply dressed businessman. He entered Karma Massage. The chauffeur then got back inside the car and kept the engine running. I took a few more photos.

The bill was dumped on my table. I glanced at it: £4.50, what a rip off.

'Cash or card?'

I looked up. 'I, umm, I have cash.' I fished through my rucksack and reluctantly gave him a fiver.

Not waiting for my change as there wasn't much time, I rushed outside and knocked on the driver's window. The window rolled down.

'Can I help you?' He was much older than I expected.

'Why are you parked outside this address? Do you usually come here?'

'What's it to you, young lady?'

'The man that's entered that building over there. Can I have his details?'

'Excuse me?'

'You heard me. I need his phone number. His name. Anything you can give me.'

He chuckled to himself, leaned back and rolled up the window. I rapped on the window with my phone. 'I need to talk to you.'

He opened it a crack. I found the picture of his boss on my mobile entering the building and showed him. 'Please open the window so I can explain,' I said, in a calmer voice. 'Don't look so worried. I won't bite.'

Surprisingly, he did as I asked.

'Look, I'll be out of your way if you just give me your boss's details. Come on. Please?'

'Why would I do that?'

'It's personal. I can't say. But it's important.'

'I can't give you my client's number. I'll lose my job.'

'I won't say it was you. How would he know? Anyway, the guy's a scumbag. Why are you protecting him?'

The driver looked at me blankly.

'You got a wife? Kids? Grandkids? Then you know what your boss is doing is morally wrong. Come on. If you give me what I ask for, I'll be on my way. You'll never see me again and your boss will never know it was you. I promise.'

Unexpectedly, the driver got out of the car. 'Not a word you got this from me. Okay, lady?' He pulled his mobile out of his pocket.

'Not a word.'

Sucker. I couldn't believe it. He'd given me what I'd asked for. His client's full name, Joshua Bolt, his phone number and even his home address in Surrey. The chauffeur had no loyalty to him. And why would he? What an absolute piece of shit Joshua Bolt was. Most evenings after work, he was driven to Laurence's establishment for a 'massage', after which he'd be driven back to his wife and four kids. He despised Joshua and said that if I had any sense, I'd stay away from him too.

Ha! Not bloody likely.

It was perfect. Now I had something solid to work with.

I dialled the number which I'd taken down the night before, and hid out of sight, in the shadows, waiting.

CHAPTER THIRTY-FIVE

Frankie

I'm staring at a new message from my Instagram troll, and this time they've included a picture. A picture of the outside of my house. There's a silhouette framed inside my bedroom window, a person with their head bowed. That person is me, and I'm looking at the phone in my hand. It must have been snapped yesterday morning. *Holy shit.* A day before the security was installed. The message is from *@youaregoingtopaybitch.* The handle has changed, but I know it's the same person as before.

Watching you, watching me.

My nerve endings are on fire, prickles of heat pulsating inside my veins. My home used to be my sanctuary. My haven. Despite the added security, I still don't feel safe. Rushing around the place, I make sure all the external doors and windows are locked, all shutters closed, the systems that were installed, working. I switch the lights on in every room. Every street sound is exaggerated, every noise making me jumpy and on edge. In my room, I bend the shutter in half and take a look outside. It's hard to see in the darkness with only the glow of the streetlamps and Christmas decorations. Whoever took the photo must have taken the shot from the opposite side of the road, next to the lamppost. The thought that someone's watching me makes me shudder. I check the Highbury Security app on my phone and notice that the external camera fitted outside my house is only facing the front door and doesn't cover the road. Damn it. Closing the shutter, I pull away and go downstairs.

I do what I promised myself I wouldn't do this week, and like an addict, I scroll through all my social media accounts to check what has been said, to see if I can spot any clues to my mystery stalker. Have they left any breadcrumbs? I find nothing. When I'm searching, I can't help but read all the comments made about me, about Lynda, about our past together. The rumours haven't died down and the online community are turning on me, impatient with my silence. Leading the way is Kelsey. My blood boils further. My follower count has gone down, Kelsey's up. I'll deal with *her* and all the online backlash at a later date.

But first things first, I need to get Sol off my back and see whether the messages are connected to him. Just because he was standing in front of me when the other message came through doesn't mean he isn't responsible. He could have a timer on his app which sends messages out on a schedule. I've used one when I've wanted to stagger my content.

I'm tempted to give him what he wants — the painting — maybe then it'll all come to an end. I wish Lynda was around to give me advice. She would know what to do. God, I miss her so much.

Switching onto her page, I notice that it's still blank. Grace hasn't put anything back up. I stare at the empty space, the void that was once Lynda's life in pictures now all gone and wonder whether Sol sold her the stash that killed her. The thought makes me want to throw up. My hand hovers over Grace's number.

Wanting to hear a familiar voice, even if it's a hostile one, I google how to disguise your number when calling someone. Pressing #31#, followed by my mobile number, I call. It still comes as a shock when Grace actually answers.

'Hello?'

'Grace, it's me.'

'Frankie?'

'Please don't hang up. Please.'

'What do you want?'

'How are you doing?'

'How do you think?'

'Stupid question. I'm sorry.'

'Is that all, or is there something else?'

'Laurence.'

'Excuse me?'

'I mean Sol. Lynda's friend, Sol.'

'What about him?'

'When did he come onto the scene? Do you know much about him? Have you heard from him since Lynda passed?'

'I can't do this right now, Franks. Not now. The funeral's tomorrow.'

The phone pressed to my ear goes dead.

There's an urgent rap at the door. My heart freezes. They knock again. And again, and again. I hear someone shouting my name. They're crying out for help. Without checking my security app, I rush to the door, unbolt it, unfasten the chain lock and fling it open.

Bee. She's standing on the doorstep in sobs of tears. She's in a terrible state and has a black eye.

'Something bad has happened.' Bee stumbles into the house and collapses onto her knees in front of me, sobbing, her make-up smeared down her face.

* * *

'Well, I think we have all we need. We'll be in touch as soon as the arrest is made,' says PC Davies, the investigating police officer for Camden and Islington. He flips his pocket notepad closed, places it in his blazer. I see Davies and his colleague, a young woman who looks about eighteen named PC Freud, to the front door and thank them again for their time. When I shut the door behind them, I lean my head against the wall with a sense of relief. In the end, the decision to call the police on Sol was forced upon me.

Even though it's been a couple of hours since Bee burst through my door, I'm still in shock. I can't believe he attacked her. I always knew he was a dealer and a hustler and an all-round scumbag, but I never knew he was a violent man. Bee explained to the police that she wanted to help me out. She could see that I was desperate and didn't like the way Sol was threatening me. She wanted to speak to him about it, to reason with him. He invited her into his establishment so they could talk. She refused and stayed on the doorstep. They got embroiled in a row and that's when he punched her in the face. Miraculously, she has a witness, a businessman named Joshua Bolt who stopped opposite in his chauffeur-driven car to get a coffee from a local café on his way home. He saw the whole attack unfold in front of him. The police took down the witness's name and number and also Sol's business address.

The same building Lynda and I lived at.

I can't believe Bee did this *all for me.*

I had to show the threatening messages he'd been sending me to the police to back Bee up. It's something I should have done from the get-go. My cowardice fills me with deep shame. From now on, no more burying my head in the sand, wishing things resolve on their own. Hopefully the police have enough evidence to have him arrested and locked up.

I enter the kitchen to find Bee sitting at the table, looking mousy. She's hunched, twiddling her fingers. What if he'd done worse?

'Why don't I run you a bath? Maybe get us a late-night take-away?' I say.

'That would be nice. Thank you.' She beams, kicking her legs like a child.

'It's the least I can do.'

I run the bath for Bee and message Stefan asking him to come over, after which I order an indulgent takeaway for three. I don't tell him the ins and outs of what's transpired over the phone.

As the bathroom steams up, I feel the tension in my body releasing. Not all my worries have disappeared, but it's a start. My thoughts turn to Lynda. The funeral is tomorrow. A day I'm dreading. Maybe once we bury Lynda and that scumbag has been arrested, I can put all this nasty business behind me and begin to heal.

Twenty minutes later, Bee is singing to herself in the bath and Stefan is at my front door. In the hallway, he holds me tight in his arms and I sink into his chest, bursting into tears. I'd been holding it in for Bee's sake all evening. It feels good to let it all out.

'What's happened?'

'Bee. She . . . She was trying to help.'

Stefan lets go. We stand facing one another. 'What did she do?'

'She went to see Laurence.'

'Laurence?'

'Sol. Soliman. His real name is Laurence Soliman. And he's a very bad man.'

190

'You keep saying this about him, but won't explain . . .'

I can't look at him.

'Franks.' Stefan steps back.

'He's from my past. From Lynda's,' I whisper. 'He used to sell drugs when we were living in the bedsits. I had no idea then that he was my landlord too! Anyway, I told all this to Bee. I thought maybe that the messages were connected to him somehow. I needed someone to talk to. I was stressed. Felt overwhelmed.'

'Slow down . . . I can't keep up. Messages? What messages?'

'Stefan! Come on, we've spoken about this before. The Instagram messages I've been getting. My mystery stalker.'

'You never told me how serious it was getting. You never told me you thought it was Sol. I mean Laurence, or whoever you say he is.'

'I still don't have proof it's him.'

'I'm getting lost here. I don't understand. What the hell has Bee got to do with all this?'

'Ssshhh. She's upstairs having a bath,' I whisper.

'A what —)? Franks. You know she can't stay with you forever. She's not your responsibility.'

'I know, I know. But she's done so much for me.'

'How?'

'After I told her about my suspicions, she decided to find Soliman herself. I had no idea she was going to do this. I didn't ask her to get involved. I just needed someone to talk to. Anyway, she found him. Approached him. Asked him to leave me alone. And he . . . well . . . I can't believe I'm saying this. But he *attacked her*. He attacked her, Stefan! Punched her in the face. Assaulted her. She has a witness. We've called the police on him. Hopefully he'll be arrested.'

'Right, well . . .' He looks to the floor.

'I know. Poor Bee.'

'You should have opened up to me. Not a young girl. A girl who can't handle herself and is stupid enough to approach a dangerous man. You should have come to me. I would have sorted it.'

I look into his grey eyes. 'I didn't know how violent he was.'

'I know she's helped you out in some way, and that's very honourable of her, but remember, she's not your responsibility. I'm here now. I'll take care of the situation.'

'Bee will stay here a few more days until things calm down. She needs a break. I owe her, Stefan. I can't just ask this young girl to leave. She has nothing. I'm going to help her find someplace else to stay. She'll be fine. Just a few more days.'

'Good. It's the right decision.'

His gaze turns away from mine. He looks past me, up the stairs. Something hardens in his eyes. I look up too.

Bee.

'Oh, hello, Stefan. I didn't know you were coming over.' There's sarcasm to her tone.

She stands at the top of the stairs with her hand on the banister. She steps forward, out of the shadows. I've no idea how long she's been there for or how much she's heard.

She takes her time coming down the stairs like she's playing a lead role in some movie. It's all very theatrical and dramatic and very, very uncomfortable. Bee's hair is tied up in a towel and she's wearing my favourite kimono dressing gown with the bird motifs. Strange. Did I give it to her? I don't recall doing so. It is possible, as I was in a bit of a haze as soon as the police left.

'Frankie, is the takeaway here? I'm bloody starved,' Bee says, smiling from cheek to cheek.

She pushes past us and heads into the basement like she owns the place.

Is it me, or is she behaving like nothing's happened?

CHAPTER THIRTY-SIX

Frankie

After our takeaway, we leave Bee to watch TV in the snug and Stefan and I go to bed. We don't make love. Instead, we hold onto each other, not saying much. His heart beats against my ear.

'Tell me everything, Franks.'

In his embrace, I open up. Not fully. Never fully. But enough for him to understand what's been going on.

'It's not only Lynda who used drugs. I also dabbled with it. Something I'm ashamed of. Laurence — I mean, Sol — he wasn't just our landlord, he was our dealer too. Lynda introduced me to him. He'd come over with a bag of brown — heroin — and it wasn't long before I was hooked as well. But something happened that made me snap out of my slump, a wake-up call so to speak, and I forced myself to clean up. It wasn't long before I moved out and never saw him again.'

I pause.

'That day in the gallery, Grace asked if I knew who he was. She was suspicious of him. But I didn't think much of it at the time because, let's face it, Grace is suspicious of everyone she meets. But there was a familiarity to him I couldn't quite put my finger on.'

'But you didn't put two and two together?'

'No. He looks so different now. And it's been years.'

'And what with the different name. Why would you make the connection?'

'Exactly. Anyway, that night, I received my very first message from my stalker. Coincidence much?'

'What do all these messages say?'

'That's the thing, Stefan. Whoever's sending the messages is threatening me about my past. They obviously know about my drug use somehow.'

'But you can't tie Sol to them.'

'No, I can't,' I say. 'The other day, when I realised who he was, I invited him over. I wanted to get to the bottom of why he'd appeared in my life. In Lynda's.'

'Oh, Franks. Why didn't you tell me?'

'Maybe it was a stupid thing to do, but I had to take control somehow.'

'So, what happened?'

'He threatened me. He said he wanted Lynda's painting in exchange for his silence. It's worth over a million now, I'm sure of it. Isn't it, Stefan?'

He doesn't reply.

'Did you speak to him about its value the day you invited him for lunch?'

Stefan stays quiet. I lie on his chest, listening to the sound of his heart thumping.

Trepidation washes over me.

'Whoever's sending the messages is basically threatening me with exposure about my past. The same as Sol,' I continue.

His silence continues.

I brush off my unease. 'The problem is, when Sol was with me, I received a message at the same time. So I can't connect them for sure.'

A dark thought flits into my mind. *What if Sol has an accomplice?*

Stefan's heart's racing, so I know he's alert and not fallen asleep. I lift my head and stare into his soft grey eyes to check if he's okay. He strokes my face, pulls me close into him and kisses me hard. We make passionate love, after which he falls asleep.

I stay wide awake, tossing and turning.

* * *

'We're going to be late,' Stefan shouts from the hallway. He's been waiting for me to get my act together for over twenty minutes now.

'One second,' I say as casually as possible, the opposite to how I'm feeling inside.

Locked in the bathroom, I lean over the toilet bowl and spew my morning coffee out. My stomach muscles contract, my body quakes and my mouth tastes like the gutter. I'm coming to the realisation that my recent spell of vomiting may not be a stomach bug after all. In fact, I'm two weeks late for my period. The thought fills me with a paralysing fear.

I'm going to be sick again. Bile comes up this time. I dry heave what's left and wipe my mouth. My head's in a spin as I hold onto the edge of the toilet seat.

'Franks, is everything okay?'

'Just a moment.'

I've woken in a state of anxiety. Everything's piling on top of me. I don't know whether it's the funeral and saying goodbye to Lynda that's making me feel worse than ever, or because I've yet to hear back from the police about the arrest. The lack of sleep doesn't help. I know stress can make someone late, but what if . . . *what if?*

I'm also angsty after receiving a cryptic message an hour ago from *@youaregoingtopaybitch* saying, *Tick, tock. Tick, tock.* I don't know who to trust anymore.

The walls in the bathroom close in.

Staring at my reflection, I notice that I'm waxy pale and my eyes are sunken. I wash my face and re-brush my teeth and tongue. Taking the bleach, I pour it inside the toilet, flushing the remnants of my vomit away. If only I could flush away my problems at the same time.

On the way to the church in our Addison Lee car, Stefan is quiet, his head buried in his phone. It makes me jittery.

I think about the possibility of a baby forming inside of me. Am I ready for this? *Is he?*

'Stefan, I received another message from my troll.'

'Ignore it, Franks. My guess is, it's a sad internet nutjob needing to get a life.' He doesn't even look up when he speaks. It's like he's talking about the weather.

Turning my attention to the outside world, I look out the window as the taxi weaves in and out of one long traffic jam, making me queasy.

I pray Sol has been arrested.

CHAPTER THIRTY-SEVEN

Frankie

We arrive at the funeral. The gate to the churchyard squeaks as Stefan pushes it open. He takes my hand and leads me up the path towards the church. Snow cloaks the ancient gravestones that have sunken into the earth on either side of us. Up ahead, there are two crow-like shadows dressed head to toe in black, smoking. Plumes of smoke mix with car fumes from the congested roads of the East End. It turns my stomach. I swallow the bile down. When we approach, I notice they're Lynda's arty friends, the Drayton Twins. Stefan nods in acknowledgement. I keep my eyes glued to the ground as we step inside.

The smell of incense, candles and fresh flowers hits me as soon as I enter. We make our way down the aisle. I see the backs of the heads of the people sitting down. I scan everyone, searching for Sol. A few people are wearing flat caps. He's not here. Of course he's not. They've arrested him, I assure myself. Perhaps they've called Bee about it, expecting her to pass the message on to me. I'm worrying over nothing.

No sooner do I breathe a sigh of relief than I eye the coffin ahead on the altar. My body tenses. White flowers spelling Lynda's name are laid on top. They are classy and delicate and dainty and twee and not her style. I'm sure she would have had something inappropriate and funny to say about them. My knees give way and I semi-collapse into Stefan. He puts his arm around me for support. I force one foot in front of the other as he guides me to the second row, where there's a gap. I take a seat behind Grace. I have an urge to touch her, somehow thinking that the contact will make me feel closer to Lynda. I place my hand on her shoulder and squeeze. Grace turns around to look at me. Her eyes are red and swollen. I sense a pain greater than mine. She gives me a tight smile.

'Why did this happen?' she asks.

I'm stunned into silence. It's difficult to know what to say and how to reassure her. Will we ever know? I remove my hand and Grace turns to face the vicar, who's clearing his throat. I wipe tears from my eyes. Organ music plays, filling up the quiet crevices inside the church.

I miss my friend.

* * *

The funeral passes in a fog of sombre hymns and poems, cries and sniffles. Grace makes an emotional speech which brings the congregation to tears. Stefan doesn't cry. After the ceremony, we all get into our arranged cars and follow the hearse to the cemetery in Tower Hamlets where she'll be buried.

The mood by Lynda's plot is sober and dark. Time evaporates and everything's a hazy blur of quiet noise and muted pastel colours. Tears are shed and there are bursts of respectful laughter too, breaking the painful silences. There's a light scattering of snow. It makes everything look serene, like we're living life inside a Monet painting. We huddle around the gravestone. Some people have black umbrellas to shield from the weather. Stefan takes my hand.

The moment comes when Lynda is lowered into the ground. I want to be sick. With heads bowed, people approach the coffin in pairs to throw a single white rose onto it. When it's our turn, Stefan pulls me to the foot of the hole. I don't want to go. Tears cascade down my face and it's hard to see. We throw our roses together.

I whisper, 'I should have done more.'

I want the ground to swallow me up instead of her. Life is cruel.

As earth is thrown on top of the coffin, Grace screams, 'Nooo!' and collapses onto the wet ground in a heap. She's hurting and it's unbearable to witness. She claws the earth, screaming, and has to be carried away to calm down.

There's a snow shower. Everything turns silent. I look up to the sky and a blanket of white envelopes me, large snowflakes falling onto my skin. I sense someone staring at me.

I turn my gaze and look across the grave, past the other mourners, and sense someone's penetrating dark eyes. They catch mine and pull me towards them.

Sol.

I don't understand.

He continues to stare with a dead expression as everyone starts to disperse, heading to the Stag's Head for the wake. I'm hot, despite the temperature. I grip onto Stefan's arm for support. Has he spotted him too? Sol looks behind him. I look to where his eyes have landed, past the plots and outside where all the cars are parked. There are two marked police cars blocking the entrance. Uniformed police wait by the large oak tree.

Sol strides towards the back of the plots, away from the police and congregation, his walk turning into a light jog, then a sprint. I look over to the lane. Two new police officers have appeared in the graveyard and one is pointing towards him.

It happens so quickly. A chase breaks out. One of the officers catches up with him and tackles him to the ground.

The disturbance gets the attention of the other mourners, and everything feels like it's in a movie scene. Grace has come back and is looking as confused as everyone else. She turns to me for answers.

'What's happening?' she asks.

'They're arresting him,' I say.

'But why?'

'He's a dealer and a very dangerous man. I think he may have had something to do with Lynda's death. He may have sold her dodgy H.'

Grace spits on the ground. 'I knew there was something not right about him. I asked Lynda but she just laughed it off, giving me some cock and bull story that he was an old friend.'

'You think you know somebody . . .' Stefan says pensively, shaking his head.

'They better lock him up and throw away the key,' Grace adds.

All three of us watch as Sol is handcuffed and escorted to a police car. When he catches my eye, he winks. A shiver travels down my spine. An officer lands their hand on his head as he is forced inside the car. Finally! The nightmare is over.

My phone buzzes inside my coat pocket. It's from Bee.

Your 'Sol' problem should be solved today. You can thank me for setting this situation up with a celebratory glass of wine later.

I check to see if anyone is staring in my direction. The police are preoccupied. Sol's safely inside the car. I delete Bee's message on my phone.

What the hell does she mean by *setting this situation up*?

CHAPTER THIRTY-EIGHT

Bee

With a satisfying pop, Frankie uncorked the wine that I'd taken from the wine fridge. The bottle had a French label with cursive writing on it, Chateau something or other, and looked expensive. She smelled the cork and smiled, but her eyes were sad and puffy.

She poured me a large glass. *I could get used to this.*

Her glass remained empty. It bothered me that she wasn't pouring for herself. I thought we were going to spend the night celebrating the arrest. The funeral was done and dusted, and I'd been waiting hours for her to return home. At least that slime Stefan wasn't around, which was something positive. Apparently, he had something urgent to deal with after the funeral.

It was just the two of us sat by the table with Lynda's painting still on her wall, thanks to yours truly. From now on, every time she'd look at the painting she'd think of me.

Frankie was wearing her funeral suit and looked classy, and I'd just come home from a satisfying day at work, making her lots of money. I'd been swept off my feet all day.

'Why aren't you joining me?' I asked.

'It's been an emotional day. I think I'll pass.'

My jaw tensed. Fucking Lynda. It was supposed to be our night tonight, not hers! *Ours.* I drank, trying to mask the foul mood that was threatening to ruin everything.

'Bee, can I ask you something? What did you mean about setting up the situation with Sol?' Frankie whispered, looking around the kitchen, like we weren't alone.

Finally, the subject was back on me and what I'd done.

My cheeks flushed. The smile I had earlier found its way back. 'I had to do *something* to get him off your case.'

'But what *exactly*?'

'I did what anyone would have done to help a friend out. He's a piece of shit and he deserves what he gets.' My hand went to my bruised eye.

Frankie parted her lips to speak and then closed them, thinking twice. She looked around again. 'I mean, I am grateful that he's not around anymore.'

'Job's a good 'un, then.'

I drank more. God, it tasted good. The wine slipped down my throat like velvet.

'Well, knowing he's under arrest makes me feel a lot more . . . how can I put it? Relaxed.'

'There you go.'

'And I haven't received any creepy messages on Instagram since, thank goodness.'

'You think it was Sol sending them?'

'What do you think?'

I shrugged. 'I mean, it must have been him. Look at what he did to me.'

Frankie sighed and made her way to the counter, flicking the kettle on. She turned to face me, placing one foot over the other. 'You know I'm so grateful to you.'

'I know. You said.' I drank more.

It was smooth and silky and tasted like the blackberries I used to pick from the overgrown bramble bush outside my tower block. The fresh tangy flavour would explode in my mouth and was like nothing I'd ever tasted before. Back then, I was starved of fresh food.

'I'm curious. Have you managed to find a place to stay yet?'

Something snapped inside of me.

Was she going to throw me out after what I'd done, while I sat there with a fucking black eye? I drained the glass and poured another, filling the glass to the rim.

'I haven't had a chance to look, what with work. I also had to take care of the "Soliman situation" for you.'

'I understand. Of course. Of course. I understand. How insensitive of me. There's no pressure. You can stay until you find your feet. I can help you out with anything you need.'

The kettle clicked. Frankie opened the cupboard. She pulled out a white cup, throwing a herbal teabag inside.

'Bee, have you seen my mug? The one that says, "Queen of Islington" on it?'

Shit. 'Never even noticed it.'

'Huh. That's strange.' Frankie shook her head, picked up a white cup instead.

'Is it special to you?' I probed.

She sat down. 'Yes. Very. That mug was from Lynda. I should have taken better care of it.' She blew onto her herbal tea, tears threatening to spill from her eyes.

Fucking Lynda this, fucking Lynda that. I was going to implode if I heard that name one more time. She was gone. Dead. Six foot under.

'Shall we talk about work?'

'Okay.' I sat upright, grinning.

'You've been doing a marvellous job. I'm impressed with how you've handled yourself this week, with our clients, on the phone, the bookings. You're a self-starter, proactive, and it makes a change. I know the gym is safe in your hands. Goodness me, you even managed to pacify Amanda, our trickiest client. Which reminds me, I owe her a coffee.' She sighed. 'Anyway, I've been very impressed, I must say. It's been great to take a step back and allow someone else to take the reins for once.'

'Thank you. I've really enjoyed work.' I was giddy from the attention.

But it also worried me, because I didn't want Frankie to have power over my emotions, like Dotty used to. I wanted our relationship to be different. To be equal. However, I was such a weakling, one compliment and I knew I'd do anything for her. Deep down, I was at her mercy, just like I used to be with Mum.

'I'm glad to hear it because I wanted to offer you the reception role permanently. And perhaps now that you have something full-time, and which pays pretty decent, you can view some properties. I can help you with a deposit if you like. Pay me back when you can.'

Her words came at me all at once. I was having trouble digesting them. I had a job, a permanent job, but — and it was a big but — she was still insisting on me leaving the house. I tried not to focus on the negative and stuck to the positives. So much could change in a week. So much *had* changed. I had plenty of time.

Even though she didn't know it yet, she was tied to me. We were connected.

And I wasn't going anywhere.

'What do you say, Bee? Do you accept my offer?'

'Of course. Yes. Of course. Thank you.'

Fresh excitement built up inside.

'Can I put a load of washing on? I don't have many smart things to wear. In fact, if I'm being honest with you, this is pretty much the only smart thing I own. I should get out of it and put it in the wash for Monday.' I was sticky under my arms.

'Sit down and enjoy your wine. You've earned it. And of course you can put a load of washing on — whenever you like. But do it later. You don't need to do it now.'

'Thank you.' I sat back down.

Frankie filled my glass, the bottle almost empty. I felt the fuzzy effects from the wine.

'Look, tomorrow is Saturday, and I don't have any plans during the day. I don't want to mope about thinking about poor Lynda, so why don't I take you shopping? You can pick a couple of outfits for work. Maybe we can get a bite to eat afterwards? I could do with the distraction.'

'But I don't have money.'

'I'm going to pay you cash for this week's work. Sssh. Don't tell anyone. Official pay cheques will start from Monday. You'll get the money owed to you tomorrow. But even so, the shopping spree and lunch are on me. My way of saying thanks. You know. *For Soliman.*' She whispered his name, like he was in the room listening.

'But Frankie, you've done so much already.'

'It's the least I can do. How about we don't mention Sol anymore. I don't want to think about him. I want to move forwards.'

Suited me fine. I nodded in agreement.

Her face was filled with warmth. 'Let's talk about your new role instead. Now that you're going to be a permanent member of staff, I need to make you official. Paying you in cash, off the record, has been unprofessional of me. Only temporary. I assume Mia took care of all the details — your National Insurance number, full name and home address. It should all be filed at work.'

My chest fluttered in panic. Why was life so shitty? Of course Mia hadn't taken my details down.

'The thing is, she never asked.'

'Oh, Mia. I could wring her neck sometimes.'

Backed into a corner, I paused, not sure how to play it.

Maybe it was the effects of the wine, I don't know, maybe I was fed up with running away from myself. Whatever it was, I decided that it was time for some brutal honesty. Well, part honesty, anyway. I couldn't disclose everything. Not yet.

'Even if she did ask, I wouldn't have been able to give her my details.'

'Excuse me?'

'My full name. My home address. I can't give this information to you.'

She cocked her head to the side. 'Why ever not?'

Because then you'd know.

I inhaled deeply, looking away from her. 'You see, my home life . . . it wasn't the best. In fact, it was terrible. My mum. My stepdad. They were abusive towards me. Now that Mum has died, I want to stay anonymous. I need a fresh start. A new name. A new identity. I can't afford for him to find me.'

Frankie sat quietly, not moving.

'They were bad people. Both of them. But particularly Mum. She was cruel.' Real tears welled up in my eyes. 'I think she tried to drown me as a baby.'

For once, I was telling the truth, or what I believed to be the truth. I did have a hazy memory of drowning as a baby, which I'd pushed to the back of my mind. It was grainy — no sound, just sensations. The vague impression of not being able to breathe was all I had, like someone muzzling me, a hand over my mouth and nose, pushing me into the water. Me crying, breathing water into my lungs.

Was it a memory or a wild fantasy I'd come up with to make myself feel better about Mum and Reg, to justify why they'd never loved me? Why *she'd* never loved me. Because she didn't love me, did she? She could only love herself.

Tears ran down my cheeks. I found myself crying without any effort. Embarrassed, I covered my face with my hands. My bruised eye hurt as I wept. Any moment, Frankie would console me, maybe put an arm around me, like I'd done for her. Unusually, I was craving physical contact. For years, I had nothing and now, now I had her . . .

The sound of a chair scraping across the floor acted like a circuit breaker. I looked up and sniffed. Frankie was standing, looking pale as a ghost.

'I'm so sorry, Bee. I've come over all queasy. If you'll excuse—'

Without finishing her sentence, she ran past the snug, towards the downstairs toilet. I heard the bathroom door slam shut, then the sounds of vomiting.

She didn't even comfort me.

CHAPTER THIRTY-NINE

Frankie

The morning's shopping trip passes pleasantly and is exactly what I need to take my mind off everything. Bee's been a nice distraction and shopping for her has given me the excuse to concentrate on the happiness of someone else instead of focusing on my worries. I feel bad for leaving her alone last night, but her revelations startled me.

The thought of being a Mum kept me up all night. I don't know how Stefan's going to take the news. *Where the hell was he after the funeral?* All evening, I couldn't get hold of him. Maybe it's a good thing we didn't speak, because I don't know how I feel about the pregnancy yet. I'm confused and can't pin down a solid stance. Am I happy? Sad? Mad? Afraid? Is it too soon to feel anything other than grief for Lynda? She's still very much an open wound.

On one hand, I'm filled with terror when I think about having a baby. But then, on the flipside, if it's a false alarm, I know I'll be disappointed. *What's that telling me?* I've never seen myself as the nurturing type. After running away from home, I didn't believe I had it in me. I've always had the fear of being just like *her*, Mum.

And I hate my mum.

But this could be my chance to prove that I'm nothing like her.

Maybe it's what I need to ground myself and take me away from all the materialistic things that have been coating my life like sticky goo. Insignificant stuff that has been filling the big gaping hole, giving me a false sense of meaning and worth, such as my obsession with social media, trying to stay on trend and relevant. Wanting and needing the likes and clicks for validation and love. It's all fake. Meaningless.

Maybe I can be a good parent, with or without Stefan's help. It's a sobering thought.

I glance up from the menu of my favourite brasserie in Islington and stare over at Bee, who's reading hers. I think back to the look of pure joy on her face as she emerged from the changing rooms in Zara, wearing one outfit after another. It was wonderful to watch. I've witnessed a change in her. She's transitioned from an insecure, nervous girl, coming from a troubled home, into a quietly confident and self-assured young woman. Maybe too self-assured at times. Sometimes a little spiky and unpredictable, which catches me off guard. After having what seems a troubled upbringing like mine, it's nice to know that I'm the person who is giving her a helping hand. Everyone deserves a break.

Bee hasn't registered that I'm staring, so I take this moment to gaze at her fully. I'm fascinated by the way her bony fingers wrap around the menu with her short fingernails and peeling nail varnish. She seems unaware that she's reading the menu out loud under her breath and biting down on her lip at the same time. I like the shape of her long face and thin nose, and her pale blue eyes sparkle under the restaurant's fairy lights. She seems familiar to me, as though I've known her all my life, but I can't quite pinpoint where and why. I turn my attention back to the menu, dismissing the thought.

Today, I'm craving carbs and contemplate ordering the French classic, croque monsieur.

The waiter approaches. 'Yes, madam?'

'Bee, have you decided?'

'I'm not sure. The menu's in French, and I didn't do very well in my GCSEs.'

She makes me smile. I hated French too. In fact, I hated school so much, I couldn't wait to leave. I cover half my mouth with the menu and giggle. The waiter, who is obviously French, pulls a snooty face.

'Well, I'm having a croque monsieur, if that helps.'

'What's that?'

'Basically, it's a posh cheese-and-ham toastie.'

'You're kidding me, right? Well, that's my bloody favourite. Sorry. Excuse my French.'

This time, I belly-laugh. She looks confused by my reaction. I don't think she's clocked the pun.

'Madam?' He's getting impatient.

'Oh. Yes, we'll order two croque monsieurs, sparkling water and a green side salad to share.'

He takes our menus and leaves in a huff. She places her hands on her lap and looks around the half-empty restaurant, walls covered with enamel pictures of Paris.

'Thank you again for today.'

'Like I've said, it's not a problem. The outfits are on me, a way to repay you for . . . *you know what*,' I whisper.

I can't help but stare into the void of empty seats around me. Even though Sol's been arrested, and the troll's messages have ceased, I can't shake off the sensation of being watched. I didn't realise what a profound effect this has had on me.

I should take this as a warning sign. It's a good time to stop all my social media activities now that I may be pregnant. Pass the baton onto a younger, fresher person, like Kelsey. Goodness knows how many more deranged people there are out there reading my posts, knowing where I am, who I'm with, watching me from afar. Or up close.

Bee smiles broadly and I notice her chipped front tooth. Again, I get a burst of familiarity. Something about her face. Her mannerisms. There's something about what she said last night that has been niggling away at me. *The drowning incident.* Another bizarre coincidence between us? Is this why she seems so familiar to me, because of our shared experiences? I want to get to know her better.

'Can I ask about your mum? You said she passed.'

She looks shocked, so I smile reassuringly at her.

'Yeah, she did.'

'Why are you still running, then? Why change your name and identity? Surely she can't harm you anymore.'

'Uhm . . . I . . .' She looks around the restaurant.

'You can trust me, Bee.'

'You know, I dream about her at night. It's like she comes for me. It's hard to explain . . . I mean, I worry that you're going to think I'm mad if I say any more.'

'Try me.'

I see pain behind her eyes. Her face is weighted with hurt; I sense it oozing from her every pore. I reach my hand over to hers and place it on top, giving it a squeeze, then pull away.

'Sometimes I think she's still here with me, watching my every move,' she says. 'Sometimes I wonder if she's dead at all. Is the whole thing a hoax? Because it feels like she's still alive, you know? I mean, I know she's dead. I watched her on her deathbed.

I watched her take her last breath. I watched as she struggled . . .'
Bee chokes up. 'I'm sorry. I can't . . . It's too difficult to talk about.'
She shakes her head.

The temperature drops and the mood shifts.

A dark cloud hovers above us.

CHAPTER FORTY

Bee

Damn Frankie and her fucking questions about Dotty. The last thing I wanted to do was sit at the restaurant and think about Mum. But it was too late. The impression of her was all around me. Suffocating me.

The last time I saw her, she was at the hospice, so frail and broken she didn't resemble the tough woman I used to know. Even though I'd psyched myself up for the visit, it was still a shock to see her that way. Her skin was blotchy and transparent, you could see the purple blood running through her veins. Her eyes were glazed, like no one was home. Her trademark flame-red hair gone. Her foul breath stunk the room out and smelled like death.

'Hello?' Her voice was hoarse. All those years of smoking had caught up with her.

Dotty tried to lift her head to look at me but couldn't manage it. Her eyes fixed to the ceiling. I approached the bed and leaned over her so she could take a look.

'You came.'

Dotty's pinkie finger lifted off the bed in acknowledgement. But then, her eyes widened with fear.

'Do you like my hair?' I spat.

'Fran . . . Fran . . . Francesca?' I hadn't heard Dotty ever say that name before.

Watching her struggle, like the name was choking her, made me laugh out loud.

'No, Mum. It's me,' I smiled.

Dotty stared wide-eyed in horror.

'Thought I'd surprise you and wear a wig. Do I resemble her?'

'What?'

'It's Bee, Mum. Not Francesca. Bernie Bee. Your other daughter,' I said through gritted teeth. 'Do I look like Francesca?'

'How did you . . .' Dotty wheezed and spluttered.

'I found the letter. The one that you wrote but never gave to me. The one hidden in your jewellery box, like. The letter that explains I have a relative living in London and that she now goes by the name of Frankie Fitz. A social media influencer. The letter that says Frankie left home when I was born. You left an address at the bottom, telling me where to find her.'

Dotty shook her head. A tear trickled down her cheek. I knew it wasn't one of remorse, but one of regret for not hiding the letter properly.

'Were you going to keep her a secret forever?' A red mist of rage circled around me, like a swarm of angry wasps. 'What's wrong? Cat caught your tongue?'

'Bernie . . .' Dotty said, her chest rising and falling.

She was struggling to breathe.

'You never wanted me, did you? Never loved me.' I yanked the pillow from behind her stupid bald head. 'Did you love her?'

'I love . . .' I didn't know it then, but those were going to be Dotty's last words.

'You love no one but yourself.'

The red fog entered my brain, my body, clouding my thoughts. I clutched at the pillow, white knuckles exposed. On automatic pilot, the pillow came down onto Dotty's face. I pressed as hard as I could, feeling her bony face through the cushion.

Dotty's arms had a mind of their own, thrashing around hopelessly, her legs jerked and kicked for a bit. Then everything calmed.

The red mist faded, and for the first time, a sense of peace washed over me.

It was over.

CHAPTER FORTY-ONE

Frankie

'So . . .' I say as chirpily as possible, after an uncomfortable quiet spell. 'I'm going to buy a Christmas tree this afternoon. I don't usually bother, but I'm feeling festive this year.'

Bee shakes her head and looks at me, like she's just realised I'm sitting opposite. This girl is a space cadet, worse than Mia. One minute, she's present, in the room, engaged and attentive, and the next, she's in the clouds, someplace else, staring into space with a vacant look in her eye.

'That's so exciting,' she says. 'Can I help you decorate? It'll be so much fun. Maybe we can drink hot chocolate while we do it? Listen to carols!' She squeals as she bounces on her chair like a child. 'I've always wanted to do that with somebody. Somebody special, like.'

Bee's mood has done a complete U-turn in a matter of seconds and she's now animated and upbeat. It's sweet and endearing, if not a little odd. However, what she's saying is not what I had in mind at all. I was imagining decorating the tree with Stefan.

'I was thinking about presents,' she continues, a flurry of excitement. 'I have some ideas about what to buy you, but I'm not entirely sure. I don't want to share my ideas though because it has to be a surprise. I'm sure you'll love the main present. Once I get my first proper pay cheque, I'm going shopping. I want to spoil you. Spoil you rotten. My way of saying thank you for giving me a job and a roof over my head, like. For helping me when I've been at my absolute lowest. Sorry. I know how you hate me saying 'thank you' all the time. Sorry.'

Her eyes turn to the ceiling as she continues fantasising. 'I can see it now. The presents under the tree. Waking up together. Do you think stockings are a good idea? We can hang them on the fireplace, like in the movies. I can't wait until Christmas morning. The look on your face when you open your present.'

My heart sinks.

I cross my hands on the table and lean forward. I mean, it was only yesterday that I was talking about giving her extra time to find a new place, but there was no mention of her staying as long as the holiday period. That's two weeks away.

'Bee. My darling. This all sounds very nice . . .'

I pause. My insides are twisting. I know I'm going to upset her, but what can I do? Like Stefan has said before, she's not my responsibility.

'I don't know how to say this, but . . . I think you're forgetting that you won't be living with me for much longer. You'll be in your new place and will have made friends. And although I've loved having you around, I think this year I'd like to celebrate Christmas with Stefan. Make it an intimate affair. You see, it's becoming serious between us.'

She looks shocked. Even I'm surprised by my own revelation. I mull it over in my mind. Me and Stefan. An item. Possibly a family? Although terrifying, the idea doesn't repulse me.

I mustn't overthink the situation. I'll invite him over to decorate the tree and tell him about the potential pregnancy. Maybe we can take the test together? We can work out the logistics after the results.

Bee's face has tightened. She's upset by this news.

Yes, I like her. Yes, I want to help her. Yes, I am very grateful to her for helping me out at work and with the whole Soliman situation. Yes, I identify with her. Yes, we are similar. Yes, I'll help her as much as I can. Yes, she's very familiar to me. But I don't want to be responsible for her.

I'm not her mother.

'Bee, my darling. Like I mentioned yesterday, I'll help you find a new place to live. It'll be fine. You can do a house share with people your age. You don't want to be stuck with old fogies like me and Stefan all day long. You're young. You should be out and about, enjoying life. Partying. Meeting boys. Or girls, or both, why the hell not? And I promise I'll help in every way I can. If you need an advance for a deposit on a place, just ask. A good reference, just ask. Whatever you need, name it and you got it.'

'I, umm . . .' She stands and grips the edge of the table with both hands, knuckles turning white.

'Are you okay? Are you ill?'

'I need the loo. Sorry.' She scurries towards the back of the restaurant.

I wonder whether I should go after her. Was I being too harsh? Should I invite her to decorate the tree with us tonight? Should I be doing more?

No. No. No. This all feels wrong. What I should be doing is backing away from her. She's too dependent on me. Bee can't rely on me for her happiness. She has to learn to stand on her own two feet. I'm doing all that I can for her within healthy boundaries.

I pick up my phone and am about to fire out a message to Stefan when I notice he's messaged me. I also notice three missed calls from Mia. I sigh out loud. She called yesterday, but I didn't have the headspace to answer her because of the funeral. I still don't have the headspace. Why is she pestering me so much all of a sudden? She probably wants her job back. But I can't trust her after the bracelet incident. Besides, that position is now filled.

I ignore Mia and open Stefan's message.

Can I come over tonight? Stef

Where were you last night?

Don't hate me, but I was with Vic.

What? Why?

I'm sorry. She was in a bad way. She hasn't taken the news about us very well.

But I needed you, Stefan.

I know. I'm sorry. That's what I told her. I told her that I love you.

Love me? I hold my breath. *He loves me?*

After a short spell, I type back. *Come over, Stef.* I take a moment before I write the rest of the message: *I love you.* I hesitate not knowing whether I should send. Doubt clouds my mind. I've never said the words to him before. Do I even mean them? Does he? In fact, I've only ever said those words to one other person, but that was a lifetime ago — when I was sixteen. A painful memory I'd rather forget.

My hands shake. *What the hell?* Send.

When I look up, Bee's standing over me. I see a flicker of annoyance and something else I can't quite put my finger on spreading across on her face. Bee's features have contorted and twisted, and she looks unrecognisable to moments earlier. It's anger. That's what it is. She's angry at me and it's unnerving.

'Who's that?' she snaps, pointing to my phone.

Her tone is shocking. This time I can't look past it. 'Bee, please take a seat.'

She slumps down in a grump.

'Can I remind you that my business is my business alone, and I don't have to answer to anyone,' I say, sitting upright like a headteacher.

Bee's eyes widen. Her face changes from one of bitterness and contempt to one that's hurt.

I soften a little. 'Maybe you're being protective over me. Maybe this whole business with Soliman has been unsettling for you as well, which I understand. Maybe you're upset because I brought up your mother and you're still grieving, in your own way. I don't know what the reasons are for this outburst. But you must know, you cannot speak to me in such a hostile way. I'm trying to help you as best as I can.'

She's looking everywhere apart from at me.

'Bee? Are you okay?'

She nods, biting her lip. Tears form in her eyes.

'Look, if you want to know who I'm messaging, it's Stefan. He's coming over later.'

She shifts in her seat. Her face contorts again, and her tears dry up. 'I'll make sure I'm not around, then. I wouldn't want to be in the way,' she says tightly.

I half smile, forcing myself not to say any more.

I'm baffled. Is this reaction justified? She's making me feel like I've done something wrong. She stares with a stone-cold look on her face.

The waiter arrives with our food, placing the plates and drinks on the table. With her head bowed, she doesn't say any more about it, and we eat in silence.

What do I know about this girl?

CHAPTER FORTY-TWO

Bee

Red. I saw red.

Stupid bloody bitch. Dumping me like that. Rejecting me. Discarding my feelings like I didn't even matter. Like I meant nothing. Like I didn't exist. Like I was a nobody.

A nothing. A FUCKING NO ONE.

I'd gone out of my way to help her out, saving her from that creep, Sol. How could she treat me in that way?

The realisation hit me like a hammer to the eye. The pair of them were the same. *Dotty and Frankie.* They were self-obsessed. They didn't care about me. They didn't want me. They didn't love me. Unwanted and unloved, that's who I was. Who I'd always been and will always remain.

The rage that had been building up over the years towards Dotty was now focused in one direction. A flying dart towards the bullseye. Frankie. My fucking sister who abandoned me when I was born. Left me to rot in that tiny flat.

I bit down on my bottom lip until I tasted blood and stared at my plate of stupid toasted cheese and ham, which I didn't like anyway, trying my best to contain my anger from spilling up to the surface.

But the uncontrollable mist had already formed around my eyes. *How idiotic of me to even believe that we could be a family.*

I thought about blurting the truth out there and then, over our croque whatever the hell it was called, but I didn't think I could handle another knock-back. I didn't know how I'd react. The thought alone made me want to stab myself in the heart. *Or stab someone else.* I placed the knife on the table. Having to stay calm, I forced myself to think clearly. But it was tricky. Dotty was all around. Laughing. Mocking. Taking pleasure in my misery and rejection.

I didn't want you and neither does she. Poor little Bernie, Bernie Bee. I didn't want you and neither does she. Poor little Bernie, Bernie Bee. I didn't want you and neither does she. Poor little Bernie, Bernie Bee.

Making tight fists, I wished Dotty away, but she continued to tease, *I didn't want you and neither does she. Poor little Bernie, Bernie Bee.* While Mum laughed, Frankie droned on about decorating her fucking tree, pretending like the last half-hour didn't happen, acting as though she wasn't even bothered about kicking me out before Christmas.

As I sat there, trembling with anger, another memory flashed in my mind from when I was ten. It was Dotty's birthday, and Reg was throwing her a party at the flat. He made sure it was after hours, so I was sent to my room, hungry and rejected, and told to go to bed. I put my PJs on and turned on the soft light so I could chat with Bee, my imaginary sister, the only real friend I had, while the party thumped through the walls.

We were sisters, Bee and I. Imaginary sisters.

We had the same long hair, the same eyes, the same smile. We even wore the same clothes. That night, we sat on the bed talking about Charlotte, a girl who we both hated at school. Dotty threw open the door. I sat to attention, biting down on my lip. I could tell she was drunk by the way she swayed — never a good thing.

'Who are you talking to, Bernie?'

'No one,' I said.

'*Who* are you talking to, Bernie Bee?'

'No one, I swear. No one, Mummy.' She yanked my ponytail hard. 'Ow, you're hurting me.'

'Well, why can I hear talking?'

'My sister, I was talking to my sister.'

'What the . . . what the hell are you talking about, Bernie Bee?'

'I'm sorry, Mummy, I'm sorry.'

'I'll teach you to talk shit about having a sister. I'll teach you. Where are the scissors?'

She found the pair in my desk drawer and cut off my ponytail. She held my long, plaited hair in her hand and waved it around. 'Poor little Bernie, Bernie Bee.'

On Monday morning, Bee told me to take the scissors into school. She was angry. As instructed, I lured Charlotte into the outdoor toilets at breaktime and cut off a strand of her hair. The following day, her big sister Taffy waited for me outside school. She tied me up to the gates using elastic bands.

I snapped back to the present. Frankie was paying the bill, using a gold American Express card. She was so rich, she didn't even look to see how much the meal cost. It made me sick to my empty stomach. I clenched my fists tighter. The fury surrounding me grew heavy and dense, bloody and red. It was only a matter of time before . . . before . . .

I had to let off steam somehow.

Pulling my phone out of my pocket, I texted Charlotte. *Tell Taffy I have her clothes. I'll be at yours in an hour.* I got up and stumbled out of the restaurant, barely able to see. I was so angry, so disorientated, it felt like birds were pecking my eyes.

* * *

I focused on the wreath hanging on Charlotte's door while I waited for her to answer. It was pissing down with rain and I was soaked through, which only made my mood worsen. I cracked my knuckles and pounded again. As usual, she was taking her time. When the door flung open, Charlotte greeted me with a soft smile. She seemed happy to see me, which confused matters. She looked at my hands and clocked that I was holding a Zara bag.

'Brilliant, you brought her stuff.'

'That's not Taffy's.'

Her smile faded and her brow creased. Charlotte closed the door slightly and stepped back inside. 'Where's . . . where's her clothes, then?' she stammered.

'That's not a nice way to say hello to your friend, is it?'

'But you said you had it.'

'Aren't you going to invite me in so we can talk about it?'

'Not a chance, Bernadette.'

I stared at Charlotte's small pea-shaped head and flimsy hair and wracked my brain trying to remember if there was ever a time where she was a good pal. She was never kind to me. Even after all the covering up I did for her at secondary school while she shagged everything in sight like a dog on heat. I used to pretend to her dad that she was with me when she was whoring herself around town. She never even thanked me. She'd always been selfish. Always. Her and her fucking sister.

'Okay, so I'm going to go now. Nice seeing you again, Bernadette.'

'My name's Bee,' I spat through gritted teeth.

She rolled her eyes. 'Whatever. You'll always be kleptomaniac Bernie to me. Always.'

Charlotte was about to slam the door in my face, but she hadn't realised that my foot was already inside, preventing it from closing.

I dropped the bag filled with my new clothes and forced the door open.

'Are you alone?'

'What? Yes. Taffy isn't here. I'm . . .'

I squeezed myself through the gap and smiled, entering her home.

'Charlotte. I think . . . I think . . . something bad is gonna happen.'

With one strong shove, I pushed her to the floor and closed the door behind me.

CHAPTER FORTY-THREE

Frankie

The garden centre is packed when I arrive and there aren't many Christmas trees left to choose from. The best, taken. I think back to how early Amanda put her decorations up and it makes me feel heavy. Maybe I'm not cut out to be the domestic type. I swipe Amanda and the looming coffee date from my mind and decide not to ponder on my choices too much. I find one that is semi-decent and wait in line for it to be wrapped in plastic netting, after which, I pay for a selection of black-and-gold baubles and a premium for it all to be delivered to my home.

I'm not feeling festive anymore. My mood has dipped since lunchtime. Something about Bee's behaviour isn't sitting right. Something about the way she looked at me across the table has been unnerving me all afternoon. Her blue eyes turned stone cold. The way she asked who I was texting was alarming. She didn't even realise she'd overstepped the mark. Then she left abruptly without thanking me for the meal and clothes, just mumbled something about seeing a friend in Hackney! *She's acting like I owe her my life.*

It makes me question her emotional intelligence. It makes me question a lot of things about her. Thank goodness she's looking for a place to live. I pray that she's got good news when I see her.

To top off my depleting mood, Mia has been calling all afternoon. I've no idea what's gotten into her either.

By the time my Addison Lee pulls up outside the nurseries, I'm experiencing sharp abdominal pains. My frame of mind has darkened. I'm fighting a depression I haven't had in years. When I was a teen, I used to get depressed for weeks on end, never knowing how to shift my mood. It was only when I discovered exercise that things changed for the better.

It's pouring down and it's washing away the snow, turning the pavements into black mush. I jump into the cab. My cramps are bad, and I wonder whether it's period pains. I think about the pregnancy test in my handbag. Stefan's delayed at work and won't be at mine for a few hours yet. I wipe my teary eyes. I've no idea why I'm so emotional today.

My phone rings, startling me. Pulling it out of my handbag, Mia's name flashes on the screen.

I answer. 'Mia, why have you been ringing?'

'It's urgent.'

'Can't it wait? I have so much going on right now.'

'No, not really. It can't wait,' she says bitterly.

'Look, I'm sorry things ended the way they did. I'm sorry that you lost your job.'

'Stop! I don't want to hear it, Frankie.'

'So why are you calling?' I'm taken aback by her abruptness. 'It doesn't sound like you've moved on from what's happened.'

'For goodness' sake, this is not about me. This is not about my job, even though I am pissed off about that. This is not even about Amanda and the bracelet — and I'm definitely pissed off about that. This is about *Bee*.'

'Excuse me?'

'Okay. Hope you're sitting down.'

'I am.' I look out the cab window.

'Since Bee took over my role, I've been receiving awful messages, scary stuff, from an anonymous Instagram account saying things like *I'm going to make you pay* and *I wish you were dead*. The messages have been getting worse by the day.'

I sit upright, the phone shaking in my hand.

'I asked a techy friend of mine to look into them for me. I asked her to dig around a little bit. Luckily, she knows someone that works at Meta Platforms UK and they traced the IP address for her. She couldn't find a specific address, but she did come up with a street name. It's in Islington.'

My pulse quickens.

'Upper Street, Frankie. The road is Upper Street, where our gym is located.'

Panic engulfs me. I already know what she's going to say next.

'I'm sorry to have to tell you this, Frankie, but I think Bee is the one sending me threatening messages. And she's sending them from work.'

Silence passes.

'Frankie? Are you still there?'

'I, umm . . . Are you sure about this, Mia?'

'I can't be one-hundred-percent certain. But I did call up Martha the other day and asked her to log onto the desktop at work when Bee wasn't around. Low and behold, Instagram came up in the browser history a ton of times. Not only that, the dates and times that Bee logged onto the site coincide with the messages that I received.'

'Oh my God.'

'I bet my life it's her.'

I swallow. 'I've also been receiving threatening messages. I thought it was someone else, then I wasn't so sure. Maybe it's been Bee all along.'

My body is trembling.

'Frankie? Are you there?'

'Okay, Mia. Thanks for letting me know. I'll be in touch.'

'Frankie, watch your back.'

I hang up.

Turning my mobile in my hands, I gaze outside and reflect on all the nasty messages I've received over the last couple of weeks. I think about the sensation of being watched all the time. It all started around the time I met Bee. Sol wasn't my troll after all.

I've been such a fool.

As the taxi drives me home, I check my security app to see if she's returned home. There hasn't been anyone near my front door for the past half an hour. I breathe a sigh of relief. Outside my house, I jump out of the cab and race up the doorsteps. I'm struggling to get the key in the door. Once inside, I switch the alarm off and listen in the hallway, just in case she's messed with my security. It's quiet. I muster up the courage to shout out her name, but only silence greets me. Taking the stairs two at a time, I enter her bedroom.

Who is this girl?

Standing in the doorway to her room, I assess my surroundings to see if there's anything amiss, if there are any signs or clues, anything at all that will tell me something about her, but the room is immaculate. Nothing has changed or moved and there's nothing of hers on display. It's as though I haven't had a houseguest at all. *Maybe she's left?*

Flinging open the doors to the wardrobe, I'm disappointed to see clothes inside. *All of her clothes.* She must have collected the rest of her belongings from the gym. I inspect them one by one. Cheap. Tacky. Faded. I approach the chest of drawers to take a look inside. More cheap, tacky, faded items. Apart from the clothes, there's nothing personal that belongs to her to give me an inkling of who she is or why she's entered my life.

Who is this girl?

I slump on the bed, frustrated. *Think, Frankie, think.*

My ears prick from a slight noise. A creak on the stairs, getting louder. Someone is in the house. I sit on the bed, holding my breath, unsure what to do. The only people who have a set of keys for my home are Stefan and Bee. Stefan's set were given to him months ago, in case I was ever locked out.

'Frankie, I have a present for you,' the voice sings.

It's Bee. Of course it's her. Stefan's never used his set before and he's already mentioned that he's going to be late.

A sense of imminent danger floods my system. I pull my phone out and dial 999, but don't hit the call button yet.

'Frankie? Where are you hiding?' She's on the landing.

My senses are heightened.

'There you are.' Bee bursts into the room, making me jump.

She's holding a tasteless plastic wreath. 'Thought I'd make a contribution to the decorations. My way of saying thank you for everything.' She's speaking like nothing has happened between us.

Frozen on the spot, I hear myself say, 'That's very kind of you.'

'What are you doing in my room?' She looks around.

'Oh . . . I . . . I wanted to see if you were here.' I stand and rub my hands down my leggings.

'Well, I'm home now, so you don't need to worry.' She grins.

CHAPTER FORTY-FOUR

Frankie

'Did you have any success?'

'Excuse me?' Bee asks.

She comes closer. I manoeuvre myself around the room. We've done a dance and I'm now standing by the doorway while she's sitting on the bed. She places the wreath next to her and looks at it as though it's a cute puppy. It's unsettling.

'You said you had a friend in Hackney with a spare room. Isn't that where you've been?'

Bee's grin dries out as she looks me in the eye. She's cold and soulless. Her stare chills me to the bone.

'The room's not available.' Poker-faced, she narrows her eyes. 'Charlotte's promised it to someone else. She said that there's nothing she can do about it and that her hands are tied.' This comment makes her chuckle.

A build-up of tension charges the atmosphere in the room.

Bee appears unstable. I wished I'd noticed before. When I met her, I mistook her awkwardness and intensity for vulnerability. I believed she needed someone to give her a break. That someone being me. I missed all the red flags. All the erratic comments

232

and micro-behaviours she displayed over time. They were warning signs. And I missed them all!

My legs are buckling. I grip the door frame for support. 'Bee, I don't know how to say this but . . .'

'You want me gone, don't ya? I know you do. You want to kick me out on the streets, just before Christmas, like,' she spits, her eyes flaring with anger. '*You* said I could stay longer. *You* said I could take as long as I needed. *You* said I had a job and a place to stay.'

'I know I said all those things. I'm sorry. My circumstances have changed. I can't offer you the job and I can't offer you a place to stay anymore. I'll give you money. You don't need to pay it back. I have cash, or I can do a transfer today. You can book yourself a cheap hotel room, it doesn't have to cost the earth. I can help you look now if you like.'

'Are you calling me cheap?'

'No. You're taking my comments the wrong way.'

'Well, I'm not cheap.' She rises, her arms stiff by her sides.

'Bee, stop focusing on the wrong thing. I didn't call you cheap. Now, please understand that our arrangement must end today. You can't live here. I'm not just kicking you out in the cold. I'm going to give you some money to help you out, like I promised. Take the clothes I bought you. Take the money.'

'Why can't we stay together?'

'Because I know!'

She's motionless. She looks at me confused. Surely she knows what I'm referencing. Could Mia have gotten it wrong?

'What exactly do you know?'

'I know about the Instagram messages you've been sending Mia. The messages you've been sending me.'

Her face drops.

She looks to the floor and taps her foot. 'I guess it was going to come out sooner or later,' she says, shrugging her shoulders, like she's hardly done anything wrong at all.

'So it *was* you!'

Bee stands. 'Let me explain, like.'

'How could you do this to me? To poor Mia?' I shake my head in disbelief. 'The messages. They were . . . horrible. Disturbing. Why, Bee, why?'

'It's complicated.'

'How?'

'I'm angry, okay? I'm angry about something *you* did. Something from the past.'

'Me? What the hell have I done to you? I don't even know you!'

'Oh yes you do.'

'What?'

The girl's delusional.

'Well, if you give me a bloody chance to explain, like, I can tell you everything. And I mean everything. No lies. No more bullshit, I swear.'

Do I want to hear more lies? 'I don't want to know anymore. It'll be excuse after excuse and I'm exhausted from it all. To be honest, I want you gone. Out of my life. Please pack your belongings. You can use one of the suitcases or gym bags under the bed, I don't care. Take anything you need. Meet me downstairs in the kitchen and I'll give you money, as promised, so you can get a hotel room, or an Airbnb if you prefer. I'll give you enough cash to tide you over for a week or so. I'm sorry, that's all I can do to help. You're getting off lightly. If you don't go, I'll call the police and tell them about the threatening messages. But of course, I don't want to do that. I still want to give you a break. A chance in life. So, if I were you, I'd take my offer and go. And never come back.'

I can't bring myself to have her arrested. Something about her face. Her familiarity. She's troubled and needs help, not a prison sentence. I leave her to sort herself out. In the landing, I sense her dark presence behind me and whip round to see if she's followed me, but she hasn't. I breathe a sigh of relief. This explains why I've been so paranoid lately. *It's been her all along.*

In the kitchen, I fire a text to Stefan, asking him to come as soon as he can. I'm weirded out and could do with backup if things turn nasty. She's desperate and I know what desperation can lead to. I think back to the dark shadow outside my house after Lynda's show and seeing her at the gym leaning against the window before I hired her. She came out of nowhere the day Mia was looking for a cleaner. The messages. I think about the picture she took of me standing by my bedroom window from across the street. That's why Bee's familiar. She's been everywhere.

She's an obsessed fan.

As I wait for Bee to pack and leave, my mind goes into practicality mode. I need my house key back. I need to change the punch code for work and security code for the alarm at home, so she doesn't have access. I need to speak to Mia about coming back. Hopefully she hasn't found another job.

My phone rings. It's Stefan. 'Hey, I'm being held up. I can't get to you for a while.' He sounds breezy and relaxed.

'Oh, Stefan,' I whisper. 'It's Bee. I've asked her to leave.'

'You're well within your rights to ask her to move out. You're not her mother. You can't be responsible for her.'

'I'm worried.'

'Why? She'll be okay. She's a grown woman. Good riddance, if you ask me. She's so intense to have around. You know, I was going to mention this to you at some point. I've caught her looking at us strangely a number of times. I think she's jealous.'

'It was her.'

'What do you mean?'

'The messages on Instagram. It wasn't an online troll. It wasn't Sol. Or an accomplice of his. Or even Mia. God, at one point I thought it was Vic. Or you. Can you believe it?'

'Me?'

'It was Bee. She's the one that's been stalking me.'

He sighs loudly on the other end. 'Makes sense. I knew something wasn't right about her.'

'She's upstairs. I'm hoping she's packing. How soon can you get here? I'm spooked.'

'Why are you spooked?' Bee says, making me jump out of my skin for the second time. She's standing at the kitchen entrance; her head is cocked, and she has a deranged look about her.

'Stefan, I gotta go. Bee's walked into the kitchen. See you soon.' There's no suitcase. 'Are you packed?'

'Answer my question first. Why are you spooked?' She steps closer.

'Bee, can't you see? The messages you've been sending. It's not a normal thing to do to someone. You shouldn't be sending cruel messages to people. It's not right. It's worrying and stressful for the person on the receiving end. Can't you see that?' I swallow hard. 'How long have you been following me for?'

'Online?'

'In real life, Bee.'

'Oh. It's hard to distinguish between the two.' She laughs animatedly.

'Why, Bee? Why?'

'I have something important to tell you.' She chuckles nervously. 'Maybe if I show you, you'll understand.' Bee's holding a crumpled piece of paper. 'I know you're going to change your mind once you know the truth.'

'The truth?'

Bee hands the paper over. 'Please sit down.'

'What's going on, Bee?'

'So impatient all of a sudden. Now, I said sit the fuck down and read the letter.'

I look at the piece of paper in my hand.

'It's from Dotty.' She smiles, revealing her chipped tooth. 'Our mother.'

CHAPTER FORTY-FIVE

Back then

Life was caving in. I was suffering from chest pains, head and body aches, feeling unwell from the lack of sleep. I was physically and mentally exhausted, not to mention full of raging hormones. I had no one to turn to. No friends and no support at home. Depression had gotten hold of me. The only way out I could see was to get the hell away from the flat, away from them, away from her.

And if I couldn't do that, then I'd have to kill myself.

It was one of those mornings and the baby hadn't stopped crying. She'd been wailing through the night. With the pillow pressed hard over my head, it was as though the cries were coming from the inside of my brain. My nerves were frayed.

Even though the cot was by her bed, Dotty was none the wiser. She'd popped two sleeping pills the night before and seemed to be having a nice lie-in. Not that she ever bothered going to the baby, ever. Her motto was to let the baby cry it out. 'She'll soon tire from her own noise,' she'd say, sucking on a cigarette, blowing smoke in my face.

That morning, Reg had left early. He'd taken extra work at the local supermarket, stacking shelves. Usually workshy, all of a sudden he was holding down two jobs and dealing drugs on the side. The baby continued to cry while I tossed and turned. It was no use; I knew she wouldn't settle unless someone went to her. I kicked the duvet off and made my way into Dotty's room.

There was Mum in her splendour. Black lacy nightie, legs over the covers, earplugs in and eye mask on, yesterday's red lipstick smeared. The room was hazy from smoke and smelled like an ashtray. I drew the curtains and opened the window for fresh air. I pulled the screaming baby out of the cot, holding her a good few inches away from me. I stared into her blue teary eyes. Her face was red and puffy. She felt breakable in my hands.

I should have sensed something for her, anything, at least a little pity, but looking at her, I was emotionally paralysed. Since the day she was born, I'd hollowed out.

A toxic poo smell hit my nose. I turned her body around and noticed that she'd soiled through her baby grow. No wonder she was unhappy. Cursing Dotty under my breath, because of course it was all her fault, I carried the baby to the bathroom trying my best to avoid touching her bottom. I lay her on the changing mat. The taps squeaked as I turned them to run a bath. The bathroom soon filled with steam. The water poured out and the splash zoned me out, the heat making me drowsy. I was so sleep-deprived, it didn't feel like I was awake at all.

I tested the temperature with my elbow and stripped her down, rolling her dirty nappy up and leaving it outside. Gathering the baby in my arms, I lowered her into the lukewarm bath. Her short, flame-red hair spread out in the water like little spikes.

It must have been soothing because she calmed. The only noise was coming from the hum of the rattily air ventilator. She splashed her chubby arms and legs about, gurgling. The poor thing didn't have a choice about which family she was born into. It was the luck of the draw — and she'd drawn the short straw.

As she played, I watched the way the sunlight poked through the window and danced on her white skin. When she smiled, she revealed only gums. I noticed she had little dimples in her chubby arms and legs. I soon became mesmerised by the magic someone so small could create.

As time passed, I found myself warming towards her. Maybe having a new family member wasn't such a bad thing after all. Maybe she was what I needed to get me through the tough times at home. Maybe we needed each other. I realised then that I could love her. And she could love me back.

Despite never being shown love by Dotty, I was sure we could both work it out.

The idea teased me for a while as I knelt on the floor stretching over the bathtub, holding her in my arms. My knees began to hurt, and my legs cramped up. I'd no idea how long we'd been in the bathroom for, but the water felt cooler. I repositioned myself, spreading my legs further apart so I could sit on my bum, but I was still uncomfortable, so I pulled myself back up and tried to reposition my legs to the side. And that's when it happened. As I moved, my body jerked and my arms opened, my grip released, and the baby slipped away from me.

Under the water she went.

The baby became still at the bottom of the bath and she looked like a doll. Staring through the ripples of water, her blue eyes captivated me.

I watched her, hypnotised.

'WHAT ARE YOU DOING?' Dotty screeched, breaking the weird spell I was under. 'The baby. Get that baby out of the water!'

Dotty barged me out of the way and leaned over the bath. She pulled her out.

'You stupid, worthless bitch. What the hell are you doing?'

My world shattered like broken glass, the reality I was in breaking into smithereens.

Shaking my head, I was unable to comprehend the horror I found myself in. The gravity of what I'd done, what I was about to do, what I was capable of doing.

I pulled myself off the floor and looked toward the baby in Dotty's arms. There was no sound coming from her mouth. The baby was blue and motionless.

Dotty tipped her upside down and suddenly, like a rebirth, an ear-splitting scream belted from her tiny lungs, out through her pencil lips. She was alive! Oh, thank God, she was alive. Then I heard another voice. I cowered into the corner as he entered.

'What's going on?' Reg asked.

'Francesca tried to drown Bernie,' Dotty relayed to Reg.

'I didn't mean . . . It was an accident . . . She slipped . . .' I covered my face with my hands to protect myself. I knew what was coming next.

Wallop.

Even though I hadn't registered his blow, I felt the effects immediately. My right cheek and eye were swelling up and my jaw felt dislocated. I squinted my eyes shut.

The next blow to the face, I registered. It was so powerful, it made me fall to my knees. The room span around me. I could taste blood in my mouth and had to fight to stay conscious.

I wanted to protect her. I wanted to protect the baby from the life she was destined to have.

She was better off dead. *I was better off dead.*

'Get out! Get out of my house!' Dotty shrilled.

'And never come back,' Reg said.

CHAPTER FORTY-SIX

Bee

Frankie was shaking. It was probably from shock. It wasn't every day a person was confronted by their long-lost sister. I was like a Jack-in-the-Box surprise.

Boo!

I waited for the news to sink in and for her to say something, but she didn't do or say anything. She just sat there trembling, staring like a zombie. She was lucky I was the patient type.

'Are you okay?' I asked after a while, annoyed that I had to ask her how she was doing. Hadn't she enough time to think it through?

'I, umm . . .' Frankie, who usually had a lot to say for herself, was lost for words.

Getting prickly under the skin, I needed her reassurance. I needed her to tell me how much she'd missed me over the years and how glad she was that I'd found her.

'In Dotty's letter, she says you can explain everything.'

'I . . . I don't know . . .' Tears rolled down her cheeks.

The crying bothered me.

'Dotty?' she asked. 'So, she's dead?'

Maybe part of the shock was finding out that our mum had died. She'd come around pretty soon. She'd embrace and tell me she loved me. It wouldn't take long to get over the death. I knew she hated Dotty as much as I did.

'Yep. Dead.'

'How?'

'Cancer. Nothing could save her.' My body rushed with adrenaline when I relived the moment I felt Dotty's face through the pillow while she took her last breath. 'Mum gave me the letter and said that I should find you and that you'd explain everything. So, explain, like.'

'I don't know how to . . . I don't know . . . I . . . Oh, Bee . . . Bee . . .' She paused, then repeated my name over and over. 'Bee. Bee. Bee.' She laughed.

Was she mocking me?

'Bee. Bee. It's so obvious. Now I understand. Bee. Bernie. Bernadette. How stupid of me. Why didn't I see this before? Why didn't I make the connection ages ago? There was always some-thing familiar about you. Oh God, no. I can't believe this is hap-pening to me. I mean, I haven't seen you since you were a baby. I can't believe this . . . Am I dreaming this all up? Am I going to wake up from this nightmare?' She cried into her hands.

Nightmare?

'Are you really who you say you are? I mean, how can I trust you? After all that you've put me through. The messages. The stalking.'

She looked around the kitchen, talking to herself like I wasn't there.

'But you have the letter. You have the letter from *her*. I'd recognise that poisonous handwriting anywhere. She was poison. Poison. And of course, now you've told me the truth, I recognise your eyes. The same pale blue eyes as when you were a tiny thing, staring back at me in the bath. Oh God. Why? Why now? Why did Dotty have to . . . Why? *Why?'*

She burst into loud sobs.

My patience was wearing thin. A red mist clouded my vision.

The kitchen disappeared, and I found myself teetering on the edge of a cliff, looking down into an empty void, imagining falling, falling, falling to my death. My skull cracked, my bones broken, my limbs ragdoll-like. Dumped. Unloved once again. One step and it would all be over. Dotty's laughter surrounded me. *Poor little Bernie Bee. I didn't want you and neither does she.* I wasn't good enough for her love. Was I good enough for Frankie's love? *Jump. Jump. Do us all a favour and jump!* the red fog inside my brain teased.

'STOP YOUR SELF-OBSESSED SNIVELLING!' I slammed my fist on the table.

Frankie looked up at me with her bloodshot eyes as I stood up.

'You owe me, Frankie. Now, explain.' My body shook from fury. It took all the will in the world not to smash her head in.

'I can't explain any of it. Not yet. I need time to gather my thoughts. I need space to think. Space away from you . . . You're everywhere. Everywhere I look. Right in front of me. Everywhere I go. You're there when I close my eyes. And I can't . . . I can't . . . BREATHE. You're suffocating me, Bee.'

'ARE YOU BEING SERIOUS?'

'What's going on?' A familiar voice said, cutting the loaded atmosphere.

Panting wildly, I turned towards the direction of the voice. *Fucking Sol.* What the hell was he doing at the house?

CHAPTER FORTY-SEVEN

Frankie

'You should learn to shut your front door, sweet ting. You never know what type of riff-raff you might attract into your home.'

'Oh shit,' says Bee, turning to me, eyes wide.

'Nice to see you gals together. Maybe now I can kill two birds with one stone.' He belly-laughs.

I'm bewildered. First Bee and now Sol.

'I . . . I saw you being arrested,' I stammer, aware that there's panic to my voice. 'You were arrested in front of me.'

'Got bail. Your boyfriend came good in the end, ya know.' Danger flashes across his black eyes.

'Excuse me?' I ask, swallowing hard, not believing what I'm hearing.

'Stefan, that boy of yours. Gotta hand it to him. Paid my bail money, pronto. Straight after the funeral.'

So that's where Stefan was. Not with Vic, like he said. *Is there no one I can trust?*

'Why would he do that?'

'He wants to keep me quiet about the little ting we have going on.'

'What thing?'

'Stef was gonna try and convince you to sell me the painting. And he wanted a hefty cut for it. But what Stef didn't realise was, he was being used. I needed him to get to that skag-head Lynda and to *you*. After she died, it was fair game. The painting was the prize. The value went through the roof. The deed had to be done and done quickly. No more fucking about. Poor Stef, he didn't realise I was gonna just take what was rightfully mine. I had no intention of paying you or him.'

He sniggers.

'You owe me, remember? You owe me your life. It was going so well, until this little bitch got involved.'

Ice runs through my veins.

Bee's stance is animal-like, ready for attack. Her eyes are red, burning with rage; her hands are poised like claws. Her eyes flit from me to Sol.

'I knew your boyfriend was a pathetic loser. You see, Frankie? You've got bad people around you. No one's looking out for you. No one. Apart from me,' she spits. 'ME!'

'She has a point,' Sol says. He struts into the room like he owns the place.

A rush of adrenaline courses through me. I fumble with my mobile to dial the police, but my stupid screen is locked. With trembling hands, I use face ID to unlock the screen. My phone doesn't recognise my panicked features.

Quick as a flash, everything changes. Sol approaches and swipes at my hands, throwing me off guard. My phone hurtles across the floor. The screen breaks and glass scatters on the tiles. I'm being pulled back by my hair, which forces me to my knees. Sol has me in his grip and is towering over me at my back.

'Don't you hurt her.' Bee's face changes shape, twists into a ball.

Sol laughs at her. 'Now, why would you think I'd hurt her?'

'Because of what you did to me!'

'You're believing your own lies, little girl. Frankie . . .' He pulls my hair hard and my neck snaps back. I'm now looking at him upside down. He shakes his head at me. 'She's right. You need to be careful who you let into your inner circle.'

'I don't understand.' I can barely get the words out of my dry mouth.

'She set me up, that little skank. Somehow, she smashed up her own face, found a witness and set me up. Called the police and is having me done for GBH. Maybe I should have her working for me. She's good. I mean, she's great.'

He loosens his grip and I collapse on the floor. I reach for my neck and cough.

'Good,' I splutter. 'I'm glad she did. You're trouble. You should be in jail for selling the bag of drugs that killed my best friend!'

He sniffs. 'You can't prove that it was me. You got nothing on me. Nothing. She's been on and off the skag for years.'

'Why are you here, Sol? What do you want?' I ask futilely

'Believe it or not, I'm not here to cause any harm. I'm here for what's rightfully mine. So, if I can just take the painting, I'll be out of your hair. I have buyers from Dubai waiting for it.'

He steps back and turns to look at Lynda's artwork.

'Nooooo!' Bee screams, charging towards him.

Out of nowhere, she rushes at him with such power, she somehow manages to push him to the ground so he's on his knees. She's splayed on top of him, pounding her fists on the back of his head and body.

'Leave my sister alone!'

She's frenzied, a wild animal. Gnawing, screaming, clawing at him. He's cowering in a foetal position. But he's laughing. Finding the whole thing funny. I run for my phone to dial 999, but the cracked screen won't allow me to unlock it. I press the side buttons hoping that it'll activate an emergency call, but it doesn't do anything. I run over to the pair and try my best to prise her off him, but she's like a crazy banshee, arms thrashing, legs kicking.

'No, Bee. This isn't the answer. You'll only make things worse.'

While she's lashing out, she catches me in the face, and I'm thrown back from the impact. Sol uncurls himself off the floor and swats Bee off him like she's an insect.

With my mobile in my hand, I stand. 'Don't come near us, Sol. I have the police on the phone right now.' I'm hoping he doesn't realise I'm bluffing. 'Bee, move away from him before you do something you regret.'

Bee's making weird hissing noises. She steps a couple of feet back.

I turn to her. 'It's okay, I got this. The police are coming.' Then I look to Sol, and he in turn looks towards the painting and then back at me. All three of us are in a triangle, a standoff. I sense the cogs in his head turn. Will he snatch the painting off the wall and flee? I point the phone at his direction again.

'The police are on their way!'

A flurry of voices coming from upstairs in my hallway breaks the tension and all three of us look towards the exit.

'Hello? The door was open. Hello? Hello? Is anyone home?'

Bee looks at me confused. Sol looks alarmed.

'Your delivery is here. Where do you want it, luv?'

The bloody Christmas tree delivery. There's a pause. All three of us look at one another.

'HELP!' I scream.

And just like that, Sol runs.

CHAPTER FORTY-EIGHT

Frankie

The door slams hard. Sol has left. The painting's intact, still on the wall. I sit down, feeling exhausted, twiddling my fingers, while Bee deals with the delivery guys and the Christmas tree. I can hear her animatedly explaining to them that we were all having a bit of fun. She sounds jovial and comfortable in this role she's playing. No one would suspect what just went down.

My face tingles, my brain is discombobulated, and my body feels numb. Everything has an artificial glow to it.

My never-ending nightmare. *Sol. Two-faced Stefan. Bee's news. Dotty's death.*

With the delivery guys gone, Bee comes bouncing into the kitchen, brushing down her trousers with her hands. She fills the kettle with water and switches it on.

'Now, shall we have a cup of tea before we decorate the tree, sis?'

The innocence has returned to Bee's face. She's grinning childishly. I see her long features, her thin pencil lips and cracked tooth. Her greasy hair falls in front of her face and she blows it away. Her pale blue eyes are smiling too.

My legs tremble beneath me as I stand. I cross the room, unable to feel them. As I approach her, she looks hopeful, tearful

249

almost. I force myself to avoid her glare and open the jar of sugar on the worktop. Inside is a large stash of cash in an envelope which I've kept for emergencies. I'm not sure how much is inside. It could be anything up to £3,000. I don't bother counting. I don't care. It's only money.

The kettle comes to the boil.

Bee's smile fades as I hand the envelope to her. She shrugs it off, so I place it on the counter next to her.

Still avoiding her, I say, 'There's money inside. A lot of money. It should see you through the next few weeks if not more. Please take it. I'm sorry. That's all I can do for you.'

Her features tighten.

My body shudders. Francesca from Folkestone is dead, along with everyone else associated with her. 'Nothing's changed, Bee. You need to leave.'

'I can't believe you want me gone,' she spits. 'After all that's happened. After what I've done. After knowing the truth.'

'I'd like you to leave as well,' a breathless voice says.

We both turn to the door.

Stefan!

'Hope you don't mind, Franks, I let myself in. You sounded desperate. I came as quickly as I could. Is everything okay?' he asks, inching in, his arms stretched out in front of him.

'This is family business,' Bee hisses. 'This doesn't concern you. You're not family. I am. Now fuck off.'

'Family?' Stefan freezes. 'Has she completely lost the plot?'

The room closes in. I need her to leave so I can figure out what to do next. I need him to leave too. I need to be alone.

'Bee, you have to go,' I say.

'What?' She whips around to face me. Her eyes widen. 'You want me to go and not him? After his betrayal.'

'What . . . what . . . what betrayal?' he stammers.

'Stefan, not now. I'll deal with you after. But first, I need some time to think.' I find strength somehow to straighten myself up. 'I want you out of my house,' I say to Bee, this time with authority.

'Why should I go? Why not him after what he's done?'

'Franks?' Stefan says meekly.

'Not now,' I say through gritted teeth. 'Stefan, stop asking questions and just do me a favour. Can you bring her stuff downstairs? Use the suitcase under the bed in the spare room if she hasn't packed. She's leaving today. Right now, in fact. She's leaving right now.'

'Of course. I'll do anything for you, Franks. Anything.'

'I'm not going anywhere. Fuck you and fuck your pathetic boyfriend.'

'I've called the police. They're on their way, Franks,' Stefan says. 'I didn't know what else to do. You sounded worried. I'm sorry. I'm so sorry.'

I wonder what he's apologising for.

Stefan scurries upstairs, leaving me alone with Bee. I brush the annoyance I feel towards him aside and head towards the table. I catch a glimpse of Bee's pleading eyes. I'm reminded of the awful day I let her go in the bath.

How could I have let go of her? *How can I let her go now?*

'If you want to avoid the police, Bee, you better take your stuff and go. And go quickly,' I say mechanically, like it's not me at all. 'Otherwise, I'll be forced to tell them about the messages.'

'You can't abandon me in this way. I'm your *family*.'

She's right. *We are family.*

Someplace in my mind, I've been yearning for her to come back. Over the years, I've often asked myself what she'd look like, what type of an adult she was becoming, but as soon as the thought entered my head, I'd shut it down. But I also can't believe that she's waited this long to tell me who she is.

The deception. The dishonesty. All those hateful messages.

'Why are you doing this to me?' Bee's voice breaks. And so does my heart.

* * *

Everything happens in a rapid blur. Stefan brings her belongings down. Bee leaves her set of keys on the table and snatches the envelope. When she's asked where she wants to be dropped off, she mutters an address in Hackney. Stefan arranges the taxi. She yanks the heart necklace from around her neck and throws it at me. It lands by my feet.

'You'll regret this, I promise.'

'Bee?'

'You're just like her. Exactly like Dotty.'

She exits, leaving her pendant on the floor. The door slams hard.

'Well, that was a tense half-hour. Thank goodness she's gone, hey, Franks?' Stefan's voice is muffled, as though I'm under water. 'By the way, I didn't call the police. I lied to get her out of your house. Bloody internet nutjobs. What did she mean about family? What was she talking about? She's delusional, that girl. Most stalkers are, aren't they? Maybe we should call the police after all. At least fill out a report.'

'Bernie Bee,' I whisper her name under my breath.

Thick, ugly, revolting guilt knots itself around me like bindweed.

'How did the pair of you meet? She was your cleaner or something like that, wasn't she?'

Stefan's grating. I tune him out and notice the discarded necklace on the floor.

'What a peculiar girl,' he says, shaking his head. 'Very peculiar.'

I gather it in my hands and inspect it, turning the pendant over. There's an engraving on the back. A date. A date I know well.

12.10.89.

My birthday. Dotty bought it for me when I was younger. It was the nicest thing she'd ever done. I left it on my bed the day I was kicked out. Bee hates me as much as Dotty.

CHAPTER FORTY-NINE

Frankie

The kitchen is airless. The walls close in; I feel compressed. The necklace slips from my hands. As I stand, everything around me sways.

'Franks, are you okay?'

Ignoring him, I unsteadily cross the room, stepping over my necklace.

'You look pale. Sit down and let me get you some water.' Stefan hurries to the fridge, glass in hand.

The ice cascades out of the water dispenser on the fridge door. My stomach convulses and I dry heave into thin air. I rush to the bathroom and lock the door behind me.

Running the tap, I stare at my reflection in the mirror above the sink. I think about how easy it was for Bee to slip from my fingers in the bath when she was a baby. Questions I've avoided all my life pop up in my mind. *Did I let go on purpose? If Dotty hadn't found us, would she have drowned?*

There's a sharp sensation in my stomach. I grip the basin and double over in pain. I squeeze my legs and rush onto the toilet, pulling my leggings and knickers down.

My period has come. *Oh, thank God, I'm not pregnant.*

* * *

Stefan has opened a bottle of wine. Two glasses of red on the table. He hands me a glass. I take it and sit down.

'Everything okay?'

'Stefan, we need to talk.'

'About Bee?'

'No. First we need to talk about you. Your dealings with Sol.'

'I swear, Franks. I didn't know who he was. I swear on my life. He came into the gallery one day, admiring Lynda's paintings. He said he was an art dealer. Had connections all around the world. We got chatting. He seemed to move in the same circles as me. Sol said he used to know Lynda a long time ago. He explained how he'd been searching for her earlier pieces, in particular *Passion and Fire*. The one that you have on your wall.' He points.

His brow is beaded with sweat. He takes a huge lug of wine.

'So I got him together with Lynda. How was I supposed to know who he was? She didn't say anything to me. *He* didn't say a word. And, well, you didn't either. Because at first you didn't recognise who he was.'

'Let's focus on the painting, Stef.'

'I told him I knew who had it. I told him that I would help him get it for a healthy price. I thought I was doing you a favour. I thought maybe you'd want to part with it, make some money. Obviously, I overinflated the value. He thought he was getting a great deal out of me.' With another large gulp of wine, he finishes the glass and pours more for himself. 'Sol seemed keen to view it. He even dropped off a deposit for it at the gallery.'

'Stefan, how could you? How could you think about making money when Lynda overdosed? After Lynda died you should have stopped. And how could you invite him into my home to take a look without my consent?'

'I didn't know who he was . . . I thought you'd agree to sell and that would be the end of that. I'd get my cut. You'd be happy with the money. He'd be happy with the painting.'

'And we'd all live happily ever after.'

'Well, kind of, yes.'

He attempts to take my hand, but I push him away.

'I swear, Franks, I wasn't being shady. Well, I was thinking about profit, because that's what I always do, but I'd never betray you. Never! It looks far worse than it is.'

'So much has happened over the last few weeks. I'm not sure who to trust anymore, Stefan. I don't know what to believe.'

'I promise you, you can count on me.'

'Explain this to me, then. Why did you bail him out? How could you do that to me? To Bee? For all you knew, he was a violent man. You knew he was a drug pusher all those years ago when you paid for his bail money. And you believed that he punched Bee in the face.'

'I owed him the money, Franks. He called asking for his deposit back. He said if I didn't bail him out, he'd spill the beans about our arrangement. I didn't know what to do. I wanted him out of my life. Out of your life. He said he was going to disappear. I just paid him. I'm sorry I'm so gutless.' He hangs his head.

'Oh, Stef.'

'I can't believe I bailed him out.'

'You're such a fool.'

'I'm sorry, Franks. Truly I am. For everything.'

Stefan bursts into tears, but I can't bring myself to console him.

He quietens down and a silence lingers around us.

Yes, Stefan is a fool, but I've known him long enough to know that he's not a malicious person. He got himself in a pickle with Sol and didn't know how to get out of it. Now it makes sense why he was so quiet about the painting when we were speaking about it in bed. He should have told me there and then.

The wine goes down my throat easily.

'I guess you're not up for tonight, then? Shall I message them to cancel?' he says, breaking my thoughts.

'Up for what?'

'The Habibs' event.'

'Who?'

'Farah and Ali Habib, the couple from Dubai. They're hosting a charity dinner. Remember? You met them at Lynda's exhibition.'

'Is that tonight?'

'I understand if you're not feeling up for it. I'll call now.'

I drink more. The alcohol floods my system. It's warm and comforting.

'The Habibs' event is tonight, you say?'

'Uh-huh.' His eyes flash with worry.

'Any chance you were hooking them up as a third party to buy the painting off Sol?'

'Franks, I thought I was helping a friend out. He said he wanted a quick sale. They wanted the painting too.'

'This just gets better.'

'I'll cancel.'

'NO! No, don't. I'd like to talk to them.'

Stefan looks to the ground.

'The painting's cursed,' I say under my breath. It always has been.

'What?'

'I'm going to sell them Lynda's painting myself. The quicker I get it out of my house, the safer we will all be. Until Sol gets sentenced and jailed, that is.'

I finish my glass of wine and pour another.

I'll use the money to set up a trust fund for Bee. At least then I'll know she'll be set up for life.

CHAPTER FIFTY

Bee

The smelly Uber pulled up outside Charlotte's. I had to leave
Frankie's; I had no choice. The red mist was out of control. The
driver didn't even attempt to help me with my luggage. He just
popped the boot open and I took care of the rest. Already in a
dangerously bad mood, his non-cooperation wound me up more.
If it were Frankie riding the cab, I'm sure he would have gone out
of his way to help her.

Now, red was everywhere I looked.

I slammed the passenger door as hard as I could and wheeled
the suitcase towards the house. Her front door looked sad and
bare. The Christmas wreath, which was once hanging below the
knocker, was now on Frankie's bed, ripped to shreds. I pulled
Charlotte's keys out of my rucksack and unlocked the door, praying Taffy hadn't come back from her trip down south.

In the hallway, I stood still and listened. Not a sound. I left
my luggage by the entrance and locked the door from the inside. I
popped my head through the lounge. A full cup of tea which had
gone a murky brown and a half-eaten cheese-and-pickle sandwich
were left on the coffee table. A blanket was thrown across the sofa

258

and socks were dashed on the floor. Exactly how it was left the last time I was there.

The galley kitchen smelled stale. The sink was piled with dirty dishes. The counter had a chopping board with bread and a slice of dried-up cheese on it. A knife lay in an opened pack of spreadable butter which had almost melted. The fridge was open, empty inside apart from a pint of milk. I picked it up and sniffed it. It was off. I filled the kettle and searched the cupboards for herbal tea — camomile, wasn't that supposed to be calming? I paced as I waited for the water to boil.

My thoughts returned to Frankie as the mist hovered around me. She'd dumped me. The letter did nothing. The fact that we were family did nothing.

Dotty laughed. *I didn't want you and neither does she. Poor little Bernie, Bernie Bee. I didn't want you and neither does she. Poor little Bernie, Bernie Bee.*

'Shut up!' I punched the wall as hard as I could. 'Shut up. Shut up. Shut the fuck up. You're dead. I made sure of it. You're fucking dead.'

The pain in my knuckles took a moment to come, but when it did, it made my eyes burn and the nerve endings in my hand throb. Blood dripped onto the tiled floor. I licked my hand, tasting metal. *I didn't want you and neither does she. Poor little Bernie, Bernie Bee.*

'SHUT UP, I SAID.'

The kettle clicked. A loud thump could be heard from upstairs. Dotty's voice faded into the distance. *Thump.* There it was again. *Thump. Thump.*

The banging had become so loud, it was shaking the kitchen ceiling. I held my breath and looked around not knowing what to do.

Thump.

I bounded up the stairs two at a time. *Thump*. The bedroom doors were shut. *Thump. Thump*. Taffy's bedroom door shook. The noise was coming from inside. Twisting the handle, I opened the door slowly. The room was dark and stuffy. The curtains drawn and windows shut.

On the floor was Charlotte.

She was lying on her back with her hands above her head, tied to the bed leg. Her feet strapped together with duct tape. Her mouth stuffed with a sock. She'd been kicking the door and had made a dent in it. I switched the light on.

'Surprise, I'm back.'

She blinked a few times and shook her head. Her eyes filled with terror.

I placed my finger to my lips. 'Shh.'

Charlotte thrashed her tied legs about and caught the side of my shin as she kicked. I grabbed both her feet with my bloodied hand and pulled them up towards my torso, so she was raised half off the ground. 'You're not being very clever, are you?'

Tears mixed with snot streamed down her face. I let go, allowing her legs to slump to the floor. She twisted herself around trying to turn over, but she couldn't fully because her hands were tied to the bed. She was making such a spectacle of herself, that it made me feel sorry for her. I stepped over her body, placing one leg on either side of her torso and leaned over, staring into her eyes. She stayed still.

'That's better.' I sat on her tummy. 'If you promise not to make a sound, I'll get you a glass of water.'

She nodded.

'Promise?'

'Yes,' she murmured.

Don't ask me why, but I didn't want to kill Charlotte. It wasn't her that I was mad at. I mean, she'd pissed me off in the past, and so had her sister, and she was paying for it now. But I didn't want the girl accidentally dying on me and causing me more complications.

As I left the room and started down the stairs, my phone buzzed in my back pocket. A bell noise sounded. I'd set up my notifications in the taxi earlier so I would immediately be warned if Frankie had posted anything on her social channels.

Smiling like the cat who got the cream, Frankie was staring at me on my screen, dressed in a figure-hugging silver dress, with a glass of fucking champagne in her hand.

It was only an hour ago that she'd found out that I was her *sister*. It was only an hour ago that she'd discovered that Dotty had died. It was only an hour ago that she'd chucked me out of her house.

And now she was celebrating?

Not only was she celebrating, but she seemed to be flaunting it to the whole world.

Did I mean nothing?

I was erupting. Exploding from rage. Red, all around.

Trembling from my core, I sat on the bottom step and searched the history on all her social accounts, poring over photo after photo, post after post, looking at pictures of Frankie Fitz throughout the years. Frankie at an awards ceremony. Frankie at a shop opening, cutting ribbon. Frankie in a double-page spread of a gossip magazine. Frankie doing a podcast, radio show, a live event at a shopping centre. Frankie in a market in Morocco, on safari, posing on a beach in Thailand. Frankie at a fancy restaurant, nightclub, rooftop bar. Frankie at a festival, indoor concert, hanging out with stars backstage and onstage. Frankie working out at her gym. Frankie doing the downward facing dog, sun salutations, pigeon and tree. Frankie skiing, Frankie boxing, Frankie cycling, Frankie running. Frankie dancing, singing karaoke, doing the fucking Macarena. Frankie at a homeless shelter, at an animal rescue, at a charity dinner for mental health!

Frankie. Frankie. FUCKING FRANKIE.

A fury took a hold of me so strong that my whole body became consumed. Violence filled my every atom. I went back to her latest post and scrolled down from the image, reading the comments.

> *What a fabulous dress. You're looking great tonight. Cheers, Frankie, good to see you back!*

With fingers like fire, I tapped. *Frankie is a skag-head whore. Frankie left her baby sister to rot in an abusive household. Frankie loves Frankie and no one else.* On and on I went, replying to every single remark. Verbally defecating on her pages. But it wasn't enough anymore. There was no sense of satisfaction. Someone had to pay.

Someone always paid.

I thought of Charlotte, squirming on the floor upstairs, hopeless and vulnerable.

My mind conjured up ways of killing her. I could pound her head in. Kick her to death. Slice her in two. Stab repeatedly.

I picked up my rucksack which was hanging on the banister and flung it over my shoulder, leaving the rest of my stuff behind, and forced myself to leave the house

With the taste of blood already in my mouth, I wanted more.

But it wasn't Charlotte's blood I wanted.

CHAPTER FIFTY-ONE

Bee

I leaned on the lamppost across the road from Frankie's and rubbed my temples. My head was banging from an intense headache that had built up since leaving Charlotte's. Everywhere I looked was coated in a red film. A neighbour's cat circled my legs, begging for attention, it's tail upright and happy. I booted it away and watched it scutter across the road with its tail between its legs. It hid under a car.

My eyes refocused on Frankie's expensive home. White doorsteps lead up to her smart navy door with the fancy brass knocker. It reeked of money and wealth and status. Stank of self-importance. The shutters on the windows were closed, which meant Frankie was still out enjoying herself. She was too busy lapping up the limelight with her phony friends and posting on her accounts to worry about what she'd done to me.

Luckily for me, Frankie was careless with her security. I let myself in using the extra key that I'd cut a week before, switched off the alarm using the same code as the clinic, the same digits on the back of my discarded necklace. In the kitchen, I spotted two empty wine glasses on the table and an empty bottle. *Bitch.* Did she pop the cork as soon as I left?

An idea came to me.

Pulling things out of drawers and cupboards, throwing stuff on the floor, I searched for scissors. The plan was to destroy everything she owned, the stuff she cared about, wait for her to come home so I could see her pathetic reaction, then I'd destroy her.

Stomping up the stairs, I left a trail of muddy footprints on her pristine carpet in my wake. I flung open her bedroom door and looked around, holding the scissors in my bruised hand. There was so much red clouding my vision, I was barely able to see.

Everything in the room was neat and tidy. Sterile and cold, like her. One wall had fitted wardrobes filled to the brim with designer clothes. I pulled item after item out, shredding her stuff to pieces. After I finished, I took the scissors to her bed and tore into her Egyptian cotton sheets and duck feather pillows, stabbing at her mattress as hard as I could.

It was a massacre.

Next up was all her sportswear and underwear which were stacked inside her chest of drawers. All ripped within a matter of minutes. Only the bottom drawer left. When I opened it, there weren't any clothes inside — instead, dozens of notebooks. I picked them up and sat on the destroyed bed with clothes and feathers all around me to inspect them. They were diaries. The dates ranged from when she was a child right up to last year. *This could be interesting.* I decided to start with the earliest one. Flicking through the pages with babyish bubble handwriting, I stopped at a random entry and read.

> *Reg and Dotty took me to the seaside today. It was crap.*
> *They ignored me all day and kept kissing each other with*
> *slurpy tongues. Yuk. I was so sick of them. I went to the*
> *seafront, knowing they wouldn't even notice me gone! I went*
> *as far as I could and stood by the edge of the water watching*

*the swimmers, some with armbands, while my feet got wet
from the lapping waves. I hated the water and the sea and
wondered why I had to live so close to it. I closed my eyes and
imagined myself being eaten up by a huge great sea monster
that lived at the bottom of the ocean.*

*Would Dotty and Reg even care? Would anyone rescue
me?*

*When I opened my eyes, I realised that I'd wet myself.
I didn't mean for it to happen. It just did. It made me cry
and some people laughed at me and pointed which made
it even worser.*

I hate Reg. I hate Dotty. I hate the sea.

The bloodied red fog which had been accompanying me
started to fade and there was a crack in my vision. My headache
had calmed a bit too. I could sense the young Frankie's loneliness
on the pages. Life must have been tough for her as well. Damn
Dotty and damn that useless piece of shit, Reg. They'd always been
selfish. I lay on my front and closed my eyes for a second, trying
to imagine what it was like for Frankie as a child.

But before I got too carried away with empathy and foolishly
backtracked on my mission, I had to remind myself that she'd left
her life in Folkestone and left me behind to rot. She now had it
all and I was the one that had *nothing*. No one. And she chucked
me out of her house, abandoning me a second time! No. There
wasn't any room to feel sorry for her.

I threw the book on the floor and picked up another one,
which was written a few years later.

*Everyone at school hates me. The girls think I'm a chav
and call me flea bag because my clothes are second-hand
and the boys don't even look at me twice. Posh twats. Why*

did she send me to that school? Why didn't she send me to the local where all the kids on the estate go? Now I'm the loser with no friends and only have a stupid imaginary sister to talk to. How tragic is my life?

But I met someone today!!!

He asked me if he could kiss me on the beach and I said yes. His name is Daniel. He was wearing a Joy Division t-shirt and looked cool, not like the drips from around here. I let him do other stuff too. Lots of stuff. It was exciting. I hope I see him again next time he visits his dad.

Intrigued by the diaries and conflicted with an upheaval of emotions, I was compelled to carry on. I picked up another one.

What the fuck does that fortune teller know? 'I see you drowning in the sea.' Idiot.

I wanted her to tell me that I was going to make something of my life. I wanted to know about all my riches and successes. I wanted to hear anything but doom and gloom and bloody death.

Was my life worth nothing?

And Dotty slapped me when I got home. Waste of time and money.

The next one I picked up was when she first moved to London and met Lynda. She talked about heroin, calling it H, and talked about meeting Lynda's dealer, who she never mentioned by name, only by the letter L, who I believed to be Soliman who used to go by Laurence. She kept repeating the same sentence over and over again with each entry.

I have to forget. I have to forget. Forget what? Her homelife in Folkestone? Me?

I took another book and then another, skim-reading sections, looking for any mention of me or any mention of regret, while I battled with my empathy. But there was nothing. No mention of me whatsoever. It was like I didn't exist.

A couple of years down the line, when she was in her mid-twenties, the tone to her entries suddenly changed. Life seemed to be going her way and she sounded more like the Frankie I knew. The Frankie I now loathed.

> *They love me. They bloody love me. I have so many likes.*
> *So many new followers. It's brilliant.*
> *I've got to keep this up. I've got to post more photos of me.*
> *The followers respond better to pictures of me rather than*
> *boring exercise videos. I'm so excited about the future and*
> *I'm bursting with ideas. I can't stop now.*
> *I won't stop until I make it.*

A photograph fell out of the last diary. I picked it up. The picture was old and grainy, and the edges were ripped. Two women stared back at me, standing side by side, both sour-faced. Both unhappy. I recognised one of the women. I'd recognise that long face anywhere, that glamorous hair and cigarette holder. It was Dotty, but a younger version of her. As always, she looked like a film star with her red hair, red dress, red-painted fingernails, offset by her piercing blue eyes. The hand holding the cigarette rested on another young woman's shoulder. A young girl, not much older than sixteen. Tall, lanky and awkward-looking with sad blue eyes.

This girl had short red spiky hair and was pregnant. Heavily pregnant.

Frankie.

Frankie was pregnant.

CHAPTER FIFTY-TWO

Frankie

We're in Novikov in Mayfair, an expensive Asian fusion restaurant and rooftop bar overlooking the City of London. The Habibs have hired the whole venue for their fundraiser, all expenses paid. The guests are a different level of rich, cloaked in self-importance, dripping in jewels and expensive designer wear. The lighting is moody, the décor opulent and eclectic, giving off Buddha-Bar vibes. The deep house pumping through the speakers is a bit too loud, making it hard to have a decent conversation with anyone unless you're shouting or on the rooftop, which, incidentally, is freezing because only a few of the heaters are working.

Not that I want to talk to anyone tonight.

Some people brave the terrace to take their selfies with views across the city. As promised, I took mine two hours ago with the hosts before dinner and posted it. I didn't want to, but I felt obliged. Let's face it, that one selfie was the only reason I was invited. To help raise their profiles in London. I also spoke to them about *Passion and Fire* and the deal is done. They'll transfer the money on Monday and Stefan will arrange for the painting to be sent to their home in Dubai. Thank goodness.

I'm slouched on a sunken velvet sofa in the chill-out zone. I look around, feeling numb. This isn't my scene anymore. The veil has been lifted, and I see everything for what it is — insincere and fake. The laughs, the smiles, the niceties. Scratch beneath the surface and you'll notice everyone's insecurities, the sly looks, checking what others are wearing, what they're posting. We're putting on a show, each and every one of us, displaying our most glamourous, best selves to others, who in turn are doing the same to us. None of it is real. Posting for the world to gawp at. *Look at me, everyone, I'm having the time of my life. Do you wish you were me?* Upload content. Check for likes. Scroll. Scroll. Scroll.

All night, I've had a strong sense of non-reality, like I'm locked inside a reality show, having to put on my best act for the cameras. The shell that's me has been going through the motions, smiling at people and chatting if need be, but on the inside, I'm broken.

Stefan's sitting next to me and is in a drunken conversation with another man. A silver fox with jeans too tight and a white linen shirt. Lots of money, no style. They're drinking expensive whisky. I'm on my fourth or fifth glass of champagne. The drink hasn't helped, and I don't want to be here.

I thought maybe I could bury my head in alcohol and forget, just for one night, but I can't. All night I've been seeing her pale blue eyes in front of me, the shocked look on her face when I asked her to leave. She was crushed. My own daughter, crushed.

I tap Stefan on the shoulder. 'I'm not feeling great. I'm going home.'

'I'm not surprised with the amount you've drunk tonight,' he shouts over the music into my ear.

I recoil. 'Stefan, this isn't a joke.'

'Shit, Franks. I'm sorry.' He stands to attention.

Unexpected tears trickle down my face. I wipe them away and hide my face. *I know I've made a mistake sending her away.*

'I'll get our coats and order a taxi,' he says.

I don't have the will to argue with him about coming back to mine.

* * *

On the way home, I pluck up the courage to text my daughter. *Please forgive me. I was in a state of shock. Please give me one more chance.* Bee appears online and reads my message but doesn't reply. The whole journey home, I'm silent, resting my head against the cab window. Stefan, being too drunk to notice my heartache, thinks I'm unwell.

The taxi pulls up outside my house, which is illuminated in the dark night. The shutters are open, and the lights on every floor are on. An ominous feeling floods my system. I try my best to stay calm. The fact is, I don't remember much after Bee left, everything is hazy.

The door is unlocked. Stefan's standing behind me, drunkenly chatting about the deal he helped set up with the Habibs. He has no idea that this will be our last night together.

We step inside. The alarm doesn't sound. It's been switched off.

None the wiser, Stefan goes upstairs to use the bathroom. I inch into the kitchen and a scream catches in my throat, sobering me up.

Stefan shouts from up the stairs. 'Franks, quick!'

'Oh my God. I've been broken into,' I say in disbelief.

Whoever it is has ransacked my kitchen. Nothing is left unturned. Chairs are thrown, the vase on the table is in pieces, the flowers that were inside trampled on. Every cupboard, every drawer has been opened, all the contents thrown out. There's broken crockery and glass everywhere.

Stefan appears, shaking his head. 'The upstairs. It's destroyed. Everything is destroyed.'

I pick up a piece of glass off the floor.

'DON'T! Don't touch anything. Leave it for the police. I'll ring them now. Maybe it's Soliman. You should check the external camera.'

Stefan heads to the patio doors and pulls them apart. A whoosh of icy air rushes into the room. I cuddle myself as I step over debris, looking around. He makes the call to the police. My hand goes to my mouth when I turn my head to look at Lynda's artwork. The painting is ripped to shreds. Not only that, there's writing on the wall next to it. Writing in what looks like blood.

You're a fraud, Mother!

'Hang up,' I say.

'What?' He turns to me, looking bemused.

'Hang up the fucking phone.'

'But, Franks . . .'

'Now! Do it.'

He does what I ask and comes back into the room. I point to the writing on the wall.

'I've got to find her.'

Our eyes meet. 'Frankie, please make it make sense. Look at what she's done. Look at your house. Your things. The painting. She's destroyed it. She's destroyed the painting! Bee's not stable. I'm calling the police again.'

'No!' I flick his hand and his phone falls to the floor. 'No, I said.'

'But she's no one to you. Just a crazy stalker.'

'She's my daughter, Stefan.' I burst into fresh tears. 'She's my daughter. And I let her go.'

His mouth drops open. I know I should explain everything to him, but there's no time. There are no messages on my phone from her. I check my Instagram post and read the comments she made. *Oh, Bee.*

I call someone I've wanted to avoid since the day I was kicked out.

Reg answers.

'That girl's a wrong'un, Francesca. She's always been a wrong'un.'

Angry bile rises up my throat. 'She needed love, Reg. Something you and Dotty knew nothing about.'

'We gave her love,' he slurred.

'Yeah, right.' He must be off his head because I can't believe the crap coming out of his mouth.

'Bernie. She was different. From when she was a young'un. She was distant. Detached. Sometimes, she'd have this look in her eye that would make you crap yourself. When Bernie was on the turn, I'd joke to Dotty that we needed to hide for cover.' He chuckles to himself.

I laugh too, but at the absurdity of his words. *As if any of this is true.*

'She's a dangerous person, 'Cesca. I knew it. And deep down, Dotty knew it too. But she was in denial. Kept her home, away from trouble, she did. Tried to protect her from doing harm.'

I sense the nervous tic going in his eye. He's a liar, a drunk and a useless piece of garbage. 'Bullshit, Reg. Dotty kept her prisoner!'

I'm so mad, I want to hurl the phone among the wreckage.

'You and Dotty. You were the ones who were cruel. Mean and unloving. Don't forget that I lived with you for sixteen years, until I was forced out by *you.* I was so confused when I had her. My hormones were all over the place. I was only a kid myself. What did I know? You kept me away from her. My own child. You kept me away.'

'You tried to drown her.'

'That was an accident, I swear. I didn't know what I was doing. I'd never intentionally hurt her. I would never . . .' A lump appears in my throat.

But I've hurt her now.

My cracked phone pings in my hand. Ignoring Reg blabbering on, I take a look at the message.

If you care about me, Mother, you'll meet me tomorrow at 6pm. Folkestone Harbour Arm.

CHAPTER FIFTY-THREE

Frankie

It's dark when the train pulls up on the platform. The sky, starless. It's not long until it's Christmas. A group of people block the carriage door with their luggage, squeezing themselves off. They're probably visiting family. It makes my heart ache knowing that families are getting together all over the country for the festive season and mine is in ruins. I check the time: 4.25 p.m. I push past the passengers in my way. Folkstone has changed and is now a gentrified town due to the influx of Londoners buying homes by the sea. The high street is filled with gastropubs, bars and art galleries. Glistening under the sparkling lights, they even have a Christmas tree.

But I don't care about the changes. All I care about is Bee.

A big thunderclap makes me jump. The heavens open and the rain comes down. I haven't been back since I was sixteen. I run.

The sudden downpour pelts my eyes, blinding me as I race towards the flat. I've gone back in time — I'm not Frankie anymore, I'm Francesca, the awkward, shy teenager. Being back is doing weird things to me, evoking the same feelings of not being wanted and not being good enough to be loved. The loneliness. The sadness. The abuse from Dotty — and her lapdog, Reg.

I speed up, trying to outrun these negative emotions that are stirring within.

I'm not leaving Folkestone without her.

My stomach lurches when I see the twin grey towers, side by side. They're exactly the same as I remember, just more weathered. The playground at the foot of them is run down. A few teenagers are kicking about, like they're up to no good. The surrounding area is barren.

Pushing my distressed thoughts to the back of my mind, I find the courage to approach Winfrey Tower, the one I used to live in, and press for a lift to take me up to the tenth floor. Neither of the two lifts are called. I stab at the buttons, but no lights appear above the shafts. They're not working. I take to the stairs and don't stop until I reach the very top. The whole stairwell reeks of urine. Loud music and shouting can be heard from a couple of neighbouring flats. As I hurry along the narrow corridor to the last flat, my courage diminishes.

I'm surprised to find Reg's front door ajar. He must be off his head again. I compose myself before I enter, straightening myself up, pushing the door open with my fingers

'Hello? Anyone home?'

There's no response. Reluctantly, I enter the small open-plan kitchen and living space and am instantly claustrophobic. The place is a mess and smells. Dirty and unkept. On the sofa under the open window, I see Reg passed out. Flat on his back, one arm hanging down, the other splayed across his chest. An empty bottle of cheap vodka with a Russian label is on the coffee table. He's sleeping off the booze. I shudder. Some things never change.

As I inch closer, I notice something and my breath hitches.

Blood.

A pool of blood on the threadbare carpet. My eyes follow the trail like breadcrumbs, up towards his body. Blood drips from his right hand. Blood splotches on the coffee table, blood across his chest where his other arm lies. I shrink into myself, realising what I'm looking at.

He's slashed his wrists.

I make it just in time to vomit in the sink. I splash my face with water and force myself to face the horror. There's a piece of paper on the floor, a pen beside it. His suicide note. Dotty was his life, so it comes as no surprise that he didn't make it after she died. I tiptoe towards the crime scene and pick up the note with my fingertips.

> *You got what you deserved. Just like Dotty.*
> *Yours lovingly,*
> *Bernie Bee x*

Oh, Bee, what have you done?

Panicked, I do the unthinkable and scrunch up the note, sliding it inside my coat pocket. I leave in a hurry, pulling the hood of my jacket over my head to conceal my face.

CHAPTER FIFTY-FOUR

Frankie

The wind is wild, and rain hits me horizontally. I race towards the harbour, puddles splashing up my legs. The black sea comes into view. The uneasy feeling I've been carrying with me since returning to Folkestone is worse now that I'm by the water. My mind floods with the memory of me and the boy I met at the fair. Daniel. The night I lost my virginity. Bernadette's father. How young and naive I was back then. How I craved attention.

That night changed my life forever.

Along the promenade are bars and restaurants filled with revellers despite the weather. I stare at the people inside, laughing, drinking, eating, enjoying light conversations, and I think about how normal their lives appear. I think about how normal my life appeared before I met Bee. And how I didn't recognise the deep-rooted loneliness within me. I filled the hole with pointless activities and fake love from an invisible online community.

She's all I ever needed.

My thoughts travel to the flat and Reg. I make excuses for her. *She didn't mean to hurt him. She wasn't thinking straight.* I finger the note in my pocket and wonder what she meant about Dotty. I dismiss the darkness enveloping me.

Bee had a troubled childhood. I should have been there for her. I should have saved her from them.

Whatever she's done, I'll take the blame. It's all my fault anyway.

Sleet's coming down so fierce, it's burning my cheeks and I'm drenched through. I take the steps down from the promenade towards the beach and then slip down the dunes. The tide's out. The sea's choppy and waves crash the shoreline. The beach is deserted. I want to cry.

Where is she?

I check my phone to see if she's contacted me, but she hasn't left any messages. I check my social media accounts, but there's nothing new. Instead, Stefan's clogged my phone up. I know he's hurting from our break-up, but I don't have the headspace to deal with him anymore. It was never going to work between us. I text Bernie to tell her that I'm here. She appears online.

Typing. Typing. Typing. Come on. Come on.

Look to your left. Next to the boat.

I can just about make out the silhouette of a rowing boat and a small person next to it. It's weird, but now that I know she's my daughter, I can recognise her skinny form anywhere.

Fear grips me. Surely, she won't row out to sea? My phone lights up the dark night.

Are you going to join me or are you going to just stand there? I'm going out, with or without you. Your choice.

CHAPTER FIFTY-FIVE

Frankie

They say that a mother would do anything to save their child. That they would die for their child.

But would they?

Would my mother have saved me? Dotty couldn't see past her own ego, her own needs, to take care of me. She took comfort in seeing me upset, seeing me squirm; it gave her a sense of power. Her whole existence was one big performance. Fake. Is this who I've been modelling myself on? Have I been like Dotty all along, fake and selfish, only out for myself? It's been about me for twenty odd years of my life. Poor Bernie never got a look in.

But I'm not my mother.

Running against the beating winds towards my daughter, I realise that I can make up for all the hurt I've caused. Up close, she looks fragile, a little girl lost. She's standing in the knee-high water and is struggling to take the boat out to sea.

'What are you doing?' I shout. 'Are you crazy?'

'Are you coming with me or not?'

'No. Wait. Stop.' I rush into the freezing water, grip the edges of the boat and try my best to haul it back to the shore. She's pulling against me. 'You can't do this, Bee. You'll die.'

'Watch me.'

'I won't let you.'

'You can't stop me, *Mother*.' She spits the word out.

I'm sixteen again. I've just given birth and have been sent out by Dotty to buy nappies for Bernie. The fairground is on. The Gypsy van is decorated in brilliant reds and golds and is parked up on the edge of the fair. I enter. The fortune teller's eyes sparkle as she reads my palm.

'I see your death. Drowning in the sea.'

My recurring dream flashes in front of my eyes. For years, I didn't know who the other person on the boat was, but now I know. My daughter's been haunting me for years.

Bee gets inside the boat, takes the oars and rows out into turbulent waters while I'm trying to pull it back. The sea is too violent, too strong, and I lose my grip. The boat is taken by a huge rush of water and disappears behind a wave. I force myself deeper in. Waves crash over my head. I'm finding it hard to catch my breath. Somehow, the boat comes back into view and I hurl myself onto it, throwing myself inside. She rows us out as we rock back and forth. Scrambling around, I sit on the bench opposite her and hold onto the sides.

'Let's go back. We can talk about everything on dry land,' I shout.

The sea's angry, unforgiving. I sense its fury with the pair of us. We've both done wrong. *Forgive Bee and take me*, I pray. She lets go of the oars and I breathe a sigh of relief.

'I've still got reception,' she yells, fiddling with her phone. She points it in my direction. The flash is on and blinds me. I blink away tears and rain. 'I'm live streaming you, Frankie. Say hello to your followers.'

'What?'

'I said, we're live. Say hello to your fans.'

Everything turns surreal. Soft around the edges. Rationality is out the window and is replaced by a bizarre set of circumstances only I can foretell. The soothsayer at the fair. Bernie slipping from my hands in the bathtub. My recurring nightmare. All of it, coming true.

The storm's merciless. The flashlight moves around like a laser beam. I hold onto the edges, terrified.

'Hello, everyone, thank you for joining us. It's going to be a bumpy ride for tonight's Q and A with Frankie Fitz.'

'Bee, you have to stop this madness. Put the phone away and get us back to shore before it's too late.'

'I'm sure everyone wants to know about this dark past you keep talking about. What happened to you when you were sixteen, Frankie? What made you run away from home?'

'I'll tell you anything you need to know. I owe you that much. But please promise you'll row us safely back to shore afterwards.'

She shrugs her shoulders in a childlike way.

'I fell pregnant. I had a precious baby girl named Bernadette. She was the most beautiful thing I'd ever seen; I could hardly believe that she'd come out of me and that I'd made her.'

'If she was so perfect, what went wrong?'

My mind travels back to the day I blocked out in my mind. I start to relive it.

'As soon as I gave birth, the nurse took her away from me. I didn't get to hold her in my arms. She wasn't breathing, you see. There were complications with the birth. Nurses were all around her. They laid her on the table in the corner and made a fuss of her. Then all of a sudden, I heard the wail. She was alive. Relief on the nurses' faces. A commotion erupted after that. Dotty was outside the room, banging on the door, demanding to be let in so she could see the baby . . .

'I don't know why, but they gave her the baby to hold first instead of me. Dotty always had a knack of getting her own way. Dotty came over with Bernie in her arms, and I wanted to die. From that moment on, my own daughter felt tainted. She wasn't mine. Dotty had claimed her. By the time I came home, I didn't want anything to do with Bernie. I didn't feel anything for her. Nothing. I was dead inside.'

She's quiet.

The flash on her camera burns the backs of my eyes. The boat's tossing around. I look towards the oars.

'Why didn't you love me?' she cries.

'I did love you, Bee. I do love you, and I'm sorry for leaving you with them.'

'But you never came back. Even when you made it, you never came back. Even when you had all that money, all that fame. You could have come back and rescued me. Why didn't you come back?'

'I blocked you out of my mind. Blocked out what I'd done to you. It was all so terrible. I couldn't live with the pain, so I blocked everything out. Tried to reinvent myself. I was selfish, okay? Totally selfish. And I hate myself for it.'

'What did you do to me?'

The boat is in a tug of war with the water. For a brief moment, I forget about my debilitating fear and reach out, taking an oar. I grip it with both hands. 'Take the other one. We need to get to shore.'

'What did you do to me?'

'Something bad happened that changed everything.'

'What happened?'

Bee's piercing eyes penetrate mine. She's still the same as when she was a baby.

'*What happened?*' she spits.

Looking around, I notice the RNLI rescue team making their way towards us. From the shore, I see lights flashing and a police boat coming out too. Shadows of people along the beach. The wind is swirling around us and we're trapped inside.

'When you were a baby, you nearly drowned because of me.'

'What?'

'You nearly died because of me.'

'So it's all true. I did almost drown as a baby. And it was you? Not Dotty. It was you all along.'

'I don't know what happened that morning. I wasn't thinking straight. I was exhausted. My hormones were all over the place. I let go of you in the bath. Maybe it was an accident, I don't know. Maybe I believed I was saving you from an awful life with them.'

'Saving me? You tried to kill me!'

'But I'm going to make it up to you and save you today.'

A foghorn breaks the spell. I look towards the RNLI rescue boat. 'They're coming for us. Look.'

'Save me from what?'

'You know what I'm talking about.'

'You mean Reg? What I did to Reg?' She laughs. 'And Dotty? Will you cover for me when it comes to *her*?'

'Bee? Don't! Don't say another word. People online are listening.'

'I smothered Dotty with a pillow and killed her. Did you know that? I hated her so much. I hated Reg too, so I sliced his wrists. And I hate you even more. But mostly, I hate myself. Because I'll never be good enough for ANY OF YOU. I'll never be good enough. No one wants me.'

She's my daughter, my flesh and blood. She's my responsibility, always has been. I don't care if she's done terrible, unimaginable things.

'No one wants poor Bernie Bee.' She drops the phone over the boat.

My body tenses. She looks overboard into the black. I reach my arms out to her.

'Bee?'

'No one wants poor Bernie Bee.'

The sea is turbulent, making her sway precariously. I'm terrified for her.

'I'm here now. I'm going to take care of you. I'm going to take care of everything,' I say, a last-ditch attempt.

When she looks at me, her normally blue eyes turn metal black as her pupils dilate. Panic explodes inside of me.

Everything unfolds in slow motion. Bernie jumps over the edge and disappears under.

'No . . . Bee . . . BEE . . .' I scream. 'NOOOOOOOO.'

My mind smashes into fragments of glass, scattering everywhere.

It should have been me. The recurring dream. The soothsayer. *It should have been me!*

CHAPTER FIFTY-SIX

Frankie

Chaos unfolds around me. I watch as though it's not happening to me but to someone else. I'm disconnected, in a million pieces, and I don't think I'll ever be put back together again. The rescue boat is up close. People in black wetsuits and masks dive into the deep. I'm being dragged out of the rowing boat, and somehow, I find myself on a larger one. I'm taken to shore.

I scream out her name.

It should have been me.

They cover me with a silver blanket. I'm numb. Stefan appears by my side. He tries to console me, but I push him away, crying out for Bee. Police are waiting to question me. Tape cordons off an area of the beach. There are spectators gathered. Lights appearing as hands. They all have their phones out, filming what's going on. I gaze blankly at the crowd.

I turn to the officer approaching me. 'Where's Bee? Did you find her?'

'They're looking for her,' he says.

I see him pat my hand, but I don't feel it. 'How did you all know?'

'Her friend Charlotte raised the alarm in London. Her sister came home and found her tied up and beaten. We've been looking for Bernadette all day. And then your boyfriend Stefan called up to say that you were missing and that she was involved somehow. And of course, when Ms Bernadette Firth started to live stream the event, tagging your name, we were able to pinpoint your whereabouts.'

The way he says her name, so formal, it makes me want to scream.

She's more than just a name. She's more than just a suspect. She's more than just a person of interest for thousands of people following the story online, like it's a soap opera.

She's my Bernie Bee.

She's everything to me. Everything.

EPILOGUE

It's been a year to the day since Bee disappeared. Her body was never recovered.

My life hasn't been the same since. Nothing brings me joy. Nothing. Endless time and regret are all I have left.

I stopped posting my life online the day she went missing, but I've kept all my accounts open, just in case . . .

Stefan and I didn't make it. He's back with Vic and seems happy. I ended most of my friendships and shut down nearly all of my gyms — apart from my flagship Islington store, which is keeping me afloat thanks to Mia.

Mia and Amanda are the only people I see nowadays. They take it in turns to check up on me, bringing me groceries and opening the shutters in the house, bringing in the light. As soon as they leave, I close them again and envelop myself in darkness. Mia's content to sit with me, making sure I eat, while she goes over what's happening at work. She's kind and thoughtful. That's why I'm leaving her the gym and the house in my will. Amanda likes to fill me in with all the latest celebrity gossip. We drink copious amounts of coffee, she talks non-stop, and I zone out listening.

Every single day, I cry.

The waves break my thoughts. I shake away any doubts left in my mind and find myself taking a few steps in barefoot. There's wet sand between my toes. I feel alive for the first time in a year. I'm live streaming on Instagram. Correcting what should have happened a year ago. It should have been me, *not her.*

Is my Bernie buried beneath the waves? Will we be reunited?

Swallowing the salty air, it tastes good on my tongue and is invigorating. The winter sun is low and bright. The gulls squawk around me. Folkestone Harbour Arm is behind me, the sea in front. It makes me laugh when I remember how frightened I was of it when I was ten, standing where I am today, wetting myself from fear. There was never anything to be afraid of.

The mist sprinkles my face. I'm now waist high and my legs have numbed.

I feel a presence behind me. I turn around, but there's no one there. Waves crash. The power of the endless expanse of water beckons me further in. I close my eyes and take a few more steps, holding my phone above my head, pointing the camera down.

My mind becomes quiet as a tomb.

I take one last breath before I submerge myself and it's finally all over.

But my phone buzzes in my hand.

My eyes spring open. My heart flutters inside my chest. A wave smashes into me, splashing my phone. Adrenaline surges through me as it buzzes again. I have a notification.

I have a notification.

I've got to get out of the water before my phone breaks. I cut the live stream and scramble out of the waves, battling against the angry surf that is now determined to take me. I must reach the shore.

Breathless, I collapse onto the beach. Trembling all over, I open Instagram messages. My body tingles from the rush. Then I see it. Among hundreds of other messages.

@youaregoingtopaybitch has contacted me.

I can't open it quick enough. The phone reception keeps cutting out. There's an image which needs downloading. The actual message keeps buffering. *God damn it, download.*
DOWNLOAD.

Finally, the message and image appear simultaneously. There's a picture of me. On this very beach. Taken moments earlier when I was getting my feet wet. The comment attached says,

Watching you, watching me.

I turn my head . . .

THE END

ACKNOWLEDGEMENTS

A huge thanks to the wonderful team at Joffe Books, who are amazingly creative and supportive.

Thanks to my brilliant editor, Becky Slorach; truly the nicest person to work with. Thank you also to the marketing team at Joffe, Tia and Sasha. I'm forever grateful for my proofreader Clare Coombes and copy editor Matthew Grundy Haigh.

As always, thanks to Maddy and the awesome team at Madeleine Milburn Lit Agency. A special thanks to the incredible Rachel Yeoh.

Much love to my beta readers, Sarah Lawton, Jenny Fraser and Angela Sweeney. A big up to 'The Six' who keep me sane when the going gets tough — what would I do without you? Other fellow writers; Sally-Anne Martyn, Daniel Sellers and Liz Webb, thanks for keeping my spirits up.

I'm forever grateful to my amazing husband, Byron and my gorgeous kids, Luciano and Arabella. I'm blessed to have you all in my life. My furry family; Ripley, Coco and Oreo, who are the best company during the day.

To all the amazing book connections I have made through social media over the last few years — thank you.

And lastly, huge appreciation to all the book bloggers and readers out there who shout out about my novels — I love you all.

THE LUME & JOFFE BOOKS STORY

Lume Books was founded by Matthew Lynn, one of the true pioneers of independent publishing. In 2023 Lume Books was acquired by Joffe Books and now its story continues as part of the Joffe Books family of companies.

Joffe Books began in 2014 when Jasper agreed to publish his mum's much-rejected romance novel and it became a bestseller.

Since then we've grown into the largest independent publisher in the UK. We're extremely proud to publish some of the very best writers in the world, including Joy Ellis, Faith Martin, Caro Ramsay, Helen Forrester, Simon Brett and Robert Goddard. Everyone at Joffe Books loves reading and we never forget that it all begins with the magic of an author telling a story.

We are proud to publish talented first-time authors, as well as established writers whose books we love introducing to a new generation of readers.

We won Trade Publisher of the Year at the Independent Publishing Awards in 2023 and Best Publisher Award in 2024 at the People's Book Prize. We have been shortlisted for Independent Publisher of the Year at the British Book Awards for the last five years, and were shortlisted for the Diversity and Inclusivity Award at the 2022 Independent Publishing Awards. In 2023 we were shortlisted for Publisher of the Year at the RNA Industry Awards, and in 2024 we were shortlisted at the CWA Daggers for the Best Crime and Mystery Publisher.

We built this company with your help, and we love to hear from you, so please email us about absolutely anything bookish at feedback@joffebooks.com.

If you want to receive free books every Friday and hear about all our new releases, join our mailing list here: www.joffebooks.com/freebooks.

And when you tell your friends about us, just remember: it's pronounced Joffe as in coffee or toffee!